Tha G-Code Gangster

Volume 1

by

Fredrick Staves

OG Publishing
Rialto, California

FIRST EDITION

First Printing 2008

ISBN 978-0-9801100-1-2

Printed in the United States of America

Published by OG Publishing
PO Box 211
Rialto, California 92377

www.OGOriginalGangsta.com

Dedication

This book is dedicated to all the real brothas caught up in the struggle of a crooked judicial system. The government may have our bodies but we and only we control our minds. We must stand tall through it all and continue to struggle for justice and freedom. We must continue to move forward and stop letting little simple dumb bullshit divide us. Together anything is possible.

My utmost Trust, Love, Loyalty, and Respect,
Gangster

Author's Note

This novel is a work of fiction. Any resemblances to real people, living or dead, actual events, establishments, organizations and/or locales are intended to give the fiction a sense of reality and authenticity. Names, characters, places and incidents are either products of the author's imagination or are used fictitiously, as are those fictionalized people, events and incidents which either did not occur or are set in the future.

Acknowledgments

First and foremost I acknowledge God for his love, grace, salvation, and his continual blessings.

To Teresa, who is the love of my life. To my four sons and my daughter, and to my mother for all her love and support.

To all the people that bought and supported me on my first book, "Some Talk It, I Live It."

To all my real homies who have stayed down for me such as: Angel, Karvin, Marv, Will, Darryl, Vann, D-Mac, Wolly-Dog, Mac 10, Big Scottie, Den-Den, Tyrone, Keebo, Lil Man, Al, Big Age, Melle Mel, and Studder Box from LPP.

I know there are other homies that feel they should have been mentioned but they need to kick back and try to figure out the true meaning of "The G Code" which is *Trust, Honor, Loyalty* and *Respect*. Once they understand what these four words mean and start living by them, then they will understand where I'm coming from.

I would also like to acknowledge all my real homies that are locked up and have been corresponding with me: Lil Black Rag, Thugg, Cebop, Lil Fee, Peddy Wacc, Big Marcellus, Bodean, Lil Ernie, Lil Man, Melle Mel, my nephew Solo, Godfather, Popeye, and Freeway Rick.

Also to the homies who are behind the wall: Bay Rob, Hoova Sam, Tweet, BeBop, Keebo, Big Jess, Smiley, Romell, Hawkeye, C-Nut, Fly, Big Gizz, Rocc, Big Fatty, Goldie, Big Ced, Rob Dog, Los, Bid D, and to all the other real homies that have been real and true to the "code".

I also like to thank all of you that have bought this book, for your support of me and OG Publishing. Thank you.

"Gangster"
Loved by few
Hated by many
Respected by all

Chapter 1
The Round Table

As NWA's "Gangsta Gangsta" rap song played through the surround sound system the War Room, six of QT's main men sat around what was known as the Round Table, bobbing their heads rapping along with NWA's song and waiting for QT to come to the head of the table to bring the monthly meeting to order.

The first Gangsta on the left side of the table was Rocc, QT's younger brother. Rocc was the third man in charge. Even though Rocc was the youngest he was one of the deadliest members of QT's G-Code Mobb. Rocc was 6' 4" tall, 220 lbs, well fit and solid. He had a bald head, brown eyes, and carmel-colored skin. The only flaw Rocc had was that he was a sucka for a fine bitch and everyone at the Round Table knew that one day, that would be his downfall.

The second Gangsta next to Rocc was Big Bam. Big Bam was one of the OGs (Original Gangstas) of the G-Code Mobb that had been created by QT's older brother Gangsta who was locked up in Folsom State Prison for murder. Big Bam was 5' 8", 250 lbs, brown skin, bald head and overweight. He dressed so clean and fresh that by looking at him you would overlook his size. He always had a big smile on his face and that was a good thang becuz when that smile disappeared the outcome almost always was deadly.

The third Gangsta next to Big Bam was Lil Man. Lil Man was 5' 5", 160 lbs soaking wet, dark skinned, dark eyes, bald head, and when he took his shirt off he looked like he was sculpted by the chisel of a knife. That physique had come from doing six straight years in San Quentin State Prison. Lil Man and QT had grown up together and as soon as Lil Man touched down, QT scooped him up and put him down with the G-Code Mobb.

The first Gangsta on the right side of the table was Goldie Loc who was one of the OGs from the G-Code Mobb as well. Goldie Loc was Gangsta's right-hand man, and had known QT for years. QT had admired Goldie and knew he could be trusted even though Goldie was from 43rd Street Gangsta Crips in Los Angeles and all of the other generals from the G-Code Mobb were from Santana Blocc Compton Crips. Goldie and Gangsta had met years ago in CYA (California Youth Authority) where they had got into it with some LPPs (Lueders Park Pirus), a Blood gang in Compton. Gangsta was fighting two of them in the school library. Goldie didn't know Gangsta personally but he knew who Gangsta was and Gangsta knew who Goldie was. Goldie didn't hesitate to come to Gangsta's aid and they had been tight ever since. Gangsta got out before Goldie and put the G-Code Mobb together and when Goldie touched down, Gangsta scooped him up and made him his right-hand man. Goldie was 6' 2", 220 lbs, light skinned, a muscular build, with brown eyes, and long hair that was always braided in corn rows. He was a silent killer. Goldie didn't talk much but when he did, people listened. Now, as with Gangsta, Goldie was QT's right-hand man.

Next to Goldie was Crip Crazy, an OG of the G-Code Mobb. He grew up with Gangsta and acquired the name Crip Crazy becuz when he started Crippin back in the day that's exactly what he was: Crip Crazy, 24/7, 365 days a year and 366 in a leap year. Crip Crazy was 6' 3", 215 lbs, and solid as a rock from all the weightlifting he'd done over all the years in and out of jail. Crip Crazy had a cocoa color complexion, bald head, and a loud mouth, but he didn't say anything he couldn't back up.

The last member of the G-Code Mobb was Boxer. Boxer was the only Mexican on the G-Code Mobb council. He grew up with QT and was also from SBC (Santana Blocc Crips). He had proven himself on many occasions and once saved QT's life back in the day. Some Bloods had caught QT slippin with all blue on with his blue rag hangin out of his left pocket. QT was coming out of the barber shop and didn't see the Bloods pull up, park, and wait for him to go through an alley by the park on his way home in the hood. QT was strapped but that didn't matter becuz the Bloods had the element of surprise. Boxer was riding his bike and happened to peep out the Bloods in the cut. Then Boxer saw QT and figured out what was about to go down. Boxer didn't hesitate. He pulled out his 9mm Taurus and started blasting on the Slobs and yelling for QT to get down. Boxer killed one Blood that day and shot another. After that, Boxer and QT were tight. After Gangsta went to jail for murder and he let QT take over the G-Code Mobb, QT scooped Boxer up and put him down with the crew. It wasn't a problem—Boxer being Mexican—becuz SBC had about ten Mexicans that were from the hood. Boxer was 5' 9", 190 lbs, brown eyes, bald head, and always wore white polo t-shirts, khakis that were too big, Locs (dark shades), Pendleton shirts, and Stacy Adams biscuit shoes.

These were the six generals assembled at the Round Table waiting for QT to enter the room and call the meeting to order. Each general had soldiers under them and homies as well, but only these six men were allowed to come and sit at the Round Table. The house that they were in was Gangsta's house located in Ladera Heights west of La Cienega Boulevard and Centinela Street — really, West Los Angeles. It was a big five bedroom, four bathroom house with a game room, family room, and of course the War Room. There was a large swimming pool with a Jacuzzi in the back yard. Gangsta also had two pit bull dogs, one solid black named Santana and the other one solid white named Blocc. They only listened to Gangsta, QT, and Rocc. They were both big chested, big headed, with their ears clipped, and it seemed like their muscles were bulging from everywhere. They were both house-trained and always stayed in the house at night. Gangsta had been given 25-years-to-life but he was appealing his sentence because he should have been charged with manslaughter becuz the fool he killed had pulled the gun on Gangsta trying to rob him. Gangsta played it off and got close enough to the fool to grab the gun. In the process of them wrestling for the gun, Gangsta shot the fool three times. The police wanted Gangsta so bad they took the opportunity to get some false witnesses to testify against him, which sent him to jail for 25-to-life, which really meant a life sentence. Now QT was running things but he still consulted Gangsta in certain situations.

As QT walked into the room, everyone fell silent. At QT's side were both of Gangsta's pit bulls. "Sit," he told them as he headed to his seat at the head of the table. Santana and Blocc sat down immediately upon command. QT was 6' 2", brown skinned, big chested and solid from working out five days a week. He had light brown eyes, a bald head, and almost always had on a Gucci, Fila, Fila BJ, Nike or La Coc Sportif sweat suit with shoes to match. The whole committee wore big gold ropes with medallions with "G-Code" in diamonds spelled out on them, and two diamond earrings in their left ear. All of them stayed strapped 24/7. QT wore a shoulder holster with a 9mm Beretta. As QT walked to his seat at the head of the table, Goldie and the rest of the Mobb stood up. Goldie walked over to the sound system and cut the music off. Once QT sat down they all sat down. Everyone at the table bought their dope from QT. Either QT or Gangsta had put them all down and their loyalty as well as their money was owed to the G-Code Mobb. It didn't matter if they could go find cocaine for a better price. Once they took the G-Code oath and was put down with free cocaine, they didn't come up off their loyalty and money — that was part of the G-Code.

"So what's been going on out there? Is everything all good?" QT asked.

QT always started on the left side with his brother Rocc and worked his way around the table to see what was going on. But in reality, he already knew everything going on on the streets, he just wanted to hear it from his generals. Rocc ran the Santa Fe apartments off Santa Fe and Compton Boulevard. The apartments covered a full blocc on both sides of the streets.

"Everything is cool in the Fays," Rocc said. Everyone called the apartments the Fays. "Money is good, the Compton dum-dums have been a little hot but we all good." Compton dum-dums were the police. "I'm still clocking about a hundred grand a week and three hundred grand on the first and fifteenth, so we good. I had to show this bitch ass nigga that came over there trying to open up shop that my Gangsta is bona fide and ain't to be fucked with."

"Yeah, I heard about that. Who was the fool?"

"Some nigga that claim he was from the old school and used to stay in the hood. This nigga opened up a spot right across from one of mine, and he was short stopping my clientele. I just pistol whipped the nigga and made him get naked and shot him in the ass."

The whole table broke out in laughter and QT asked, "What was this nigga's name?"

"Some shit like Madd Mikey or Madd Mike. Shit, I don't know," Crip Crazy said.

"I know that nigga. He used to try and claim the blocc. You got to watch that nigga, he a scandalous muthafucka. Next time you see him, it would be best to just smoke that fool and get him out of the way," QT said. "If it's like that, whoever see that nigga, get him out of the way. Rocc, you should know better anyway. Never give a nigga action at getting back. That's part of the G-Code."

"I know, Cuz, I fucked up. Gangsta taught me to never under-estimate anyone. I slipped."

QT asked, "Big Bam, what's up on your end?"

Big Bam had Santa Fe and Pine Street sowed up. "Everythang is everythang, Cuz. I got that muthafucka rolling twenty four seven, you should see those fuckin base heads. They coming through that bitch three, four, five in the morning like zombies, they be looking like the living dead. The money is good. I ain't got no complaints."

"Lil Man, what's up on your end?" QT asked.

Lil Man ran Golden Street. "Cuz, them muthafuckin Mexicans—" Lil Man looked at Boxer and said, "no offense, but them mutha-fuckin T-Flats tried to open a spot on Golden. I had to send the homies to close that bitch down. Shit, it was gun play and all. I know we going to end up at war with them fools. But other than that, money cool. We good."

"Cuz, fuck them muthafuckas and anybody else that's trying to step on our toes. This is our hood. My brother started this shit and ain't nobody going to capitalize on this shit but us. If we have to go to war with them fools or anybody else, we will." QT rarely raised his voice but he did now and everyone in the room knew he was dead serious. They all nodded in agreement. "Boxer, what's up with your end?"

Boxer had the south side of the hood which consisted of Willow, Rose, and Spring streets. He had spots on all three streets. "We all good, Cuz, the money good and ain't no problems," he said.

"That's what I like to hear," QT said. "Crip Crazy, what's up on your end?"

Crip Crazy ran the north side of the hood which consisted of Rose, Spring, McDivitt, and Willow streets. "Cuz, I'm good, you know if shit wasn't right it would cee some dead bodies somewhere around that bitch."

QT smiled becuz he knew Crip Crazy was real about what he was saying. Both Goldie and QT ran Tucker, Kay, Peck, Van Ness and Short streets, so he knew they were cool. "I already know Goldie's shit is straight," QT said. "I got a surprise for you niggas. Follow me."

Everyone got up and started to follow QT until they had to pass Santana and Blocc. Goldie said, "Cuz, what up with the dogs?"

QT turned around, smiled, and told the dogs to go upstairs. They immediately obeyed his command. Everyone followed QT out the back door to the back yard. When they got to the pool area there were ten females already naked in and around the pool. Rocc spoke first. "I love this Gangsta shit." Everyone voiced their agreement.

QT didn't have a steady woman becuz he had yet to run into one that fit his criteria to be his woman. So he had many and plenty, and didn't give a fuck about any, until that special one came along. QT wanted a street smart, book smart, and Gangsta bitch that was down for him like Santana and Blocc were — do-or-die — and of course, she had to be beautiful.

As QT watched his homies choose different women, a pretty, sexy Puerto Rican about 5' 6", with 36-inch breasts, hazel eyes, a nice fat ass, thin waist, and hair down to her ass walked up to QT. She kneeled down in front of him, pulled his sweat pants and boxers down and proceeded to give him some head. QT loved to get head and this beauty was sucking him like a pro. When QT opened his eyes, everybody was naked and was getting head or fucking or both. Big Bam had two females — one he was fucking doggy style and the other one was on the ground under the other female licking on Big Bam and the female. QT stopped the female that was sucking his dick, put on a condom, put her on the lower diving board doggy style and entered her from behind.

Two hours later, after QT escorted the females to the front door, the homies were in the back yard eating pizza and buffalo wings that QT had ordered. QT went back to the back yard and asked, "So what up for tonight? It's Wednesday Sport's Night at the Carolina West. Ya'll want to roll or what?"

QT knew that they would roll just becuz he was rolling but he asked anyway. Everybody agreed to meet up in the hood at a spot QT had on Tucker Street at 9 p.m.

Before Rocc left, QT pulled him to the side and told him, "Cuz, you watch yo ass, don't be out there slippin. Keep a couple of yo boys wit you until we get that nigga."

"Cuz, I got this, don't trip," Rocc said. "I will find that bitch ass nigga and handle my business."

After everyone left, QT way lying back in his big sauna smoking on a Lemac (Camel spelled backwards) and thinking about his trip to go see Gangsta the coming weekend. QT missed his big bro. It had been three years since QT had taken over the G-Code Mobb. He didn't want to let Gangsta down, that's why he didn't drink or smoke weed; he wanted to always be on his Ps and Qs. He knew that it was not always about the use of force; you still had to be able to combine strength and smarts with street sense in this game. QT got out of the sauna, put in an Isley Brothers tape and listened to "Fight the Power."

Chapter 2: The One

Far away from where QT was in Ladera Heights on the west side, on the east side at the Compton Police Station was Police Detective Beckman, a short, chubby, white man with blond hair, blue eyes, about 5' 8" and 200 lbs, who stood looking up at his partner, David Ross. Ross was white, dark haired, 6' 2", 210 lbs, and had brown eyes with a big ass head. They were in an interrogation room with one of their snitches.

Beckman was saying, "Look here, asshole, this gun charge is going to send your black ass back to the penitentiary this time and you know what happens to cute motherfuckers like you."

The snitch's name was Green Eyes, because of the color of his eyes. He was mixed with black and something. He had long hair, light skin, green eyes. "I told you, I don't know nothing about QT. I live in the hood and claim Crip but I don't kick it with that crowd."

"Well, you better figure out a way to fit into that crowd or your pretty ass is going to prison," Beckman said. "Shit, once you get to 4800 in the L.A. County Jail, that ass will probably be busted. You know that's the gang module and most of the motherfuckers in there are getting life for murder. I bet they would love to get ahold of your yellow ass."

Ross said, "Look, we ain't going to play with your ass. Either you work for us and get into QT's organization and give us something to bust his ass with, or your ass is grass. It's either your ass or his ass. Now, who's ass is it going to be?"

Green eyes started to cry. He knew that QT would kill him if he found him out, but he had heard the stories about niggas getting raped in 4800 and made to wear make-shift panties made out of boxers all day everyday. And also having to clean the cell and make beds like a bitch and often getting a spanking with a shower shoe for no reason at all.

As Green Eyes thought about that, tears ran down his face. Yeah, he claimed Crip but he knew if he was tested — and he would be tested in 4800 — surely he would fail. He wiped the tears from his face and asked, "What do I have to do?"

Smiles spread across the detectives' faces. They knew they were sending Green Eyes to his death if he was found out but they didn't give a fuck because the only thing on their minds was busting QT, like they had done to QT's brother, Gangsta. That's how they had got their promotions to detective. If they could bust QT, they would move further up the ladder.

Ross said, "We are going to give you money to start buying dope from one of QT's boys. Eventually, as you buy more and more you will ask to deal with QT only. Once you deal with him a couple of times, we will send you in wired and we will bust his black ass."

Beckman tossed $1,400 in cash to Green Eyes and told him, "Here, start off buying an ounce at a time. If you cross us, you won't have to worry about that tender ass of yours because we are going to kill your sorry ass. Now, get the fuck out of here." Beckman gave him his card and added, "Call me once a week and let me know how things are progressing."

Green Eyes took the card and walked out the door.

Ross said, "If we can bust QT, we are on our way to the big time."

Beckman said, "No matter what it takes, we will get his ass just like we got his brother's."

They both laughed.

QT left his spot in Ladera Heights about 7:30. He left Santana and Blocc inside the house. There was a dog door on the back door to the house in case the dogs had to do their business. QT had a three car garage with a black 500 SEC Benz with Centron and Pirelli tires on it with the AMC kit. He also had a black 911 Porsche Turbo Carrera and a black Ferrari. QT chose to drive the fin hunned (500 Benz).

QT had on a Fila sweatsuit, a pair of Fila shoes, his 9mm Beretta in his shoulder holster, his presidential Rolex, chain and medallion with G-Code on it in diamonds, a pinky diamond ring on each pinky finger, two 2-carat diamond earrings in his left ear, and a gold rope bracelet to match the rope on his neck.

When he pulled up to the spot on Tucker, Crip Crazy, Goldie, and Big Bam were already there. It was 8:30. QT knew the others would be there soon. The spot on Tucker was his bachelor's spot: two bedrooms, one-and-a-half baths, a big back yard where he kept all seven of his Low Riders and also where he had another pit bull named Crip. So all together, QT had Santana, Block, and Crip. Crip was black with a white chest, white socks, and white on the tip of his tail, ears clipped, and just as muscular and big as the other two. Crip was also trained and had the run of the back yard and the house.

By 9 p.m., everyone was there and they all had on their pieces and they drove Benzes or Porsches. Everybody rode alone because they knew that they would be going home with something. Even though everyone was strapped, there were four cars with three homies each from the hood that followed QT and the crew to the club.

When they got to the club, the line was long as usual but QT wasn't trippin becuz he never stood in line anyway. Everybody that was anybody knew who QT was. There were a lot of major players in L.A. and Compton but QT and the G-Code Mobb was one of the most feared. They parked, got out of the cars, and all headed for the front door of the club behind QT. People in line just watched. The ones that didn't know asked the others. He walked up the steps to the front door of the club, whispered in the ear of one of the security guards who nodded yes, and QT and all of his crew went in.

Once inside the club they found four tables that were occupied by some busters. Crip Crazy and Big Bam told them they had to beat it. One of them started protesting when one of his partners grabbed his arm and whispered something to him. He immediately got up and left with the rest of his partners.

The club was packed. There were other major players in the game there and the women were wall to wall. There were phones at the tables so that you could call other tables if you wanted. Whodini's "Friends" came on. QT felt like dancing so he got up and asked this fine chocolate female with long silky black hair, sexy dark eyes, and a killer body, if she would like to dance. Before QT had finished asking, she was up on her feet. They danced for a couple of songs and QT got her phone number and told her he would call her after the club was over. QT's homies were smoking chronic and drinking. QT just chilled, drinking on a 7-UP or a Coke. As QT was watching everyone, he saw Gangsta's wife, Tonya, walking over to his table.

Gangsta had married Tonya the day he got sentenced at court. He had been messing around with Tonya before he got busted. Tonya was cool, she wasn't a hood rat and she wasn't out there gold digging. She had a job even though QT gave her $3,000 a month on Gangsta's request. Tonya was 5' 8", carmel colored, and had long brown hair, a beautiful smile, white teeth, and a killer body. She sat down at the table with QT.

QT said, "What's up, Sis, you kind of bored tonight I see."

"Yeah, I was at the pad chillin and decided I would come out and relax a little since I don't have to be to work tomorrow until noon."

"What's up with my brotha?"

"He cool. We have a family visit coming up in two weeks."

"Shit, I know he happy about that. I'm going to see him this weekend. I finally got me a fake ID and got approved on his visiting list. He's been sending photos. That nigga's getting big. What they feeding that nigga in there?"

"I'm the one feeding his ass. I send him his quarterly package and four more every quarter to some niggas that don't get shit from the streets. So they get it for him for a carton of cigarettes."

"Why didn't you tell me so I could give you the money for that? You know I got you on whatever," QT said.

"I'm cool. I make good money on my job, and that three thousand you give me every month, I puts that up," Tonya said. She stood up to leave and added, "I want a dance before you leave."

Before QT could answer Tonya turned and walked away.

QT, Goldie and Boxer were all chilling at the same table when the phone rang. Goldie picked it up and the female voice on the other end of the line said, "You and two of your friends come over to table eight. I promise you, you won't be disappointed." Without another word she hung up.

Goldie relayed to the others what the female had told him.

QT said, "Cuz, ya'll go handle that shit. I'll hold the fort down."

As they got up to leave, QT was looking in the direction that they were walking. He saw this beautiful bronze skin female looking at him. When his eyes met hers, she didn't blink or look away. She just sat there and looked at him. So QT did the same thang; he just sat there and looked at her. For at least ten minutes, they just looked at each other without saying a word.

Finally, QT got up and walked over. He had started to call her table but he wanted to get a closer look at her. She was sitting by herself. Qt said, "What do you drink? I would like to buy you a few."

She smiled and said, "A few? You wouldn't be tryin to get me intoxicated, would you?"

QT said, "Fair exchange. Ain't no robbery. Your beauty has me intoxicated."

Again she smiled. "I must give it to you, you are good. Don't many men make me smile."

"I want to be the only man to make you smile. My name is QT. May I have the pleasure of knowing yours?"

"I already know your name is QT but I don't know what QT stands for. My name is Natalie. My friends call me Nat."

"Natalie. I like that, I also like Nat. The Q stands for Quint, short for Quinten."

"Quinten. I like that and I also like Quint too."

"So, can I buy you that drink?"

"You can buy me a 7-Up. I don't drink liquor."

QT said, "This is getting better by the minute becuz I don't drink either."

"So we have something in common." That made QT smile.

Natalie added, "You have a beautiful smile. You should smile more often."

"The more I get to see you maybe the more I will smile."

Tonya walked up to QT and tapped him on the shoulder. When he turned, she asked, "Can I have that dance?"

QT looked at Natalie and told her, "This is my sister-in-law,

Tonya. Tonya, this is Natalie."

They both spoke to each other and QT told Natalie not to leave, he would be back. Alexander O'Neal's "Innocent" was blasting from the speakers.

As they danced, Tonya laughed and QT said, "Why you laughing? I'm innocent."

"Yeah, right. Boy, when are you going to get you a good woman and settle down?"

"Whenever I find the one. You don't hook me up with yo friends no more."

"That's becuz all you do is hit it and leave them to cry on my shoulder."

They both started laughing. After the song went off, QT told Tonya he would get with her later and he went back to where Natalie was. When he got there, three females were sitting with her. The DJ put on "Be My Girl" by the Dramatics. QT asked Natalie to dance.

On the dance floor he held her in his arms and everything felt just right. They were the perfect fit. He smiled to himself. As his body moved in union close to hers, he started to get a hard-on. The sweats he was wearing wasn't giving him any support. Natalie looked him in the eyes and said, "I hope this doesn't happen with all the ladies you dance with."

QT replied, "Naw, baby. It ain't about the dance, it's about the woman."

After they danced, QT gave her his number just to see if she would call him and he went back to where his homies were. He was thinking to himself she could be the one. I'm not going to rush it, he thought: I have to see what she's about. She could be a gold digger.

When he got back to the table, Rocc, Crip Crazy, and Lil Man said, "Baby wouldn't even dance regular wit us but you got her to slow dance."

QT said, "That's becuz I'm the hog with the big nuts."

Crip Crazy said, "Cuz, my nuts are so big, when I take a shit they fall in the water."

Everyone started laughing. Rocc said, "That ain't shit, my dick so long when I take a shit if I don't hold my dick up and flush the toilet, my dick be going down the hole in the toilet."

Everybody was saying nigga please, if you got dick like that, you in the wrong line of business.

When the club was over, the chocolate female that QT had first danced with and got her number walked up to him. "So what's up with the rest of the night?"

QT answered, "Follow me to the pad." QT was going to Compton on Tucker because he didn't take females that he just met to his house.

She said all right and went to get her car. QT didn't want her riding with him becuz he didn't want to have to take her home in the morning.

As QT and his homies were walking to their cars, QT saw Tonya walking to her car. She passed by a nigga that tried to grab her by the arm and talk to her. He was with three of his boys. Tonya snatched her arm away and kept walking. The nigga yelled out, "Fuck you, you punk ass bitch, you ain't all that. You lucky I don't slap yo ass."

That was all QT needed to hear. His homies could see the fire in his eyes and they knew the shit was about to hit the fan. QT walked straight up to the nigga, 9mm in hand and hit him right above his eye. Blood squirted everywhere. Before his homies knew what had happened they were surrounded with guns in their faces. The nigga that QT hit was now on the ground.

QT said, "Bitch ass nigga, you gonna slap my sister." He cocked the 9mm back.

He was at the point of no return when Tonya ran up to him. "No, not here. He ain't worth it. It's too many witnesses. Yo brother needs you out here."

That's what saved the nigga's life—Tonya saying that Gangsta needed QT on the streets.

QT looked at the fool. "Tell her you sorry, you sorry ass nigga."

He looked up, beaten and battered, and said, "I'm sorry, I'm sorry."

They searched him and his homies to make sure they wasn't heated, then left. Once Tonya was in her car and gone, QT went to one of the cars with three of his lil homies in it and told them, "When them niggas leave, follow them and smoke they ass. All of them."

QT and the rest of his homies pushed back to the hood. As QT rode to the hood he thought to himself, I ain't giving no nigga action to get back at me. If I get into it with a nigga, he dead. Fuck him.

As the four fools that almost got smoked rode off in their car, the one that got pistol whipped spoke. "I don't give a fuck who that nigga is. Ain't no nigga gonna do me like this. I'm gonna kill that nigga. This shit ain't over." All the other niggas in the car agreed.

QT's lil homies got the AK47 out of the trunk of the new Camaro they were in. Keebo, Moonie and Lil Ken were in the car. Lil Ken was driving, Moonie was in the passenger seat, and Keebo was in the back seat. Lil Ken said, "Cuz, I'm going to pull up on the side of them and, Moonie, you blast the driver in the head. When the car stops we all get out and smoke they ass. We can't fuck this up. This car is new with no plates so all I got to do is get it painted."

When Lil Ken pulled up on the side of the Benz the occupants were so busy talking about revenge that they didn't see Moonie pointing the gun at the driver's head and pull the trigger. The driver's head exploded when Moonie blasted him with a .45 automatic. The car swerved to the right into a pole. Before the occupants could react, Keebo had the AK47 and Lil Man and Moonie had .45s and were walking up on the car unloading on the dummies inside. Lil Man made sure they were dead. He shot them all in the head. This didn't take more than a minute once the car had wrecked. Before anyone could ID them, they were on their way home to Compton.

When QT got to the spot on Tucker Street the only homie that was with him was Goldie. The other homies had either picked up females or had females follow them to wherever they was going. QT pulled his Benz in the driveway behind the gate so it couldn't be seen. Then he took the chocolate female that had followed him from the club into the spot.

The spot was plushed out with big screen TVs, Italian leather couches, top-of-the-line Yamaha sound system, portraits of different Gangstas on the wall, king size bed, the works. As he had baby sit down on the couch, the lil homies pulled up. QT turned the sounds on in the house. Anita Baker was in the deck, the song "Angel" filled the house through the surround sound system. QT told baby that he would be right back and to get comfortable. When QT got outside the lil homies were still excited telling Goldie how it went down.

QT asked, "Is it a done deal or what?"

At the same time all of them said, "Yeah, dem niggas history."

QT said, "Give all the guns to Goldie and go burn that car as soon as you leave here. I will buy you another one tomorrow. You can keep the insurance money. Keebo and Moonie come see me later today. I got something for ya'll too."

When they left, QT told Goldie, "Break them guns down and get rid of them. We got plenty of guns. Gangsta taught me to always get rid of a heat when it's dirty."

Goldie put the guns in the trunk of his car and left to handle his business. When QT got back in the house, baby—who's name was Tasha—wasn't in the living room. QT cut the music down and heard the shower running. He smiled and cut the music back up a little as he got undressed. He opened the bathroom door and stepped into the shower with Tasha. QT knew that she had a nice body in clothes, but the clothes didn't do her justice. Her body was as smooth as silk without even a blemish on it. To top it off, her pubic hair was shaved off. Tasha soaped up the towel and washed QT from head to toe. Without saying a word she got down on her knees in the shower and started giving QT head. She knew what she was doing too. When QT was about to cum he thought that she was going to stop but she kept sucking and sucking and sucking until QT came in her mouth. She swallowed it all and just looked up at QT with a smile.

They got out of the shower and Tasha dried QT off then herself. They went into the bedroom and QT was lying on his back while Tasha sucked him back to hardness. QT reached over to the night stand and retrieved a Magnum condom and put it on. Tasha positioned herself over QT's dick and slowly eased herself down on it. QT didn't say anything but he thought to himself, damn, this is some good, tight, hot pussy.

Tasha was moaning, saying, "Oh, daddy, oh daddy, I didn't

know...I didn't know...oh...this dick is big and strong. Fuck me, daddy, fuck me, please, fuck me."

QT started stroking up as she was coming down. Tasha tried to use her hands on QT's thighs to stop his upward thrust. QT flipped Tasha over and put her in the doggy style position. Tasha was against the headboard so she couldn't go nowhere. QT started fucking her doggy style, slamming his dick into her. All she could do was holler, "Oh oh oh, daddy, please, please, daddy."

QT said, "Who's pussy is this?"

"It's yours, daddy, it's yours, I swear it's yours."

"Bitch, you better not give nobody my pussy, you hear me?"

"Yes, daddy, I hear you. This is yo pussssssyyyyy...oh...I'm cumming!"

QT really started banging that pussy until he came. He rolled off her, took the condom off, and stuck his dick back in Tasha's mouth. She started sucking. QT knew he didn't want her for his woman but she was a good fuck and he would have her on call. Plus, he wanted to fuck her in her nice fat ass but that would have to wait for another time. QT looked up and saw Crip sitting in the middle of the door watching. He laughed and told him to go in the other room. Crip got up and went as he was told. Crip knew that when QT brought females there, not to bite them or growl at them.

So he wasn't surprised when he woke up to see Tasha rubbing Crip's back by the bed. They took a shower together and QT got his dick sucked once more. Afterwards, they got dressed and went their separate ways. QT told Tasha he would call her.

Chapter 3: Gangsta

When QT got home and walked in the front door, Santana and Blocc were there to welcome him. They knew not to jump up on QT unless he motioned for them to. All QT had to do was hit his hand against his chest and that was the sign. They both started wagging their tails and jumping up on QT. He fell to the ground and started wrestling with his two loyal friends. After playing with the dogs for fifteen minutes, QT fed them and went to the game room where he had his weights. After putting on his workout apparel, QT went to the fridge, poured himself a large glass of orange juice and went to work out.

He loved listening to the NWA's *Straight Out of Compton* while he worked out. His favorite song was "Fuck the Police." After working out for an hour, QT took a shower and checked his messages on the answering machine. There were two messages, one from Goldie saying all was good—which meant he had taken care of the guns.

The other message was from Natalie. It said, "Hey there you, I waited to take you to breakfast but I guess you didn't make it home this morning. Call me." Natalie left her phone number.

QT smiled and wrote it down. He got dressed and headed back to Compton. He was in his new Chevy Lumina that he had parked in front of his house. It was bronze color with tinted windows, a cool sound system, and had stock rims and tires. QT really never drove his other cars to Compton unless it was night and then it was in and out or he parked the car in the driveway behind the gate so no one could see it. When QT got to the spot, Goldie was parked in front and waiting on him. Goldie was the only one that had keys to the spot besides QT. Goldie was also the only one besides QT and Rocc that could touch or command Crip to do anything.

Goldie got out and opened the front gate, and then the second gate so QT could park his car in the back. When Goldie opened the second gate, Crip was standing there at attention. Goldie told Crip to go in the back and he obeyed. QT pulled in the back yard and Goldie closed the gate and went into the house through the back door. Crip followed them in. They sat down in the living room.

QT asked, "How many kilos do we have left?"

"I checked the spot this morning on my way here and there's only ten kilos left."

QT picked up the phone and dialed. A female answered. "Hey, what's up?" QT asked. "Is Carlos in?"

Five seconds later, Carlos got on the phone. "Hey, what up?"

"I need to see you tomorrow for lunch at the same place."

Carlos asked, "You want to eat the same thang?"

"Yeah, but better still, I will eat somewhere else and Goldie will be eating there."

Carlos said, "All right." He hung up the phone.

Carlos was QT's Columbian cocaine connection. That whole conversation meant that Goldie would meet him tomorrow at Carlos' spot to pick up one hundred kilos, the same number as QT got the last time they met. QT was going to start sending Goldie because Gangsta told him since he was the man and could trust Goldie with his life, to start sending him and to kick back and take less chances.

"I'm going to see Gangsta this weekend. I'm leaving tomorrow morning, that way I can see him Saturday and be back Saturday night. It's only about a six and half hour drive."

Goldie said, "You taking a freak with you to keep you company?"

"Yeah, I got someone in mind but I got to see what's up first."

There was a knock on the door. It was Moonie, Lil Ken, and Keebo. Goldie let them in immediately. Crip stood up and faced them. QT said, "Calm down, Crip. Sit." Crip sat back down but kept his eyes on them.

Keebo said, "Cuz, I need a dog like that. He ain't no joke." His other two homies agreed with him.

QT said, "Check this out. I'm promoting all three of ya'll. From now on, ya'll won't be selling rocks. I'm going to give each one of ya'll a half a bird. You can sell ounces, half ounces, or quarter pieces.

I'm giving this shit to ya. You earned it. All I demand is that you buy from me. This is not up for discussion. I don't care if you can get it a thousand dollars cheaper somewhere else. It's about loyalty, respect and honor. All we really have in this life is our name and our word. If yo name and word ain't shit, you ain't shit. Don't think you can sneak off somewhere else and I won't find out either. So do I have ya'll's word on this or what?"

Keebo spoke first. "Cuz, it's about more than the money to me. You my homie and I love you. Cuz, you got my word."

Lil Ken said, "Cuz, you my nigga. If a nigga got a problem wit you, he got a problem wit me. Money don't make me, I make money. Cuz, you got my word as well."

Moonie said, "Cuz, I don't got a real family. You and the homies is my family. Ya'll all I got. Never will I let money come between that. You got my word too."

QT didn't show it but he was real proud of all of them. He said, "Do ya know the first three rules of the G-Code?"

They nodded yes and at the same time said, "Never snitch, death before dishonor, you fuck with one you got to see us all."

QT smiled and said, "Okay. Live by it. Get wit Goldie later and he will hook ya'll up. Keebo, you go with Rocc. Moonie, you go with Crip Crazy and, Lil Ken, you go with Boxer. Goldie, let the homies know what's up."

QT went into his bedroom, opened the floor safe in the closet and took out $30,000. He went back to the living room and tossed $20,000 to Lil Ken. "That's for your car." He tossed Moonie and Keebo $5000 each. "Goldie will give ya'll some more straps." QT shook all of their hands, hugged them, and said, "Don't blow yo money and don't buy a car unless you got enough money to buy it twice, and still have yo recop money. That's real talk and don't fuck wit nobody you don't know, I don't care who brings them to you."

After the youngstas left, QT said, "I think they are going to be all right."

Goldie replied, "It seems that way but we'll see."

"Follow me to my house so I can give you that money to recop tomorrow. Take Boxer with you."

When QT got back from giving Goldie the money to recop, he called Natalie. The phone rang three times before she answered. "Hello?"

"What's up, beautiful?"

"Hi QT. I was wondering if you were going to call me."

"How could I not call you. I got to have you."

"You don't even know me, how you got to have me?"

"What are you doing right now?"

"Just relaxing. I just got out of the tub."

"Let's go to the marina to Aunt Kizzie's and eat some soul food." She asked, "Where are you?"

"I'm in Compton, off Long Beach Boulevard on Tucker Street. The address is five-twenty-three. It's off the left hand side of the street. Come pick me up."

"I'll be there in about an hour and a half," she said.

"I'll see you when you get here."

He hung up and QT went to the back yard to feed Crip.

After Natalie hung up, she thought to herself, this nigga can't live in Compton because the phone number he gave was an L.A. 213 number and Compton is a 310 number. It don't matter though because I like this nigga. I hope he's as cool as he seems to be. I'm tired of the fake ass want-to-be ballers that think I'm a gold digger or just a punk ass bitch. Shit, I'm more Gangsta than most of these bitch-made niggas that's out here in the game. I wonder why QT was pistol whipping that punk ass nigga Rudy last night?

Natalie knew Rudy and his boys because one of her girlfriends use to mess with Rudy. He was a wannabe Gangsta and a half-way baller. As Natalie was getting dressed, the TV news caught her attention. The reporter was saying, "...Four senseless homicides occurred here on Aviation about 2 a.m. It looks like a scene out of an Al Capone movie, there's so many holes in this Mercedes Benz it doesn't seem real."

All four occupants were dead and the names were being withheld until families could be notified. Natalie knew immediately that it was

Rudy because she knew his car. She thought, this nigga QT is a real Gangsta. She had already put it in her head that this was his doing. She didn't know it, but she only lived a few blocks away from QT in Ladera.

Natalie's man had been dead for three years. He was a dope dealer as well. His number one man had set him up to be robbed and killed but the robbery went wrong and the robbers ended up getting nothing. Natalie was the only one who knew where the money was. She had taken half the money and gave the rest to his mother, and moved from the valley and bought a house in Ladera. Natalie was already in her last year of college when everything went down. She got her degree in business and now she owned three Louisiana Fried Chicken franchises. She was still sitting on a total of $3 million cash that Uncle Sam didn't know about.

She hadn't had a man physically since her man was killed. She was definitely ready but no one had rubbed her the right way, except QT. She was turned on by him. After she got dressed, she got in her convertible 500 Benz and headed to Compton. She was an only child and when her mother and father found out she was in love with a Gangsta and drug dealer, they disowned her and forbad her to come back to their home. So she was on her own and wanted her own man so that she could make her own family.

When Natalie pulled up, QT was in the driveway talking to Goldie. QT didn't give her a chance to get out of the car, he got in and told Goldie he would get with him later.

Natalie said, "Oh, I can't even come into your humble abode."

"You can do that later. I'm starved, baby, let's go eat."

Natalie had Aura's song "Are you single?" jammin in the tape deck. She turned it up as they drove off. QT thought to himself how much he liked her.

He didn't say anything during the ride, he just enjoyed the music, especially when she put in the Isley Brothers' *Greatest Hits*.

Once they were in Aunt Kizzie's and seated, he asked, "So what do you do for a living? If that's not personal."

"I manage a fast food restaurant."

QT smiled and said, "Is that right? It sure must pay good for you to have that car and a Rolex watch and this Gucci outfit you have on. Not to mention those rocks on your fingers and in your ears."

"I get by. Where's all the jewelry you had on last night?"

QT replied, "I only wear jewelry when I'm going out. All I need for days like this is my gold Whittnauer watch, one pinky ring, and two diamond studs in my ear."

"Tell me this: why do all of your crew, except the guy that was in your driveway, have bald heads?"

He smiled and said, "That's just a neighborhood thang. The guy in my driveway is not from my hood."

"But he's part of your crew?"

"Why do you keep saying 'my crew'?"

"I've been around real niggas, so I know what's what."

He smiled. They ordered their food and talked some more. On their way back to Compton, she put in Chapter 8's "I Just Want to Be Your Girl." When they got to the spot, QT got out and opened the gate to let her pull her car in the back behind his. Crip already knew to be cool.

When Natalie saw all the Low Riders she said, "They are all so beautiful. I've never rode in one before. One day, will you take me for a ride?"

"I don't let just anyone roll in my Low Lows, but you are special so I can make an exception for you."

Natalie smiled. "I'm glad that you consider me special. Your dog is beautiful. Can I rub him?"

"Call him. If he comes to you then it's all right."

As soon as Natalie called, the dog immediately came to her. QT watched and said, "He likes you. That's a good sign."

"What's his name?"

"Crip."

Natalie looked at QT and said, "You too much."

They went into the house and QT told her to have a seat. He wasn't expecting any sex but he wanted to change the sheets on his bed. To his surprise, Goldie had left him a note saying he had one of the home girls come straighten the spot up and QT could thank him later. QT smiled and thought, that's my nigga. When he went back to the living room, Crip was lying across Natalie's feet on his back and she was rubbing his stomach.

"I see he trying to get in good with you. He lets females rub his head but he has never went this far. Come with me."

Natalied followed QT to his bedroom.

"Don't trip, I ain't going to try anything. I just want to relax and hold you." He cut on the sound system. Sade's smooth voice was flowing through the speakers. They took their shoes off and lay down on the bed. QT was holding her from behind, his arms wrapped around her.

"I got a brother in prison. For life," he said. "He's in Folsom and I'm going to drive up there tomorrow to see him. I was wondering if you didn't have to go to work, would you roll with me? You will have to stay in the hotel while I visit him, but I sure would appreciate your company."

She smelled real good and touching her made him hard all over again. Even though he tried to control himself, he couldn't. She totally turned him on.

Natalie turned over. Her face was only inches from his. "Yes, I'll roll with you. I don't know why, but I trust you and I feel safe with you."

Even her breath smelled good. QT didn't know what to do because usually he didn't give a fuck what a bitch thought but Natalie was different. "I will always protect you. I will always keep you safe," he said. He didn't know why he said what he said, but at the time that's what he was feeling.

Natalie moved the short distance that was between them and kissed QT on his lips. Slowly, she slid her tongue into his mouth. QT didn't like kissing but for some reason, this felt good. He slowly kissed her back. They just lay there kissing for what seemed like forever. QT's dick was so hard that he thought it might bust. But he wasn't going to rush it and he didn't want to have sex with her there in that bed. He wanted it to be special.

After all the kissing they held each other. Later, after they had slept for a while, QT told her, "I really live in Ladera. This is just a kick it spot."

She said, "I figured that much because I didn't see your Benz, and there's not that many outfits in the closet."

"Where do you live?"

"I live in Ladera too."

They both started laughing. They told each other where they lived and they both went home to get dressed so they could go out to dinner together.

As Natalie got dressed, she thought how she really wanted to make love to QT but she didn't want to rush it either. Fuck it, she thought, that nigga is going to be mine. I can see myself having his babies. If he tries to get into my panties tonight, I'm not going to stop him.

When she got to QT's house, she wasn't surprised by it. She figured that he would live in something nice like that. She had a nice three bedroom, two bath house, with a family room and a swimming pool and Jacuzzi. But this was a step above hers.

Just as she was about to ring the bell, QT opened the door. On one side sat Santana and on the other sat Blocc. QT told the dogs to go upstairs and they did.

Natalie looked beautiful. Her hair was hanging down the middle of her back. She had on a one piece cream and brown colored Coogi dress that came to about six inches above her knees, a pair of 4-inch heels, and a waistline cream mink coat. She had all the accessories: rings, watch, earrings, tennis bracelet, and she smelled good enough to eat.

QT had on a black pin-striped Armani suit. When he saw baby he told her to make herself comfortable, then went upstairs and changed into a cream-colored, pin-striped Armani suit with a short sleeve, crewneck tan Armani shirt, a pair of brown gator shoes, and all his accessories. Over it he wore a tan and brown three-quarter length mink coat.

When he got downstairs, Natalie was seated on the couch in the den rubbing Santana's and Blocc's backs.

"You just going to steal all my dogs."

Natalie smiled. "I love dogs, especially these kind. What are their names?"

"The black one's name is Santana and the white one's name is Blocc."

"You are serious about yo Gangsta."

"My Gangsta is official. Let's roll. I'll drive."

They went to the garage through the den. QT cut the light on the Benz, Porsche, and Ferrari which were sitting there shining like new money. QT walked to the passenger side of the Benz and opened the door for Natalie.

She said, "Oh, you are a gentleman too. I like that."

They went to dinner at Gladstone's on Pacific Coast Highway. All the women's eyes were glued to QT and all the men were glued to Natalie. Everyone wanted to know who they were. They thought they were a celebrity couple. Most patrons were white and the few blacks wanted to be white.

After dinner they went back to QT's house. As soon as they got inside, QT pulled her to him and kissed her softly on the mouth. She parted her lips and they explored each other's mouths. QT picked her up and carried her upstairs to his room.

They both started to undress. Natalie's body was flawless and QT wanted to explore all of it. She lay down on the bed on her back. It had been three years since she had had sex. She could tell that QT was well endowed from her feeling him at his house in Compton, but when she finally saw his manhood as he got naked, she almost moaned out loud.

QT lay on top on her and started kissing her from her forehead on down. When he got to her breasts he took his time giving both all his attention. She had beautiful breasts with dime-size brown nipples. Nat was moaning and almost ready to explode. QT hadn't even got to her honey sweetness yet. He went down from her breast to her stomach, down to her navel, then down her outer thighs to her inner thighs. Nat was moaning; it felt so good.

When QT licked from the bottom of her pussy up between the lips to her clit, then slowly, softly started sucking. She couldn't take it anymore. She started shaking uncontrollably and tried to push QT's head away but he wanted to make sure she would be his and only his.

Nat started screaming, "Oh oh oh, baby baby baby, please baby please...I'm cumming...oh...it feels so so good."

Right when Nat started cumming, QT stopped and positioned himself above her. He guided his manhood into her and she lost her mind.

"Oh baby, I love you, baby. I love you, oh, baby I love you. I don't what nobody but you. Oh baby, it feels so good...fuck me, baby, please, fuck me good...it's been so long."

Nat started bucking like a horse. "Oh oh oh, I'm cumming again!"

Tears ran down the side of her face. She knew that this was the man—her man—and she would ride and die for him.

QT was on the verge of cumming and really started pounding that pussy. All Nat could do was scream and holler and hold on to QT. It was a hell of a ride.

After he came, he rolled off. Nat's legs were still shaking. He pulled her to him and held her in his arms. He whispered in her ear, "I love you too, Nat."

The tears came like a flood. She had wanted to feel this love and hear the words for so long. Now that she had, she would never let go. This was for life.

After awhile, Natalie broke their embrace and slid down to QT's dick. She wanted to please him as well. She hadn't given head since her man was killed but she knew how and she was good at it. Slowly, she took him in her mouth and slowly, QT's dick grew larger and larger. She couldn't take him all in completely but she did give him a hell of a blow job from deep throating him to sucking and licking on his balls. Before QT could cum, he stopped her and turned her over doggy style. He mounted her and slowly began to make long slow love to her. All Nat could do was moan and say over and over, "Baby, I love you, I love you, I love you." This time they came together. QT rolled Nat over on her side and held her close to him as her legs shaked uncontrollably. He held her tight with his manhood still inside of her. Later, they fell asleep in each other's arms.

The next morning they took a bath together. Nat made them breakfast. She put on a pair of QT's boxers and a white Polo shirt. She had brought clothes for the trip but they were still in the trunk of her car. QT called Goldie to make sure everything was cool. Goldie told him to tell Gangsta he sends his love. He told QT he would hold down everything til QT got back.

QT and Nat left about 11 a.m. in his Benz. Nat told QT all about her prior boyfriend and what had happened to him and how she hadn't been with anyone for three years. QT held her hand as he listened.

When she was finished, he said, "Baby, I know this is fast but, will you marry me?"

Once again, tears ran down Nat's face as she said, "Yes, baby, I will marry you. Anytime, anywhere."

QT hadn't planned on getting married but he knew in his heart that Nat was the one for him. He was also tired of going home alone. Yeah, he could get pussy a dime a dozen but he wanted more and now that he had found it, he wasn't willing to let it go. He couldn't wait to tell Gangsta and Rocc the news. He also had to introduce Nat to his mother and sister. Everyone called his mother G-Moms because she was a Gangsta in her own right and didn't take shit from nobody. QT knew that his moms and his lil sister Lisa would love Nat just as he did. They got to the hotel about 5 p.m. They took a shower together, made love, and ordered room service.

The next morning QT got dressed in a blue and white La Cod Sportiff sweat suit with the tennis shoes to match. He had on most of his pieces, a fresh bald head that he had shaved in the shower, and his signature goatee.

Nat sat in the bed and watched him get dressed, admiring his body and good looks. When he came to kiss her goodbye, she said, "Don't let me have to come down there and beat them bitches off you. I know that they are going to be on your fine ass."

QT smiled and said, "I got a woman."

He kissed her and told her he would be back around 2 p.m. It was

7 a.m. when he walked out the door. When QT got to the prison, the front of it looked like an old castle from the 1600s with a graveyard on one side. As he parked the car, he could see all the regulars already in line, mostly females, some with kids, some alone. As QT got out of the 500 and strolled to the end of the line, the females were looking at him like he was breakfast. Some tried to look on the sly but others didn't care and was looking like "Nigga, what's up. So what if I'm going to see my man? What he don't know won't hurt."

QT got in line, blazed up a Lemac and thought about Nat. He didn't pay any of the females in line any attention. After QT went through all the bullshit of being searched, shoes taken off, filling out the paperwork, and putting up with guards' jealousy, QT finally got in. It took about two hours but it didn't matter to him, he wanted to see his brother. QT hadn't seen Gangsta in fifteen months. He loved his brother and respected him greatly. QT went to the vending machine and bought some ham and cheese sandwiches, two bags of BBQ chips, and two 100% orange juices.

About fifteen minutes after QT sat down, Gangsta appeared. The prisoners were dressed in blue jeans and blue button-up shirts and different kinds of dress shoes. You could look at Gangsta and tell he was different from most of the other inmates. He was a convict— there is a difference. Gangsta was 6' 3", broad shoulders, big chest, 19-inch arms, bald head, goatee, and had the coolest walk one could imagine. He just glided like a panther. His skin was like milk chocolate and he had medium brown eyes. His presence demanded attention.

As he walked towards QT, most all the other inmates spoke to him and their female visitors had lust in their eyes. QT stood up and they embraced, then shook hands.

QT said, "Damn, cuz, you getting bigger and bigger. Those photos don't give you justice."

Gangsta smiled, gave his lil brother a look over and said, "You ain't doin so bad yoself, lil bro. You look like you on a bust-a-bitch mission as clean as you are. What happened to the khakis, Stacey Adams biscuits and Ace Deuces?"

"I still got all that but that's my Crenshaw Skating Rink attire. This is my playa shit."

Gangsta laughed and said, "I feel you, cuz, so how has everything been going out there?"

"We are about ten million strong and that's cash, not counting the recop money. All our Mobb is straight, everybody happy and everybody getting money. The one thing I worry about is Rocc. You know he's still a cockhound and sometimes he let that pussy be having him slippin."

Gangsta said, "That could be a problem. I've been hearing about niggas getting kidnapped and tortured and murdered. Didn't cuz from Watts get got about a month ago?"

"Yeah, that was some fucked up shit, cuz. Got fucked over bad."

Gangsta's face was serious. "Cuz, you got to stay on Rocc. You know he thinks because we are his brothers niggas won't fuck wit him. It's some cut-throat niggas out there that don't give a fuck about us and nobody else, all they see is green. We both know that if any of ya'll get caught slippin, no matter what they say, they ain't going to let ya'll live."

QT said, "Fuck all them niggas. We live by the code and die by the code. A nigga got to kill me on the spot. Ain't no nigga handcuffin me, doin shit to me. He goin to shoot me on the spot or shoot me trying to take the gun from his ass."

Gangsta said, "It's a lot of hungry niggas out there. Everybody ain't getting money. You stay strapped and be careful going home at night. You know how to roll to see if a nigga is on you, don't take nothing for granted."

"Cuz, I stay on my P's and Q's. I haven't forgot nothing you taught me."

"Make sure Rocc keeps at least two homies with him all the time becuz he's reckless when it comes to those bitches," Gangsta said. "So what else is going on? Tell me something I don't know."

QT looked at Gangsta, smiled and said, "I'm getting married. Her name is Natalie."

QT ran everything down for his brother about Natalie, everything that she had told him including that she had her own money. When QT was finished he waited for Gangsta's reply.

"Congratulations, cuz. I couldn't have picked a better woman for you."

QT was relieved that his brother approved of Natalie.

"By the way, I knew her dude," Gangsta said. "He was straight, a stand-up nigga. I heard about that fucked up situation his main man put him in. That nigga still out there somewhere. The niggas that got busted for killing Ty—that was cuz's name—well, they didn't tell on Boo so he still out there."

QT said, "Who is this nigga that used to claim the hood, name Madd Mike?"

Gangsta said, "That nigga is a piece of shit. He can't be trusted and the nigga is sneaky. Why do you ask about that clown?

"He tried to open up shop in the Fays and Rocc striped that nigga naked and shot him in the ass."

"Find that nigga and smoke him. Sooner or later he will try to get some get back. What the fuck is wrong with Rocc? He knows you never give a nigga action at gettin back at you."

"Don't trip, crip, I'm on it. I'll find out where that nigga lays his head and handle it. So what's up inside this bitch?"

"Same niggas you see on the streets are the same niggas in here. Only on the street they can maneuver and get away from you. In here you got to go for what you know. I'm in control of the Compton Car so we cool. We ride with Watts, or if it's a Crip thang, we ride with all the other Crips. We cool, we got all that we need. I don't drink or smoke weed but the homies do. I still got that money hungry ass CO on the payroll so he keeps the homies supplied with weed, cocaine and heroin. They smoke the weed and sell the dope. I don't touch shit because I don't need shit—my books are fat. I let the homies use my CO so they can make them some money. the Mexican Mafia (EME), the Black Gorilla Family (BGF), the AB's (Aryan Brotherhood), the Bloods and the 415, and the police, are all against the Crips. But it don't matter—we deep and we strong and we control most of the dope."

QT said, "Cuz, you watch yo ass in this bitch becuz if anythang happens to you in here, whoever's responsible, they family on the street going to feel what I feel, and that's real talk."

"I got this in here, lil bro. You just concentrate on the shit out there. So when is the big date?"

"It's May now ... probably in July."

"I heard about you outside the club the other night. Slow yo roll."

"How did you hear about that shit so quick?"

"Soon as shit happens out there, we hear about it in here. You did what you was supposed to do, so it's all good."

"What do you mean by that?"

"Cuz, you know what I mean—no get back."

QT wondered how his brother found out about the club and the aftermath. They talked, laughed, and kicked it until it was time to go. QT hated leaving his brother behind but the lawyer told QT that he was on to something that maybe could bring his brother home. They embraced, shook hands, and QT told him he would be back soon. QT didn't even bring up that Gangsta's wife was at the club and everything that happened was becuz a nigga had disrespected her. QT figured if Gangsta knew about what he had done, then he also knew why he had done it.

When QT got back to the room Nat was looking sweet as ever with a Fila skirt on with the top to match, and some Fila tennis shoes with her hair in a ponytail. As soon as he saw her and smelled her, he wanted her. He didn't say a word. He walked up to her, pulled her towards him and slowly kissed her. He reached under her dress and slowly pulled her panties down. A low moan escaped from her. They made love, real love not lust. They made it back to QT's house around 11 p.m. They took a bath together. Nat cooked dinner for them and they went to sleep in each other's arms.

Chapter 4: In-Laws

QT woke up the next morning and he called his mother. He told her he was coming over for breakfast with a companion. QT's mom knew that she had to be special because he had never brought any female to meet her. After Nat got up QT told her that they were going out to breakfast. She wanted to cook for him but he insisted on going out.

QT's mom still lived in Compton where she had been for twenty-eight years and refused to move. Even when Gangsta wanted to buy her another house in Ladera, she refused. She lived in the hood in a modest three bedroom house, a tan stucco with brown trim. The lawn was immaculate.

When QT and Nat pulled up in the driveway, Lisa was standing on the front porch. Lisa was seventeen years old and fine to the bone. She had light brown eyes, a thin waist, 36-inch breasts, nice ass, hair that was cut shoulder length, white teeth and golden colored skin. Lisa ran to the car and hugged QT when he got out. He introduced her to Natalie and they hit it off instantly. When they went into the house, G-Moms was already setting the table with the china and food.

QT said, "Moms, this is Natalie."

G-Moms hugged her and said, "Hello, baby, glad to meet you."

Rocc came in and they sat down at the table. G-Moms said grace. Then she looked at QT and said, "Spit it out, boy. What's going on? You know you can't fool mama."

QT replied, "Me and Natalie are engaged to be married."

"It's about time, boy. Welcome to the family, baby." G-Moms knew that if QT was getting married, he really loved Natalie and she was happy for him.

Rocc said, "Congratulations, cuz. I need a lil niece or nephew to spoil. Welcome to the family."

They all ate breakfast and when QT was ready to leave, G-Moms said, "She's staying here with us. Lisa will take her home later. We got talking and shoppin to do."

QT knew moms wasn't taking no for an answer so he kissed his moms and kissed Natalie, and he and Rocc went to the spot on Tucker Street.

Green Eyes had already bought an ounce of rock cocaine from one of Goldie's lieutenants that worked on Peck Street around the corner from the spot. He called Detective Beckman.

"Yeah, this is Beckman."

"This is Green Eyes. I copped an ounce from one of QT's boys. What do I do now?"

"You fuckin sell it and keep copping until you can get to QT, you hear me? Don't worry about coming to jail because if you get picked up, I will get you out without charges being filed."

Green Eyes couldn't believe his ears. He had a free reign to sell dope. He thought to himself: fuck Beckman, I'm going to come up and get the hell out of town. Fuck that lil fat redneck bitch, I'll get this money and go to Seattle. Shit, I got family there.

Green Eyes cut the dope up into rocks and went to work slangin, no worries, no problems.

Beckman turned to Ross at the station and said, "Fuck this shit. Them fuckin feds are trying to come and step on our toes. They are starting a task force because of all the fucking gang related murders. Fuck these niggers and spicks. Let them kill each other is what I say."

Ross said, "We got to get that asshole QT before these damn feds get onto him because once they do, we are shit out of luck. Good thing for us, we've got ninety days to get that fucking nigger."

Across town in West L.A., on 34th off of Denker in Harlem Crip neighborhood. Madd Mike was recuperating from the beating and the gunshot wound in his ass. He had two younger brothers that were nobodies that wanted to be somebody. The older one's name was Jaybo and the younger one's name was Ceebo. They were rejects from Santana Blocc, and had tried to turn Harlem Crip when their moms moved to that neighborhood. The Harlems wouldn't accept them either so they were basically two busters that claimed Crip without a neighborhood. They were in Madd Mike's room discussing a retaliation plot. James Brown's "Big Payback" was playing in the tape deck.

"That young muthafucka must don't know who I am," Madd Mike told his brothers. "Cain't nobody disrespect me like that and get away with it. The bitch nigga should have smoked me. Fuck that nigga Gangsta, he got life and he ain't no threat, and QT's bitch ass is as good as dead too."

Jaybo said, "So how we going to get them niggas?"

"I got this shit covered. I don't want ya'll in this. Don't no nigga know how to creep like me. All I got to do is find out where QT lays his head. Rocc is easy. All I got to do is sick a bad ass bitch on that nigga. He's a cockhound. You niggas just stay out of Compton and don't fuck with nobody from Compton. When the shit hit the fan, them G-Code Niggas and the Santanas will be trying to figure out where I am. If they can't get me, they will get you."

Ceebo said, "Fuck that, we ain't scared of them niggas."

"It ain't about being scared, it's about being smart and living," Madd Mike said. "I got a crew ready and we will handle this shit."

When QT and Rocc got to the spot, QT called Rocc in the house. "Cuz, you know I went to see Gangsta yesterday. We talked about a lot of shit. One of them was that Madd Mike situation. Big bro said we got to smoke that nigga. Man to man, he's a bitch but he has to save face and he will blast a nigga if he can get close to you."

Rocc said, "So what's up? What I got to do?"

"Put the word out to all the OGs, twenty thousand dollars for where the nigga lays his head. All we want is the right address. Also, don't fuck wit no new bitches until we get this nigga. Gangsta said the nigga is sneaky, so we got to be cautious."

Rocc walked to the front door, turned and said, "Don't trip, Crip. I'm on it like yesterday."

When Rocc left, QT called his mom's house and told Nat to buy some jeans, a blouse and a jacket when she went to the mall. He also told her not to go home. They were going to hit Crenshaw later. It was Sunday, his Low Riding day.

QT hung up the phone and brought the dog Crip into the house. He called three baseheads that always cleaned his ridas and had them clean four of his ridas: a Crip blue-on-blue rag 64, a triple black Rag 62, a baby blue hardtop 63, and a yellow 64 hardtop SS with a white top and white interior. All of them were cut out (had hydraulics) and all of them were super clean. QT was going to roll the rag Crip blue 64, the other three he would let the homies that didn't have a rida roll. It was a ritual for the whole G-Code Mobb and the homies from SBC to roll out on Sunday nights to the skating rink and then to Crenshaw. QT usually always rode alone but tonight he would make an exception and have Nat with him. Besides, he wasn't looking to bring a freak back to the spot tonight—he had Nat and it didn't get any better.

When the baseheads were finished cleaning the cars, QT paid them and parked the cars on the street in front of the house. All the lil kids on the block would come look at the cars and each one would claim a car saying: "That's my car—no it ain't—that's my car—No, I called it first, that's my car. QT smiled becuz he thought back to when he used to do the same thing. One of the kids said "Hit the switches" then they all chimed in saying the same thing.

Gangsta had taught QT how to hit the switches when QT was twelve years old. QT got in the yellow 64 SS and pulled it into the middle of the street. The foe was super hot: it had two pumps to the front, two pumps to the back with fourteen batteries and three square dumps. QT hit the ass two times and it shot up in the air, the back wheels coming off the ground. Then he hit the front, playing with it up and down, getting in rhythm. Once he had a rhythm he hit the front. It shot up—the wheels coming about 16 inches off the ground.

The second hit, the wheels were about 45 inches off the ground and the third hit, the foe was about 60 inches up. It could have gone higher but the foe only had 12-inch strokes in the ass. The car slammed down on the back bumper, stopping the Foe from going any higher.

QT put the foe on three wheels and cut the sounds on. Parliament's "Auga Boogie" was screaming from the speakers. All the kids were in awe, saying, "No, no, no, that's MY car."

QT parked the Foe, and as he got out he saw detectives Beckman and Ross slowly driving by.

Beckman said, "Soon. Real soon."

"Not in this lifetime," QT told him and walked into the house to get dressed.

He took out his dark blue khaki suit, his blue Stacy Adams biscuits and his dark blue Stetson hat. By the time he was dressed, the homies had already started to arrive at the spot by 8 p.m. All the homies knew the dress code and they were dressed for the occasion. Whenever QT and his crew rode together, they rode deep and was always ready for whatever. Even though they were strapped they had at least three undercover cars with homies following them with the big guns like AK47s, SKSs, and Mini-14s.

By 8:30, they were ready to roll. The cars were already gassed up. It was a typical California night: warm, about 75 degrees, and there was no need for a coat—besides, QT's heater and AC worked. QT got in the rag Foe and took off leading the pack. He was bumpin "The Message" by Grand Master Flash and the Furious Five. As he drove he sang along to the song "Turned stick-up kid look what you done, did got sent up for an eight year bid. Now your manhood is took and you're a maytag spend the next few years as an undercover fag, being used and abused, served like hell until one day you found hung dead in a cell."

As QT rode, singing and rocking to the music, he really did appreciate the Low Rider movement. Just the feeling of the car dippin, top down, good music—the only thing missing was Nat and he was pulling up to his mom's house to get her. Before he could stop the car, Lisa and Nat were out the door. QT cut the music down and said, "Where do you think you going?"

Lisa said, "I want to go. You never let me go."

Nat said, "You know, I might need some company when you are talking with yo peeps."

QT said, "Get in but don't think you goin to make this a habit cuz you ain't."

QT didn't like having his sister around him and his homies becuz he knew that she was fine and he didn't want his homies—whoever it might be—come between him and his sister. He knew all his homies fucked around on their women plus there was a safety issue. G-Moms kept a tight rein on Lisa and QT didn't want to be the one to help her break it.

QT loved oldies and he put in a mixed oldies tape "The Fuzz." The song "For All Seasons" was on. Nat had never been in a Low Rider before but she loved the way the Foe rolled, dipped and bounced.

Nat said, "I got to get me one of these!"

"I got seven, what's mine is yours," QT told her.

Nat just smiled and realized once again she knew why she loved him.

They got to the skate depot in Cerritos in about thirty minutes. They all parked together and left the straps in the cars because of the sheriffs that were always posted in front of the rink. QT left two of the lil homies with the cars and instructed them to be cool and chill in the car so they wouldn't draw any attention to themselves.

Most of the homies had their own skates and the one that didn't had to skate with the rink's raggedy ass rental skates. QT had his own skates. Nat didn't have any so QT bought her a new pair inside the rink. QT could skate really good but came from years of experience. Nat wasn't a push over. Maybe she hadn't been skating in years but she knew how. The homies that didn't skate, like Big Bam, Crip Crazy, Boxer, and Goldie, just kicked it, fucking with different females, and they made sure that if anyone came into the rink they didn't get along with, they would prepare accordingly.

QT knew almost all the females at the rink, and even the ones he didn't know they knew who he was. He was having fun skating with

Nat and Lisa when a knucklehead rolled up on them and said, "I know you can't handle both of them. Let me have one."

QT tried to be cool and said, "Naw, playa, I got this."

The idiot made the mistake of trying to grab Lisa's arm and pull her to him. QT didn't think, he just reacted. It was so fast that if you wasn't right there you wouldn't have seen it. QT quickly moved Lisa out of the way and gave the idiot a quick two piece to the chin and head. He flew off his feet like he had been hit on a football field. He was out before he hit the ground. Some of the idiot's homies came and picked him up, trying to mad dog QT. That pissed QT off even more.

He said, "What's up, nigga? You got a problem wit me? Yeah, I knocked yo homeboy out."

The fool QT was talking to said, "Yeah, cuz, I got a problem wit you doin my homie like that. This Long Beach Four Corner Blocc Crips."

QT said, "What nigga? You wanna gang bang?"

Before QT could say anything else, there were about thirty Santana Blocc Crips at his side. One of the lil homies said, "Fuck yo hood, nigga, this our skating rink."

QT turned around to calm his homies down. He turned back to the nigga that was talking and said, "Yo homie was out of line and disrespectful. Either ya'll can accept what went down, or we can get into some Gangsta shit."

A nigga QT hadn't seen before walked up. He was about 6' 5", 240 lbs, and looked like he had just got out of the pen. He said, "Cuz, I apologize for these niggas. They don't know what they gettin into. I saw the whole thang and cuz was in violation." He turned to his homies and said, "Get that dumb ass nigga off the floor." He then turned around and said, "Tell yo brother Gangsta that Big Dave sends his love." He turned back around and walked off and his homies followed.

By now, the sheriffs had come into the rink but when they saw the crowd dispersing they kicked it for a minute inside, then went back outside. The skating resumed but QT wasn't in the mood. He was debating on whether to smoke the fool or not. QT, Goldie and Big

Bam went to the restroom. A minute later Big Dave walked in alone. He said, "QT, let me holler at you a minute."

QT's homies didn't budge. QT said, "You talk in front of them, these my homies."

"Cuz, me and yo brotha were driving partners in Folsom. We are homies and we always talked. He told me how he taught you and Rocc not to ever give a nigga get back, always handle yo business. I know how ya'll roll. I checked the young nigga and when I get back to the hood, I'm going to discipline his ass. You got my word, that nigga and none of the other niggas ain't got no beef with you or the Blocc. Ask yo brother about me. I do what has to be done and I get the job done. Shit, I ain't no punk but I got love for Gangsta so that means I got love for you and Rocc too. All I got is my word and my name and both of them stand on their own."

QT walked up to Big Dave, shook his hand, and said, "You got that, homie. One love."

They walked out of the restroom together. QT hoped that he hadn't made a mistake. Surely he would question his brother when he called about Big Dave. If Big Dave was on the up and up, it was all good. But if he wasn't, Big Dave would be like Abraham Lincoln: history. QT had a gut feeling that Big Dave was on the up and up because Gangsta wouldn't just talk to anybody, especially about his brothas and how they roll. Nat and Lisa were at the table waiting for him.

"What's up, baby?" Nat asked. "Is everything all right?"

"Yeah, baby, we cool."

Partners skating came on and Nat said, "Let's skate. We came to have fun, didn't we?"

QT smiled and said, "Come on, but don't try no hanky panky out on the floor."

"Yeah, right. You wish."

They skated to SOS Band's "The Finest."

After the rink was over and everybody was at their cars ready to roll, Big Dave walked up to QT and said, "If you ever need me, just holler and I'll be there." He gave QT a phone number and an address.

They shook hands again and QT said, "After I holler at my brother we will talk."

Big Dave nodded and walked away. QT pulled out first. Behind him were a total of twenty Low Riders and four undercover cars all under QT's command. Big Dave sat on the hood of one of his homie's cars and said, "Ya'll some lucky ass niggas because if I hadn't of been locked up with his brother and we were cool, none of us would have made it home alive tonight. Them niggas ain't no jokes. Them niggas Gangsta and they about money. Let's get the fuck out of here." True to his word, Big Dave disciplined his homies when they got back to their hood.

QT and his homies hit the 605 Freeway, to the 91 Freeway, to the 110 Freeway, and got off at Vernon Avenue. They dipped all the way down to Crenshaw Boulevard. As usual and true to form, Crenshaw was jumpin.

When they got to Crenshaw Boulevard Goldie and Lil Man pulled to the left side of QT and laid their cars in the middle of the street, throwing a road block so QT and the rest of the homies could make a right turn without the caravan being cut into by other cars. Once everyone had made the turn, Goldie and Lil Man hit the switches and their cars sprang up from the ground. They rode back up to their regular spots in the caravan and merged into line. It was a beautiful sight—straight Gangsta. QT loved this shit especially when they made their grand entrance.

The Shaw was packed in front of Winner Schitzel. Both sides of the streets were packed, people were standing outside of their cars, drinking, smoking, talking to females, kickin it with their homes, talking shit about who's car was the hottest. The music was bumpin, it was a hell of a scene. QT and his crew came through in a straight line with QT leading the pack. All of QT's cars were hot so it didn't matter that he was in the rag 64.

QT said, "Nat, you and Lisa hold on. I don't want ya'll flying out the car when I hit the switches."

He stopped in the middle of the street and laid the ass of the foe on the ground. He took a second to change the tape on his two knob Alpine. All his homies knew what time it was—they had done this a thousand times. Everybody put in NWA's "Straight Out of Compton." As soon as the song came on, QT eased off the brake and slowly hit the ass on the foe. After the second lick, the back wheels were off the ground. As QT pulled off, he started hitting the front of the foe. The foe was hot when it went up in the air. All QT, Nat, and Lisa could see was the stars in the sky. All eyes were on QT and his Mobb. Once QT started hitting his switches, all the rest of his homies started hitting theirs as well. It was a beautiful sight to see. It was an experience that Nat had never felt before. She was excited, happy, and scared all at the same time.

Once they got to the end of the block, QT put the foe on three wheels and so did all his homies. They made a left hand turn onto the island where Winner Schitzel was. Once the turn was made, QT let the front up, laid the ass, and slowly drove through all the looky lous. QT made sure everyone saw the mural on the trunk of the foe called "Gangstas Inc" with pictures of QT, Rocc, Gangsta and some more of his homies all G'd up with straps and standing on Rosecrans in front of the hamburger stand in the hood. The mural also had a list of all his homies that R.I.P. (rest in peace), and "Santana Blocc Crip" was written Gangsta-style in the background on the hamburger stand.

As he rode through, different homies from different hoods that he knew spoke to him. He spoke back showing respect to them as well. There were Crips from all different hoods all up and down the Shaw but where they were from was mainly Rollin 60s, Harlem 30s, 111th Neighborhoods, Main St. Mafias, Compton and East Coast's.

After they found parking they got out to check the scene. The first people QT saw were his homies Big Jess and Droopy from Main St. Mafia. They shook hands and embraced. Nat was at QT's side. He introduced her. "This is my wife-to-be, Nat. Nat, this is Droopy and that's Big Jess."

They exchanged hellos and Droopy said, "Cuz, I knew baby had to ce special cecuz I ain't never seen you rolling wit a female. And who is this other beauty that's wit you?"

QT said, "This is my lil sis and she's off limits. She's a square and I plan on keeping it that way."

Droopy said, "I feel you, homie. I'm the same way about my lil sis."

They went in front of the hot dog stand where QT was being greeted and was greeting others as they walked by.

Mad Dogg, Sleep Rocc, MooRocc, and Big F-Bone from 60s was in the street talking shit to a nigga that thought he had the hottest car; a tan 63 Impala. It was clean, but they were debating its hotness. Mad Dogg said, "Hey, QT. This nigga says he got the hottest shit on the Shaw."

QT said, "I got five thousand that say he don't."

Everyone got to oohing and aahing and placing bets at that.

The nigga in the 63 said, "I ain't got five thousand, but I got my pink slip." Everybody went off then.

QT looked at him. He knew that all his own shit was hot. As he looked in the nigga's eyes, he knew that the nigga was trying to bluff his way out of hopping. He asked Nat, "You like that car?"

She looked at the car and said, "Yeah, it's pretty." She didn't know what was about to happen; she thought they were just talking Low Rider shit.

QT looked at Boxer and said, "Go get the yellow foe."

Then everyone went crazy hollering and betting. QT looked back at Nat and said, "This is your wedding present."

But Nat didn't understand. "How much are you buying if for? I can give you half."

QT laughed and said, "I got this, baby."

The street part of the island was cleared so that the cars could be facing head to head. QT took his Stetson hat off and gave it to Nat to hold. Boxer pulled the foe in front of the tray. QT cut the foe off, put it in neutral, and put the Dayton hammer behind the back wheel so the car wouldn't roll backwards as he hopped it. He then sat in the 64, put a tape in the deck, found the song he was looking for and turned it up. It was Kurtis Blow's "These are the Breaks."

Everyone started laughing, singing, and hollering. "Go, go, go, go, go, go."

QT hit the ass on the foe and it shot up like a rocket. He looked at the nigga and said, "Take off, nigga, I can catch up."

The 63 took off. It was pretty hot but he hadn't even hit the back bumper after four hits of the switch. QT knew he had him. QT hit the 64 one time, two times, and the crowd was going crazy. The third time the 64 passed the 63 and slammed down on the back bumper. QT slammed the back bumper four times while the 63 was about an inch from touching the back bumper but never made it. QT put the 64 on three wheels, threw his hands up in the air, and looked over at Nat. "Baby, that car is yours!" Then he said, "Lil Ken, get my baby's car and park it with the rest of our shit."

QT got out and walked up to the nigga. "Cuz, where you from?"

He looked at QT with sad eyes. "I'm from Harlem 30s."

"This ain't personal, cuz, this was just business. What they call you?"

"Crazy Keith."

As Lil Ken got in the 63 and pulled off, QT went into his pocket and tossed Crazy Keith $3,000 and Crazy Keith gave him the pink slip. Some of Crazy Keith's homies were in the background talking shit. They were mad becuz not only did Crazy Keith lose the hop, they also lost money betting on him.

Killa Watt and Spookey from Harlem stepped up and said, "Ya'll niggas shut the fuck up. Cuz lost straight up."

Killa Watt, Spookey, and QT had done (CYA) time together. They walked up to QT and they all embraced and shook hands. Spookey said, "I told that nigga if he kept jumpin out in the street he was going to get run over."

QT said, "What's up, cuz? What ya'll niggas been up to?"

Killa Watt said, "Trying to get that loot, you know how we do."

"What ya'll dealing wit?"

Spookey said, "We getting two birds at a time for thirty-three even."

QT said, "Come get at me. I can give them to you for thirty even."

They looked at each other and Spookey said, "We will be ready in a day or two."

QT gave them his beeper number and said, "Hit a nigga. We can do something."

Nat had walked away with Lisa happy that she now had her own Low Rider. While they was rolling she had already decided to buy herself one. The money wasn't a problem and to top it off the 63 was one of her favorite colors, so that was cool. They walked across the street to the liquor store. Crip Crazy was with them. As they came out of the store, Nat looked over to her right when she heard what she thought was a familiar voice. As she turned to look, even though his back was turned to her, she knew it was him—the nigga Boo who had set up her man Ty.

She almost couldn't control herself as she took off across the street towards QT. Crip Crazy and Lisa didn't know what was up but they knew it wasn't good. When she got to QT, he was talking to Big Keebo from 111st Neighborhood Crips. Nat grabbed QT's arm and said excuse me and pulled him away.

QT knew that something was wrong by the way her eyes were looking, and Crip Crazy and Lisa ran up behind her. Nat reached under QT's shirt and grabbed for his Beretta. Tears started to come down Nat's face. QT looked at Lisa and said, "Go to the car. Now."

Lisa wanted to know what was going on but the tone in QT's voice kind of scared her. Crip Crazy escorted her to the car.

QT said, "Baby, what's wrong? What happened?"

Nat still had her hand on the Beretta trying to get it out of QT's waistband. QT broke her hand free and said, "What in fuck's going on?"

Nat was crying uncontrollably. She said through sobs, "I saw him…Boo, the nigga that set Ty up. I promised myself if I saw that nigga again I would kill him. This is unfinished business. I'll understand if you don't want me anymore, but I got to get that snake ass nigga."

Nat had also told QT about how Ty had been set up by Boo. QT knew that Nat had loved Ty, and that she had went against her parents for him. QT pulled her close and said, "Show this nigga to me. Just calm down. I'll have my homies get him and you can do what you want to him." QT said that thinking that once he had that nigga he would smoke him. He didn't think Nat was cut like that.

They went to where all the homies were chilling. QT called Lil Man, Boxer, and Goldie to walk with him. Boo was a loud mouth, always talking shit to somebody. He was so busy talking shit to three females in a 4-door Honda Accord that he didn't see Nat point him out to QT and his homies.

QT looked at Goldie and said, "I want that bitch ass nigga tonight when he leaves here. Follow him, bring him to the abandoned apartments in the Fays. I want the nigga alive." He turned and walked off with Nat. He couldn't stand to see anyone he loved hurting. If she wanted the nigga dead then so be it. It was obvious that the nigga didn't have the slightest idea about what trust, loyalty, respect, and honor was. This nigga was everything that the G-Code wasn't.

When they got back to the homies, QT pulled Rocc to the side and told him to make sure the disciplinary room in the Fays was cool and no base heads were around. Rocc didn't question QT, he knew he would find out everything in time.

QT and his homies kicked it on the Shaw until 2 a.m. Boo had left about 1:20, alone in his convertible Beamer. What he didn't know was he was being followed by two different cars. Usually, Boo was careful but tonight he was high on chronic and had been drinking heavily. He barely made it home. He lived in some condo in Gardena. Ever since he had fucked up and set Ty up, shit wasn't the same. It would have been lovely if they could have gotten Ty's money but the nigga went out like a real Gangsta and all Boo ended up with was the jewelry Ty had on. It was worth $200,000, and he sold everything except the Rolex watch that he was wearing.

Boo pulled into his parking space, stumbled out of the car, and was headed for his front door when he felt the barrel of a big gun to his head.

"You make a sound, nigga, you dead," Goldie said as Lil Man put duct tape on Boo's mouth and hands. They threw him in the trunk of a Buick La Saber.

QT took Lisa home but on the way he lied to her and told her Nat was upset becuz she saw a nigga that had tried to rape her. He told the rest of the G-Code committee to meet him in the Fays at the vacant apartments. They knew somebody was in for some shrewd punishment, if not murder.

When they got to the Fays, Rocc had everything in order. Only the committee was allowed in the empty apartment. Rocc had five lil homies posted, making sure no one had access to what was about to happen.

Five minutes after QT, Nat, and the other homies got to the apartment, Goldie, Lil Man, and Boxer pushed Boo through the bedroom door. His eyes got as big as bo dollars when he saw Nat there.

There was only one chair in the room. Plastic was taped to all the walls and on the floor. QT grabbed Boo by his shirt collar and pushed him down in the chair. He snatched the tape off Boo's mouth.

Boo began to protest. "Man, what's the fuck going on? I ain't got no beef with ya'll."

QT slapped Boo like a bitch and said, "Did I ask you to say anything."

"Naw man..."

Immediately, QT slapped him again. "I didn't ask you to say shit." He looked at Nat and said, "He's all yours."

Nat went over to Boo and spit in his face. She told him, "Why did you do it? Ty had a lot of love for you. If you would have asked, he would have given you anything." Tears were running down her face.

Boo tried to lie. "I loved Ty. I didn't have shit to do with that. I would have killed the niggas myself If they hadn't got caught."

Nat looked down at his wrist. Off the top, she knew that the watch Boo was wearing was the one she had bought for Ty for his birthday.

QT and the others just watched. None of them thought that Nat had it in her to smoke this fool. They thought she would cry, spit on him, slap him–but actually kill him? Naw.

When she saw the watch, any doubts that may have been creeping in her head disappeared. She walked over to QT, took the Beretta out of his hand, and checked the chamber to make sure there was a bullet in there. Then she walked right up to Boo, put the gun in his face and pulled the trigger three times.

The first shot hit Boo right between the eyes and the second and third shots hit him through the heart. She walked back over to QT and handed him the Beretta and asked if anyone had a knife. Rocc handed her one. She cut the tape off of Boo's hands and took the Rolex off his wrist.

She turned to QT and said, "I bought Ty this watch for his birthday. He had it on when he was kidnapped and killed."

"It's all right, baby. You will never be alone again. I got you."

QT turned to Big Bam and said, "Get rid of this piece of shit. You know what to do."

All the G-Code members were still amazed how Nat didn't even hesitate to smoke Boo. She did what had to be done. They didn't know her, but they knew that QT was going to marry her and now they knew that she was a ride-or-die female. She was a Gangsta as well. They knew QT was in good hands.

When QT and Nat got back to QT's house, they took a bath together. Both of them were quietly caught up in their own thoughts. When they were in bed, with Nat lying in QT's arms, he asked, "Where did you learn how to use a gun?"

"Ty taught me," she said. "We used to go to the shooting range all the time."

"So, is there any more unfinished business I should know about?"

Nat looked QT in the eyes and said, "Baby, that was something I had to do. It didn't have anything to do with you or my love for you. I love you, QT, you are my life, my future. Yes, I loved Ty but he's gone. I would do the same for you if someone hurt you, baby. I ain't no punk bitch that's just with you for the money. If anybody hurts you, I'm going to hurt them. And no there isn't anymore unfinished business that I have to handle." QT knew that he had finally found the one, his soul mate. He pulled Nat close to him, kissed her softly, and said, "I love you, Nat, that's all that matters. Me and you, baby. Me and you."

They fell asleep in each other's arms.

QT woke up the next morning at eleven. Nat was cooking breakfast and Santana and Blocc were at her side. When QT came downstairs and saw them, he said, "Are you going to steal all my dogs?"

Nat smiled. "I can't help it if they like me. They need a woman's touch around here."

As they ate breakfast, he asked, "So what's up with your parents?

Are you going to tell them about us getting married so I can meet them?"

Nat thought for a minute before she spoke. "I haven't talked to them in four and a half years. They hated Ty and didn't even know him or want to get to know him. So after Ty died, I let them die with him."

QT sat there trying to find the right words. Finally, he said, "All parents want is the best for us. That doesn't necessarily mean that they are always right. We are going to be married regardless of what anyone thinks or says. Just think about giving them a call. It would be nice if they were part of the wedding."

She looked at him and said, "Okay, I'll think about it."

"So what are you doing today, beautiful?"

"I'm going to figure out what you can invest some of your money in. I have one and a have million dollars in the bank. Legally, I can make out a loan to you so that on paper, you can be legal. That way, you won't have to explain where your money comes from. You know I have a degree in business."

"I have been thinking about a legal business. This house is in my uncle and aunt's names. They have money so this house and the one in Compton are covered, and they are paid for in full."

"So what do you like to do? It's better to start a business doing something that you like to do, that way you will be more involved."

"I always wanted to open up a music, rim, and hydraulic shop."

"Okay, I'll have the loan paperwork drawn up, and you go find a good location. Remember, location is one of the keys to a business's success," Nat said, then added, "I also have to go to my house and get some of my clothes and girlie stuff."

"Do what you got to do. I'll meet you here tonight." QT tossed Nat a set of house keys and said, "The alarm code is 7, 22, 62, 63."

"What do those numbers mean?"

"722 is my hood day, 62 is the year I was born, and 23 is the day I was born."

Nat went to her lawyer and had him do the paperwork for QT's business. While he was doing that, Nat sat and thought about her mother and father. Nat and her mother were real cool years ago, before she met Ty, but Nat and her father had been super close years ago. She really missed her parents. She wanted to share this part of her life with them, but she knew the first thing that they would ask QT was what he did for a living. They didn't know that Nat had her own franchises and was a successful business woman. She hadn't seen them over four years. She decided she would call them after QT opened his business. In reality, Nat did miss her parents tremendously. Hopefully, this time everything would work out.

Chapter 5: Wedding Bells

Three weeks later QT was having his grand opening for his first shop. He had found the perfect spot in West L.A. on Venice Boulevard. The building had just been remodeled and everything fell into place. Nat was right there by his side making sure everything was straight. She helped him acquire the different vendors and also hire personnel. The shop was named Imagine This, and sold rims, tires, hydraulics, music, and accessories.

Nat loaned QT $600,000 to get the business started. It didn't cost that much but she gave it to him because QT wanted to open another one in another city if this one did good. QT gave Nat the $600,000 back the same day she gave him the cashier's check. Nat put the money in a safety deposit box at her bank. The shop was a big hit and the wedding was one month away. Meanwhile, Nat and Lisa had become real tight and Lisa often spent the night at QT's house on the weekends.

QT had hooked up with Killa Watt and Spooky from Harlem 30s. They were buying two birds and QT fronted them two. Big Dave from Long Beach was also part of QT's crew now. None of them were on the committee but they were on QT's team.

Nat finally got up the courage to call her parents. While QT was at the shop, Nat was at home about to cook dinner. She picked up the phone and dialed the number. On the third ring, her father answered.

"Hello, this is the Davis residence. Mark Davis speaking."

Tears started to form in Nat's eyes.

"Hello? Hello, who is this on my line?"

"Daddy...Daddy, it's me, Nat."

"Oh my God, Nat! Nat, baby, is that really you? Please don't hang up. Please let me get your mother on the other line."

Nat could hear her father calling for her mother to pick up the other phone.

"Hello?" came a soft voice for the other line.

"Hi mama."

"Oh my God, thank you Jesus! Nat, baby, where are you? How are you? Baby, we so sorry we love you, oh we miss you so much. Please let us see you."

All three of them were crying on the phone. They could barely talk. They talked for an hour and Nat told them that she was getting married and she wanted them to meet her husband-to-be. Nat's mother said that they could come over tomorrow for dinner and she would cook Nat's favorite meal.

Everyone was on their way out of the shop except QT. He was about to lock the front door when Tasha walked up. QT said, "We are closing."

"I just want to look at some rims and leave a deposit," she said. "I'll drop my car off tomorrow."

One of the sales clerks turned around to take the order but QT said, "Go on, I'll take care of it. I'll see ya'll tomorrow." As they walked off, QT let Tasha in and locked the door. "What's up? What do you really want?"

"I want you, daddy. I thought you said you were going to call me. I been holding all this just for you."

QT walked back in to his office. It was a big office with two leather sofas, one of which was a sofa bed. QT told her, "I'm getting married in three and a half weeks so it's over for us."

Tasha walked up to QT. She had on a short skirt. She got right in front of him and bent over to show him she had on a g-string. "Daddy, I told you this was yours and only yours. Ain't nobody hit this since we were together."

QT didn't want to cheat on Nat but he had unfinished business with Tasha. He owed her a good ass fuckin.

Tasha turned around, got on her knees, undid QT's pants and let them fall to the floor. When she pulled his boxers down, his dick was right at her lips. She slowly started taking him into her mouth. QT thought to himself, damn, this bitch give good head.

Before he could cum, he stopped her and told her to bend over the couch. He took a condom out of his wallet. He always kept three condoms with him. He put the condom on and positioned himself between Tasha's pussy lips and slowly pushed his dick inside of her. She was wet and tight as fuck. He started long stroking her and Tasha couldn't take it.

"Oh daddy, oh daddy, please, daddy, please. I told you this was yo pussy only, daddy."

The more she hollered and moaned, the more excited QT got. Finally, he pulled his dick out of her pussy and rubbed it between her asshole cheeks. He said, "I want some of this black ass."

Tasha said, "I ain't never done that before, but I'll try anything for you."

QT lubricated her ass with her juices, then slowly pushed the head of his dick into her ass. Tasha kept moving away before he could penetrate her. He laid her on her back with her head against the arm of the couch so she couldn't get away. Then he slowly penetrated her asshole. She was screaming at first, "Oh oh please, you killin me!" as tears ran down her face. But once QT was a good three quarters inside of her, he started moving very slow and told her to move slowly with him. The pain started turning to pleasure. QT could feel that the condom had broken but didn't care—her ass couldn't get pregnant. As he fucked her ass, he shoved three fingers in her pussy. She went wild.

"Oh daddy. I love you. Oh I love you, this is yo ass and yo pussy, daddy, please fuck yo ass, daddy!"

QT couldn't hold back any longer. He started pounding her ass. When he came, Tasha said, "Oh daddy, I'm cumming too. Ohhh, I feel yo hot cum in my aasssss!" She started shaking and bucking. QT just held her and went along for the ride.

QT had a shower in the bathroom in his office so he got naked and went to shower. He knew not to use soap, just hot water, because nobody smelled like soap after being out all day. Tasha got in the shower as well. She tried to bath QT but he told her not to use soap on him. She got down on her knees and sucked QT to another nut. She swallowed it all. He got out of the shower and got dressed. When Tasha got out, he told her, "Don't ever come up here again. My girl be here. I got yo number. When I want you, I will call you."

Tasha really was in love with QT and she hadn't been with anyone else. She said, "Whatever you say, daddy, I can live with that."

QT put on just a touch of cologne. The hot water worked wonders—he didn't have Tasha's scent on him, nor soap, just a dash of cologne. When he got home, Nat greeted him at the door, gave him a big kiss, and told him the news about the dinner date at her parents' house the next day. QT was happy and hoped that everything worked out for the best, but said, "Nat, maybe you should go see them by yourself first. I know that there's a lot you need to discuss and I don't want them to be uncomfortable because I'm there."

"Yeah, I think that would be better and we can go over for dinner Saturday if you don't have anything planned."

QT said, "Naw, baby, I don't have any plans. I'm all yours."

They ate dinner and both of them wrestled on the floor with each other and with the dogs. They took a bath together and fell asleep watching movies.

In Compton, Green Eyes was sitting in the back of a squad car. He had been caught with a strap and a half ounce of rock cocaine in a sting. The police sent a snitch to buy some rock cocaine with some marked money. As soon as the snitch walked off, Green Eyes was rushed and arrested. Green Eyes saw the sergeant and called him to the car.

"You want to tell me where you bought that dope? I can get you a deal if your info is good," the sergeant said.

"Just call Detective Beckman or Ross. They will tell you what's up."

"What do you mean they'll tell me what's up? What have they got to do with this?" the sergeant asked, then added, "Fuck Beckman. I don't like his white ass anyway."

Green Eyes was taken to jail. At the station, Beckman and Ross were walking out the back door as Green Eyes was being brought in. Sergeant McBride was a brotha, about 6' 3", dark skinned, well built, and he hated Beckman and Ross because he knew they were racists. McBride had been around a long time. He had grown up in the Santana Blocc neighborhood and him and Gangsta had been homies. He was fortunate to make it into college without being caught up. After college, he applied for the force and was accepted. He wasn't a dirty cop; if he caught you fair and square yo ass was going to jail. He understood what most of the youngsters was up against, especially the minorities. He knew he could have easily gone the other way if he hadn't of made it to college. He hated snitches. He figured if you was able to do the crime then you should be able to handle the time. Don't get caught and cry like a bitch man—up and do yo time.

The only thing that kept McBride from beating the shit out of Beckman and Ross was the thought of losing his job. As McBride walked to the back door of the station, Green Eyes called out to Beckman who walked over.

"I'll take it from here," Beckman said. "He's one of mine. We are working on something big. We need this one."

McBride looked at all of them and said, "If you want him, you can have him ... after I book his snitch ass!"

He walked on past them and hauled Green Eyes into the station.

After the door closed, Ross turned to Beckman. "Who in the fuck does that nigger think he is?"

Within the hour, Beckman had Green Eyes released and no charges were filed. The two detectives walked the snitch to the front door. On their way, they passed McBride and they all smiled.

McBride thought to himself, smile now, cry later, muthafucka.

The next day, QT, Goldie, and Rocc were standing on Tucker in front of the spot when a patrol car pulled up. It was McBride in the car by himself. QT knew him, so did Rocc. McBride knew their whole family. QT walked up to the car and said, "What's up, McB?"

"What's up, QT? How's your brother doin?"

"He standing tall through it all. You know how he is."

McBride smiled. "Yeah, I know how he is. Me and that nigga use to do damage back in the day. But I ain't here to reminisce. I'm here to let you know that nigga Green Eyes is working with Beckman and also the feds will be starting a task force in Compton in a few months."

"Good lookin out, McB," QT said.

McBride said, "This was a once in a lifetime thang, for old times sake."

"If you ever need anything, just say the word."

"I'm cool, young cuz."

As McBride drove off, QT walked back to where Goldie and Rocc were. "Cuz, you know that soft ass nigga Green Eyes? That bitch ass nigga is working; he's a rat and a snitch, ain't that a bitch."

Goldie said, "That nigga tried to buy an ounce from me the other day. I told that nigga to get the fuck out my face. I don't sell dope."

Rocc said, "Don't trip, Crip. I got this. I'll take care of this nigga."

"Before you smoke his ass," QT said, "find out exactly want he knows and what he was trying to do."

Qt went in the house to call Nat. When she answered, he said, "I love you, baby, you know that right?" to which Nat replied, "You better becuz I love the fuck out of you."

He asked, "What time are you going to your parents' house?"

"I'll be leaving in about an hour."

"All right, I'm in Compton now but I'm about to go to the shop so call me there if you need me, okay?"

"All right, baby. Mwahhhh, bye bye."

QT pulled his Porsche out of the back yard and called Goldie over to the car. "Ain't no news on that Madd Mike yet?"

Goldie said, "All that we know is that the nigga lives in L.A. with his mama and two buster ass brothers somewhere."

"Stay on that, cuz, somethin don't feel right. We got to get rid of that nigga and soon."

"I feel you, cuzzin. I'm on it."

QT pulled out of the driveway and headed to L.A. He had already decided not to close the shop at night by himself anymore. It made him vulnerable. He would leave early and let the manager close, unless he had a few of his homies there with him. QT wasn't scared but he knew it was better to be safe than sorry. When he got to the shop it was kind of crowded. This had been a good investment for him and now he was about to open another one in Inglewood down the street from the Forum on Manchester Boulevard. It would be ready in two weeks, and a week and a half after that he would be married to Nat. Life was good, everything was falling into place. He just hoped everything stayed in place. Women always tried to hit on him because he was a good looking guy and not to mention he had money and they knew it. He had already put it in his mind that once he was married he wouldn't cheat on Nat anymore. So that meant he only had three and a half weeks to sow his wild oats.

He sat in his office relaxing in his big comfortable leather chair behind his desk. He had Earth, Wind, and Fire's "Reasons" playing. His manager, Paul, knocked on the door, which was open, and QT motioned for him to come in.

"Sir, we have a small problem with a young lady out here. She wants to speak to you."

QT said to bring her in. Paul came back with one of the most beautiful women QT had ever seen. She was black, but you could tell that she was mixed with something. She had an exotic look, very sexy. On the way out, Paul closed the door.

"Excuse me for staring, but you are rather beautiful," QT said. "Now, how may I help you?"

QT made her blush, he could see it in her face. Her hair was long down the middle of her back and curly. Her eyes were light green and a little slanted. She was wearing a sun dress and when standing at the right angle, QT could see right through the gap between her legs. She was about 5' 8", nice legs, thin waist, ass bulging from the dress, with nice breasts that stood up on their own. QT could see the outline of her nipples sticking out through the sun dress.

"Please, have a seat and tell me what's the problem."

She sat down and crossed her legs. "I love that record. It has meaning."

QT could tell by her body language that she wasn't mad and she had something on her mind. QT didn't say anything, he just looked at her, waiting for her to make a move. When the song went off, he got up to change the tape. He put in Cherell's "Saturday Love." He turned around to go back to his chair and almost choked as he looked at this beautiful woman butt naked with only her heels on. She didn't have a mark on her, a smooth body, and all the hair was shaven from around her pubic area. QT had on a sweat suit and didn't notice it but as he looked at her, his dick began to rise—she could see it trying to burst out of his sweats.

The female walked up to QT and said, "My name is Destiny and I have been watching you for months. I like your style and from what I see bulging in those sweats, you like my style as well."

She was inches from QT's face. She slowly massaged his dick through the fabric. QT glanced towards the door.

"I locked the door so we wouldn't be disturbed," she said.

She slowly and seductively went down to her knees and pulled QT's sweats down. He was so shocked he didn't know how to react. He wanted to pinch himself to see if he was dreaming. She took his dick in her hand and slowly began to stroke it. He couldn't believe this shit. She licked and sucked on QT's balls, one by one. He was almost weak at the knees. She then licked her way up to the head of his dick and slowly slid his dick into her hot wet mouth. QT couldn't help it, he had to moan. Destiny slowly started deep throating him. It felt so good he couldn't hold back. He blasted cum deep down her throat. She didn't gag or anything, she just kept sucking and swallowing every drop.

QT was holding her by her head with both his hands, fucking her hot mouth. After she swallowed every drop, she stood up, went to the couch and bent over. She looked over her shoulder at him and said, "Come fuck me, daddy."

QT's dick was still hard so he wasn't about to pass this up. He got a condom out of his wallet, put it on, and walked up behind Destiny. She was rubbing her clit and sticking a finger inside her pussy. When she pulled her finger out, QT could see the wetness on her finger. She immediately slid her finger in her ass. He was so turned on he didn't know what to hit first. She decided for him. She gripped QT's dick and guided it into her hot pussy. She was even tighter than

Tasha. QT wanted to plunge his dick into her roughly but he didn't want any of his employees to hear them, so he had to fuck her nice and slow. She still couldn't handle him. She started to get loud. He had to stop and get one of the pillows from the closet. He put the pillow in front of her face and pushed her head into the pillow.

"Holler into that. We don't want everyone hearing us."

He really started fucking the shit out of Destiny. He was about to cum, so he pulled out of her pussy and slowly pushed into her ass. She was hollering and moaning into the pillow. She was saying something but QT couldn't make it out. He wanted to cum in her ass so he pulled out, took the condom off, and went back in her ass. Within six hard strokes he was cumming. When he finished, he pulled out of her ass and turned her around. He pushed his dick into her mouth, and she sucked and licked him until he was satisfied. He went and took a shower and she tied her hair up and joined him. Afterwards, as he sat at his deck and she was on the couch, there was a knock on the door.

He got up and opened it. He had already sprayed some air freshener so nothing was out of place. The manager said, "So what are we going to do about her car? She didn't get the music put in here so we aren't liable."

QT said, "Fix it this time, but next time she pays. This one is on me."

Paul went back to the front and QT left the door open. He sat back down.

Destiny said, "Another place, another time and you would be mine."

"Probably, but I'm about to be married soon so this can't happen again."

"I can respect that. It's my fault I made my move too late."

"You seem like cool people and you are one of the most beautiful women that I've ever seen. I know that you are going to make some lucky man proud."

Destiny said, "That's why I love you. You are one of the real ones."

Paul came back to the office and said, "Boss, we got it. It was only two fuses blown. It's ready to roll."

QT said thanks and that she'd be out in a minute. He got up and went to Destiny and gave her a hug. "Thanks, you are special."

She took a business card out of her purse and gave it to him. "I'm always only a call away. Bye, daddy."

She walked out looking sexy as a muthafucka. When QT looked at the card. It said: Detective Destiny Stevens. L.A.P.D.

QT said out loud, "Ain't that a bitch."

Destiny grew up on the west side of Compton, QT was from the east side. They were the same age, twenty-eight. She had been on the force for seven and a half years, and had mainly worked undercover for the first six and a half years taking down drug dealers. She knew who the major players were in Compton even though she worked for L.A.P.D. She had been watching QT on her own time. She knew that he was slick and wouldn't be easy to take down. After watching him for a while, she began to like him because he was real. He was cool. He was a Gangsta. He represented his self well and he didn't abuse his power just becuz he had it. He was also respectful to women, even when ugly women approached him, he was still respectful. Destiny found herself falling in love with him. Now that she was getting a transfer to the Compton Station to be a part of the local and federal task force, she wanted to make love to him just to see if he really was who she thought he was. And now she knew, and she was going to do whatever it took to protect and warn him. She was in love with a man that she knew she couldn't have.

As Nat pulled up in her parents' driveway, her mother and father ran out the front door to greet her with tears in their eyes. They weren't going to play the tough roll; they loved their daughter and had missed her so much. It had been four and a half years since they had last seen her. Now that she was back they didn't care what they had to do to keep her in their lives. She was their only child, their princess. Natalie's father got to her first. He hugged her tight with tears running down his face. Her mother joined in on a three way hug. By now, all three of them were crying. They must have hugged for five minutes before they broke the embrace.

Nat's father stepped back and said, "Princess, you are so beautiful and we missed you so much."

Nat said, "Let's go inside. We don't want the whole neighborhood in our business."

They went in and sat down in the living room. Nat had already told them QT wasn't coming with her because they needed to talk first, but that he would be over for dinner Saturday night.

Nat's mother said, "Princess, we realize we hurt you and we are truly sorry. That wasn't our intention. We should have known that we can't choose the man for you to love."

Her father broke down and cried. Nat could barely understand his words as he said how beautiful and adorable she was and that it broke his heart for allowing his self to let her be out of his life for so long.

They talked for hours. Nat told them about having a degree in business, about her three franchises, and most of all, she told them about QT and their engagement. She also said that she didn't want to talk about Ty. She explained that, that was in the past and QT was her future. Nat told them that he owned his own business and was in the process of opening up another one.

After dinner, Nat laid her head on her father's shoulder like in the old days. They were all happy and he had already told her mother than under no circumstances was he losing his daughter again. The last four and a half years had been the worst years of their lives. Nat was a grown woman and whatever she chose to do or who to be with, whether they approved or not, they would support their princess. At least if things did go wrong, they would be there for her.

Time flew by so fast that before Nat knew it, it was 10 p.m. She had been there for five hours. She called QT at home and told him everything was fine and she was on her way home. Her parents walked her to her car. They embraced and kissed. She told them she would see them again in two days, on Saturday, at 5 p.m. for dinner.

As Nat drove home she felt relieved and elated that she had her parents back in her life. She had the man she loved and she would work on getting QT out of the game. Making sure he started those businesses was a start. Nat put Anita Baker's "Rapture" in the tape deck. She smiled and sang along to the beat as she glided down the 405 Freeway.

Moonie pulled up on Green Eyes on Peck Street just around the corner from QT's spot. Rocc had directed Moonie to pick up Green Eyes and bring him to the Fays. "What's up, cuz?" he said. "You still out here getting yo hustle on?"

Green Eyes said, "Don't nothing come to a dreamer but a dream."

"Get in. Ride wit me over to this bitch pad in the Fays. She got a bad ass sister too. I need somebody to get at her while I'm dicking her sister down."

Green Eyes wanted so badly to be accepted that he jumped in the car without hesitation. Moonie cut the sounds up. Nucleus's "Jam On It" was blasting through the speakers. They both rocked to the beat as Moonie headed to the Fays. When he drove around to the back, Rocc and about eight of his soldiers were there. When he saw them, Green Eyes got a sick feeling in his stomach.

Moonie pulled right up to where they were and parked. As soon as Green Eyes got out of the car, Moonie drew down on him. Lil Ken pushed him on the car and searched him. He had a .38 in his front pocket, a little over a quarter piece of rock cocaine, and eight hundred dollars.

Green Eyes tried to protest. "Cuz, what's up wit this shit? We all from the same hood."

Rocc slapped him like a bitch and said, "Bitch, you ain't from shit. The Blocc don't harbor niggas like you."

They dragged Green Eyes into one of the empty apartments where they bound his hands and ankles to a chair with duct tape. Tears was running down his face; he knew that they knew.

Rocc said, "You can make this easy or you can make this hard. Your choice."

Moonie handed Rocc a big pair of wire cutters. Moonie held a bat in his other hand.

"I'm only going to ask you one time what in the fuck you doing working for Beckman, and what did he want you to do?" Rocc said as he walked towards Green Eyes with the wire cutters in his hand.

"He wanted me to keep buying dope until I was able to buy from QT," Green Eyes blurted out. "Then I would be wired so he could get QT on tape and bust him like he did Gangsta. He hates QT with a passion. I swear, all I was going to do is make some money and go to Seattle where I got family. Fuck Beckman. I wasn't going to go through with that shit."

Rocc said, "How stupid are you? QT don't sell dope and if he did he would never deal with a piece of shit like you." Rocc looked at his lil homies and said, "Let this be a lesson. What's the first rule of the G-Code?"

They all said at the same time: "Never snitch."

Rocc didn't say nothing, he just looked at Lil Ken. Lil Ken pulled out a Glock from under his jacked and walked up to Green Eyes who pleaded for mercy. Lil Ken shot him in the face.

Rocc took the Glock from Lil Ken and said, "Always follow the code. Put that piece of shit in that G-ride (stolen car) out there. Leave it on Alameda and burn it up with him in it."

When Nat got home, QT had just hung up with Rocc telling him everything was cool and he would fill him in when he saw him. QT could tell that Nat was really happy about the visit with her parents and he was happy for her. Nat had a one of a kind beautiful smile that would brighten up a room. QT loved to see that smile.

On Saturday night, they went to Nat's parents' house for dinner. QT dressed average but clean in a pair of slacks, a button-down shirt, and a pair of Brooks Brothers shoes. The only jewelry he wore was his pinky ring and his gold Wittnaeur watch. The dinner went well and Nat told them that she would come get them the next evening so they could meet QT's mother. That way, they could all finish planning the wedding together. A few times QT caught Nat's father staring at him but it didn't matter to QT. It was what it was and the facts were that he and Nat were in love and would be married no matter what.

After QT and Nat left, Nat's father said, "He's from the streets. He seems like a nice young man but he has an aura about him, a confidence that says he's somebody."

Nat's mom said, "He's Nat's choice, not ours. I can tell they are really in love so all we can do is support our princess."

Nat's father hugged his wife and said, "I know, sweetie. As long as she's happy, I'm happy for her."

QT's uncle, Reverend Turner, had a big beautiful Baptist Church in L.A. on Vermont Boulevard. The wedding was held there. Rocc was best man and Lisa was Nat's maid of honor. The parents had met prior to the wedding and all went well.

Neither Nat nor her parents knew that QT had eight of his homies posted outside of the church, all of them heated. QT wasn't taking any chances.

While Nat was getting dressed for the wedding, Lisa, Nat's mother, G-Moms, and a couple of her bridesmaids were in the room with her. The wedding colors were dark blue and light blue. Nat had a beautiful white wedding gown. The day was beautiful and the sky was blue—there wasn't a cloud in the sky. Nat stood at the window and thought to herself that it was a perfect day to get married. Her moms walked up behind her and said, "It's all right to be nervous. I was nervous when I married your father."

Nat just looked at her mother and smiled and hugged her. Nat wasn't nervous at all. QT was the man she loved and there wasn't a doubt in her mind about marrying him. He was her soul mate.

Down the hall, QT was dressed and ready to go. Rocc said, "Okay, big bro, let's get the show on the road. I saw one of Nat's bridesmaids and I got to get under her dress."

The G-Code Committee was all in the room and they laughed.

Goldie said, "Yeah, I didn't know Nat had some fine ass home girls like that. I got my eye on the Latin-looking one so ya'll niggas back off of her."

Big Bam went to the door, opened it, and said, "Let's do it."

The church was packed with at least 800 people, and 300 of them were QT's homies from his hood. As QT walked down the aisle, he saw plenty of women he had had sex with. There was one there that he hadn't seen since they were in junior high school together. Her name was Patricia, his first love. A lot of major ballers from Compton, L.A., Watts, and Long Beach were there. Everywhere you looked you saw gold and diamonds.

Once QT was in position, the music came on and Anita Baker's "Angel" played throughout the church. The flower girls came down the aisle and Nat and her father were behind them. Nat was as beautiful as an angel. QT knew that he was truly blessed to have her. Even though he didn't go to church, when he was younger he was raised in the church and he did believe in God.

Nat's father passed her off to QT with a head nod and went to sit next to his wife.

As the preacher married them, Destiny stood at the back of the church looking beautiful in her own right. Tears streamed down her face as she watched the man she loved marry another woman. Destiny had checked up on Nat and knew that she wasn't a gold digger or unfaithful to QT. In fact, Destiny liked Nat, she just wished that it was her at the front of the church marrying QT instead.

Destiny wasn't alone in her unhappiness; there were a lot of women there in tears wishing that they were standing in Nat's place, including Tasha. She hadn't seen QT since the last time they had sex at his shop. She didn't know why but QT had a hold over her. She felt something for him that she hadn't felt for any other man. She didn't care if he was married, she would be there for him whenever he called and she knew sooner or later, he would call. Tasha cried again as QT hugged and kissed his new bride.

The wedding reception was to be held in Hollywood. Right before QT and Nat got to the front door of the church, he spotted Destiny. He could see that she had been crying because tears were still in her eyes. He didn't say anything, he just nodded to her. There was a line of people waiting to congratulate them, then they got into the limo to go to the reception. Two limos followed QT with his eight homies that was there to watch his back. Goldie, Big Bam, and Crip Crazy rode in Goldie's Benz ahead of QT's limo.

At the reception hall, Goldie took command and positioned every-one where they needed to be. They were all strapped. They didn't think that anyone would be so stupid as to try anything but just in case, they would be ready. The reception was packed. After QT and Nat cut the cake and had their first dance, an hour later they said their goodbyes to their family and were off to the airport headed for the Bahamas.

Crip Crazy and Lil Man escorted them to the airport after they changed their clothes and got their luggage. QT left Goldie in charge. Rocc was to make sure that Santana and Blocc were taken care of.

On the drive to the airport, Nat leaned over and whispered in QT's ear, "I always wanted to make love in a limo." QT smiled and leaned forward to press the button to put the partition window up so the driver couldn't see. He laid Nat on her back, pulled her skirt up, pulled her panties down, and slowly began to lick up her leg between her thighs.

At the reception, the party was in full swing. QT had gone all out: bottles of Moët, Cristal, and Dom Perignon were all over. QT had bought 100 bottles of each. Everyone was getting their groove on and having a good time. Goldie spotted Nat's home girl that he wanted to get at and walked up to her table. He said, "Hello, sexier than me."

She looked up and smiled. Goldie said, "You should smile all the time. You have a beautiful smile." As she blushed, he went on, "I have been watching you ever since I first saw you at the wedding rehearsal. I can't seem to get you off my mind. Now, why is that? Excuse me, allow me to introduce myself. My name is Keith but my friends call me Goldie."

She put her hand out and said, "My name is Monica."

Instead of shaking her hand, Goldie held it politely and softly kissed it. To Monica, his lips felt so soft and smooth they sent chills through her body. Monica had broken up with her man months ago. She had come home from work early and caught him having sex with a female that worked out at the gym with them. She left him and hadn't been with anyone since. Monica was gorgeous with green eyes and long sandy brown hair. She was 5' 6", with 36-inch breasts, thin waist, smooth skin and a nice round ass. She was 25 years old, originally from Brazil and had come to America to go to school but had decided to stay. She was in law school. She met Nat at the gym two years ago and they hit it off and became good friends. Monica didn't know why but she was drawn to this man. Her previous boyfriend had been the only man that she had been with—before him she had been a virgin.

There were three other females at the table and all of them were telling Monica, "Girl, you better go on and get with him, cuz if you don't, we will. Girl, we know you overdue."

Just then, Keith Sweat's "Right and Wrong Way" came on. Goldie asked Monica to dance. It was 1:30 a.m. and it was the last song for the night. Goldie took her hand and escorted her to the floor. He took her in his arms, pulled her close to him, and they moved together in union. He didn't say anything, he just danced, holding her, not wanting to let go. When his manhood started to rise, Monica didn't say a word she just held him tighter to her. When the song was over, Goldie didn't let her go. He asked, "How did you get here?"

Monica said, "I rode with one of my girlfriends. Why?"

"I want to take you to breakfast. I want to spend some time with you. I don't know, it's just something about you. I really don't trip off of women. They sweat me but you are different. I don't believe in love at first sight but now I'm starting to think twice."

Goldie had always been a smooth operator with the ladies but now for the first time he wasn't draggin, what he was saying was real. She told Goldie to wait a minute and she went to her friends and told them that Goldie would be taking her home. They got to high fivin and saying don't hurt him, girl. When they got to the car, Goldie opened the door for her and told her he would be right back. He went over to Rocc who was talking to this fine female. A thick red bone. Goldie pulled him to the side and told him he was about to roll and to be careful.

Rocc raised his jacket to show Goldie his two Glocks and said, "I'm cool. Besides, I got two of the lil homies wit me and they strapped as well."

Goldie went back to the car. Monica unlocked the door for him, he got in and they pulled off. Rocc got the female's phone number, slapped her on the ass and told her he would call her. He already had another of Nat's bridesmaids waiting in his car.

Goldie decided to take Monica to his house in Palos Verdes. It was a big four bedroom, four bathroom house with a family room, weight room, game room, swimming pool and Jacuzzi. Only the members on the committee knew where each other lived.

When he pulled up in the driveway, Monica said, "I though we were going to breakfast."

"We are. I'm going to cook for you."

Monica asked, "No one's going to wake up?"

"Naw, baby. I live here alone, me and my dogs. I have two pit bulls but they are in the back yard. They are house trained, but they only come in the house when I let them in."

Goldie's house was immaculate, just like QT's. He had big screen TVs everywhere, he even had a TV built into the wall in the kitchen. He took Monica to the den where he turned on the TV and gave her the remote, then he went to the kitchen.

Goldie took out jumbo shrimp, onions, bell peppers, jalapeno pepper, rice, and a can of red Mexican sauce that was somewhat like tomato sauce. It took about forty-five minutes to prepare. The meal was simple but good. As Goldie cooked Monica sat on the sofa thinking to herself, "He's fine, polite, lives alone and has a beautiful home, has money…the million dollar question is, why is he alone?"

Goldie brought the food to her and they ate together. He fed her the first shrimp. She was surprised at how good the food tasted. "This is delicious," she said. "Who taught you to make this?"

He said, "It's a family secret." After they finished eating, he put the plates up and came back with two large glasses of orange juice. Monica said, "I'm glad you're not trying to get me drunk."

Goldie said, "I don't want you drunk. I want you entirely sober so you can feel and understand everything that I do to you." He reached over, pulled her to him, and slowly and softly kissed her.

At first, Monica didn't open her mouth but Goldie slowly pushed his tongue between her teeth. She opened her mouth and began to kiss him back. Her mind was telling her to stop but her body needed this, wanted this. But then all of the sudden, she pulled away and said, "I can't do this."

Goldie asked, "Why not? I want you and I know you want me too."

"It's too soon. I've only been with one man in my life and I just don't give myself away at random."

Goldie looked into her eyes and said, "I'm not random. I know that you are feeling me. I'm not going to do nothing that you don't want me to do. I know that you are special. Sometimes in life you have to do something out of the ordinary."

She sat there for a minute, then stood up and proceeded to take her dress off. Goldie didn't move until she was completely naked. She was even more beautiful than he had imagined she would be. He looked at her for a minute, then he stood up and started to undress. But she walked up to him and said, "Popie, let me undress you."

Goldie watched her as she undressed him. When he was naked, he kissed her, picked her up, and took her to his Jacuzzi tub in the bedroom. They took a bath together, washed each other, then dried each other off. Goldie laid her on his California king-size bed, opened her legs, and moved between them. He slowly started kissing her. Her lips were soft and sweet. He made his way down her neck to her breast as she moaned.

"Popie, please, please, be easy. My last boyfriend wasn't even half as big as you are."

This turned Goldie on even more. He licked and sucked her perfect breasts as she moaned and moved beneath him. He made his way down her stomach to her navel, then down to her inner thighs. As he sucked and licked on her thigh, she tried to guide his head to her pussy, but he wanted her to beg. After a few minutes, Monica started saying, "Please, please, Popie, please lick my pussy, it's all yours, Popie, please, I can't take this."

Goldie started at her asshole and licked all the way up between her pussy lips to her clit and back down to her pussy. He pushed his tongue inside her pussy, working it like a jackhammer.

Monica screamed, "Oh oh oh, oohhhh ... Popie, oh, that's it, that's it." Goldie moved to her clit and slowly and softly began to lick and suck her clit, then he inserted a finger inside her pussy and one in her asshole. Instantly, she started shaking, screaming, and cumming. "Oh, Popie, what did you do? What did you do? I'm cumming! Ohhh, oh, oh, I love it, I love it!"

She tried to push Goldie's head away but he wouldn't budge. Suddenly he stopped and slowly pushed his dick into her. He didn't care if she got pregnant; he knew that she was his. Monica was so tight that he could barely get inside of her but by cumming her juices made it all right. He slowly began to push his dick in her further and further. Once he was past the halfway point, he began to slowly stroke her.

Monica began crying, saying, "Oh, oh, oh, it's so big...so big, Popie. I love that big dick. Fuck me, oh, please, fuck me. This is what I waited for."

Goldie began to fuck her by plunging his dick into her. She started cumming and Goldie pushed his finger inside her ass and really pounded her.

Monica never knew that sex could feel so good. She held on to Goldie while tears ran down her face but they were tears of joy. When Goldie came inside her, she felt it. She closed her eyes and continued to say over and over, "I love you, I love you, I love you."

After he finished cumming, he pulled his dick out of her pussy and his finger out of her ass. His dick was still hard so he slowly pushed it into her asshole. Once the head popped through, Monica started hollering, "No, Popie, NO, NO, NO! I can't take it there!"

Goldie held her tight and said "Relax, baby, it's in now just move slowly."

After awhile, the pain turned to pleasure. Goldie had two fingers in her pussy and she started cumming again. He sped up his pace and came shortly afterwards.

She started screaming, "Popie, Popie, Popie, I feel yo hot cum in my ass, oh, oh, oh, oh...I love it."

When Goldie pulled out of her ass, they lay together, holding each other for about an hour. They got up and took a shower together.

After they washed each other, Monica got on her knees and slowly sucked Goldie's dick until he came in her mouth. They went back to bed and fell asleep in each other's arms.

The next day, Monica moved in.

Chapter 6: Chaos

Nat woke up with a smile on her face. She was officially Mrs. Quinten Turner. She sat up in bed and watched QT sleep. He looked so peaceful and handsome. She loved him so much that she made a promise to herself she would never let nothing nor anyone come between them.

They were in the Bahamas, the weather was beautiful, they were in a hotel right on the beach, and today was to be their shopping day. They would shop for themselves and get some souvenirs for family and friends.

As she got out of bed the sheet came off of QT and he lay there naked. She decided to wake him up with a smile. She climbed back into bed and slowly started sucking QT's dick. She felt really excited as it grew larger and larger in her mouth. QT woke up with a big smile on his face.

For the moment, everything was going good back in the hood. Goldie had called all of the committee together at the spot on Tucker. He reminded them of the new task force that McBride had informed QT about. He told them to make sure their stash spots, where they kept their dope, were secure, and to stay on the lookout. Let the workers handle all the sales and stay out of the hood as much as possible, he told them, because they can't catch what they can't find. After the meeting, they all went their separate ways and Gold went to pick up Monica for lunch.

Even though QT had told Rocc about fuckin with new bitches

until they smoked that nigga Madd Mike, it went in one ear and out the other especially since QT wasn't there. Rocc called the Red Bone broad that he had met at the wedding reception. He had been talking to her for the last four days and even went over to her house once but he had taken three of his homies with him. Rocc told her that he would be by her apartment within the hour. He told her he was coming alone but by her living in the back she wouldn't know that he was parking in the front and leaving two homies in the car. Rocc wanted to go and hit that Red Bone before QT got back from the Bahamas. QT was due back late that night; he'd been gone for a week.

The Red Bone's name was Keisha. She immediately called Madd Mike and told him that Rocc was coming over.

Madd Mike was there within fifteen minutes. There was an alley behind the back of the apartments. He parked in the alley and went to Keisha's back door. She opened it and he went in. She sat on the sofa in her panties and bra. She was thick with big ass long blonde hair, 40-inch breasts, and a slim waist. Madd Mike tossed her $10,000 and said, "You know the plan. As soon as the nigga get in here you rub that fat ass on him, then tell him to wait—you are going to put on something more comfortable. You go right out the back door and I'll walk out of the bedroom and blast his ass. You got everything you need packed in yo car, right?"

"Yeah, daddy, I'm ready to roll. I'm going to drive down to Vegas and chill with my cousin for about eight or nine months until shit cools off."

Madd Mike was getting horny watching Keisha's fine ass sitting there in just her panties and bra. He pulled his sweats down and started stroking his dick. He wanted one last shot before she left. Keisha was a real freak. She pulled her panties down, bent over the sofa, and immediately Madd Mike pushed his dick straight in her ass. All she did was moan. Her ass was so good that he came within three minutes. He pulled out of her ass and she sucked and licked him clean. She went to the bathroom then to her room and came back out wearing jeans and a blouse. Keisha cut the tape deck on, and Enchantment's "Gloria" played through the speakers. She sat on the sofa and Madd Mike went in the bedroom to wait.

Five minutes later there was a knock on the door. She could see Rocc through the living room window. She went to the bedroom to tell Madd Mike that he had arrived, then went back to the living room and opened the door for Rocc. "I was beginning to think you weren't coming," she said as Rocc walked into the apartment.

As he passed her, he turned and squeezed her ass with both of his hands. He said, "You know I had to come get some of this nice fat ass."

Keisha backed her ass up on Rocc and grinded on him backwards. She could feel his dick getting hard. She stopped and said, "Wait a minute, let me put on something more comfortable."

As she walked off towards her bedroom, Rocc turned to see what tapes she had in her collection. He found Tone Loc and put it in. He turned it up a little as "Wild Thang" flowed through the speakers.

Keisha had picked up her car keys and her purse and was easing out the back door. She wasn't worried becuz nothing in the house was in her name nor was there anything of real value to her there. She'd got the apartment a month ago under an alias, and she had three different sets of fake IDs.

Rocc was looking out the front window thinking about how good he was going to fuck Keisha when he heard a familiar voice.

"Did you think you could disrespect me like I was a bitch and I wouldn't come for yo ass?"

As Rocc was turning around, he already knew whose voice it was. He went for his Glock that was in his waistband.

Madd Mike got off three shots before Rocc could get his strap out. The first shot hit Rocc in the back and the other two hit him in the side. Rocc dived out the front window firing his Glock in Madd Mike's direction. The bullets hit the wall about Madd Mike's head. As soon as Rocc's homies heard the shots, they bolted from the car and ran towards the apartment. As they got around the corner they saw Rocc lying on the ground and Madd Mike standing in the window frame about to shoot Rocc again.

Immediately, Lil Ken fired his Glock at Madd Mike. The bullet grazed his arm. Madd Mike ducked back in the room and ran for the back door. Lil Ken ran to Rocc while Keebo kicked the door in, strap in hand, looking for Madd Mike. He ran out the back door when he heard a car burning rubber. When he got to the alley, Madd Mike was about thirty yards away and moving fast. Keebo aimed and unloaded his 9mm 16-shot Beretta into the back window of the car. One of the bullets hit Madd Mike in the shoulder.

When Keebo got back to the others, Lil Ken was holding Rocc's head in his lap with tears coming down his face. Rocc was unconscious but he wasn't dead. The ambulance was there within five minutes. Lil Ken gave Keebo his strap and told him to go tell Goldie what happened. He'd know what to do.

Lil Ken rode in the ambulance with Rocc. Rocc was like the big brother Lil Ken never had. He swore on everything he loved that the bitch and Madd Mike wouldn't live to see another week.

When Keebo got to the spot on Tucker Street, Goldie was just pulling up from taking Monica to lunch and dropping her back off at one of her friends' house. Keebo ran up to Goldie and told him what happened.

Goldie went in the house and paged all the members of the G-Code Mobb committee with their emergency code, 1969, and left the spot's call back number. Within ten minutes, everyone had called back and was told to meet at Martin Luther King Jr. Hospital. Goldie called G-Moms and told her he didn't know how serious it was but Rocc had gotten shot and was at MLK. He was on his way there, and G-Moms and Lisa were on their way immediately as well.

QT and Nat were on their way back from the Bahamas. They'd had a great time on Paradise Island and had brought back souvenirs for everyone. As she lay with her head against QT's chest, he said, "Something doesn't feel right. It feel's like something has happened."

She asked, "What do you mean?"

"I just feel anxious and impatient...I can't really explain it."

Nat said, "We'll be home in another hour, baby. Try to relax. Whatever it is, we will deal with it together."

When they got off the plane and saw Keebo, QT knew something was wrong. Goldie was supposed to pick them up. The first thing QT said was, "What's up with my brother?"

Keebo told QT what had went down and took them straight to the hospital. Everyone was there. QT went straight to his moms who was crying. He hugged his moms and asked, "How is he? He's gonna be all right, ain't he?"

His moms said through sobs, "They had to operate. The operation went well but it's touch and go. My baby is in a coma. That's my baby in there, QT, he's in a coma."

The doctor came out and told them it was up to God and Rocc now, and that he had done all he could do. They just had to wait and see what happened. QT asked if he could go in to see Rocc. They doctor said yes but that only QT, G-Moms, Lisa, and Nat could see him.

Rocc was hooked up to all kinds of machines. It tore QT apart to see his lil brother like that. Tears were coming down everyone's faces. G-Moms took Rocc's hand and said, "Baby, it's me, mama. If you ain't never listened to me before listen to me now. You are strong, you hear me? Strong. You can get through this. I know you ain't never been a quitter. Remember when you first learned to ride a bike you fell off fifty times and got up fifty times and got back on it. By the end of the day you was riding that bike. You my baby boy and we love you so much. If anyone can pull this off, you can." G-Moms broke down crying. Nat and Lisa held her, all of them crying together.

QT walked up to the bed and took hold of Rocc's hand. Through his own tears he said, "What am I going to do without you, lil bro, who am I going to worry about? I know that you can hear me...we both got to be here when Gangsta comes home. I can't lose you, Rocc. You got to fight this. One day you will meet yo queen like I did...your soul mate. Being in love is beautiful and it's a feeling that surpasses all others. I want you to know this feeling too, lil bro. I know that I don't say it enough but I love you, Rocc, I love you." QT broke down. He couldn't stand to see his little brother like this, fighting for his life.

Nat went to him and held him tight. "He's strong, baby, he'll pull through, I know it. We got unfinished business to take care of."

G-Moms pulled QT to the side. She looked at him straight in the eye and said, "I don't care what it take. You get the nigga that did this to my baby. This ain't no gang shit, this is family. We can't allow nobody to hurt our family."

QT dried his eyes and took Nat by the hand and walked out the door. He called Goldie over and told him, "I want two homies here outside the door 24/7. Tell the committee to meet at my house now."

QT and Nat rode to his house with Goldie. QT was thinking all the way, he didn't say a word. Nat and Goldie were thinking as well. At QT's house, everyone was assembled around the Round Table. Nat stood at QT's side.

"We been slippin," QT began. "This muthafucka should have been dead. I want this muthafucka and I want the bitch that set Rocc up as well. I don't give a fuck what it takes. We all know people everywhere. Put the word out. All we want is an address. That's it, that's all. Everybody at this fuckin table is my family; you fuck with one of us, you fuck with all of us. We hurtin, so they family gonna hurt, only they gonna hurt more."

QT's pager went off. It was Spooky on the other line.

"What's up, cuz, we heard about Rocc. What you need us to do, just name it and it's done."

"I got this, homie, but I do need to find out where a nigga named Madd Mike lives. He the nigga that shot Rocc."

"Madd Mike? That nigga lives over here with his moms and two brothers off of Denker," Spooky said. "His brothers tried to claim the hood and we told them niggas to get the fuck on. I saw the nigga brothers about fifteen minutes ago. They be trying to slang chronic a couple of houses down from where they live."

QT said, "I'll meet you at yo spot in a hour." He hung up and filled everyone in on what was said. He went to a closet in the War Room, pushed a hidden button and the back of the closet opened. All kinds of straps appeared. QT retrieved two 16-shot 9mm Berettas.

Nat picked a mini Uzi 9mm with extra clip. "This is personal," Nat said. "I ain't trying to tell you how to run yo business. Rocc is my family as well, baby, we like Bonnie and Clyde; if you ride, I ride."

Everyone was surprised but no one said anything. They all wished they had a woman like Nat. QT didn't say nothing. He closed the closet and went back to the table with Nat at his side. QT told Crip Crazy to get a few of the homies and drop off two throw-away cars in the parking lot at MLK and to leave the keys under the floor mats. QT had at least thirty regular throw-away cars for the sole purpose of being used in times of war. They were all registered and up-to-date but couldn't be traced to anyone.

He told the rest of them that Goldie and Nat was going to smoke Madd Mike's brothers and for Boxer and Lil Man to post up in one of their undercover vans with the tinted windows with a couple homies at Madd Mike's house. As soon as they saw QT kidnap him, they were to at all costs not let him get away. But first, Nat would push up on his brothers to see if Madd Mike was home. If he was, Nat and Goldie would handle the brothers and QT would handle Madd Mike. He told everybody else, which was Big Bam and Crip Crazy to stay posted at the empty metal plant on Alameda because that's where they would be taking Madd Mike if they found him. After thinking for a minute, QT decided to change the plan.

"Change of plans. Get the van for me, Nat and Goldie. We're going to kidnap the two brothers. First, they will tell us where Madd Mike is, then we'll kidnap Madd Mike, and kill them all. We can't leave anyone that's a potential threat to us. Crip Crazy will meet you at the hospital in forty-five minutes to pick up the van. Everybody else get the warehouse ready. We're having company."

As everyone filed out, QT held Nat in his arms and told her, "Baby, you don't have to do this. I know that you got my back, but I can handle this."

Nat replied, "If this was regular business I wouldn't mind but, baby, this is personal, this is family."

QT walked back over to the closet and pushed the hidden button. When the back closet wall opened, he took three pair of handcuffs and a handcuff key, and said, "Let's get dressed."

Whenever QT dressed for war he put on all black: black khakis, black sweat shirt, black Nike Cortez, and his black ski mask. Nat put on some black jeans, a black pullover sweater, and some black Vans.

When they got to the hospital, Crip Crazy was waiting for them. Goldie gave Crip Crazy his car and they took the van. They were at Spooky's spot within thirty minutes. Spooky and Killa Watt were leaning against Spooky's car in the driveway. QT got out of the van and approached them.

"Cuz, I see you ready, we're ready too," Spooky said. He and Killa Watt pulled up their shirts to show QT the two Glocks apiece they had in their waistbands.

QT said, "Thanks for the love, cuzzin, but this is personal. Me and my people got this one. Just show me where these busters are."

They got in the van. Nat was driving. Madd Mike's house was only a block away. They showed QT the house and a couple of houses down from that they pointed out to QT where Madd Mike's two dumbass brothers were standing on the curb trying to sell chronic. They dropped Spooky and Killa Watt off and headed back to get the two dummies.

"Nat, just pull up. Give them yo million dollar smile and ask them where can you find some chronic. When they come up to the van, draw down on them but don't shoot unless they make you. Me and Goldie will open the sliding door and snatch they ass in."

When she pulled up, everything went exactly as planned. Jaybo and Ceebo saw Nat's beautiful face and smile, and they were thrown way off guard. Their thoughts went to sex—until she pointed the Uzi with the extended clip at them. That took them by surprise, just long enough for QT and Goldie to open the van's sliding door with straps in hand.

When they saw QT they automatically knew what time it was.

QT and Goldie quickly threw them in the van and handcuffed them. The dummies didn't even have a strap. Both of them were protesting at the same time. QT slapped one across the head with his strap. The dummy screamed as blood ran down his face.

"Shut the fuck up or it's going to get way worse," QT said. "Where's yo brother now? Before you answer that question you better think hard becuz if I don't get the answer I want..." he looked at Goldie and Goldie put duct tape over the bleeder's mouth. Goldie took out a pair of wire cutters and put a pinky finger between the blades. Jaybo's eyes got as big as a silver dollar. He was making all kinds of noises behind the duct tape.

When Goldie pulled the tape off his mouth, Jaybo said quickly, "He's in the house. He just came from Harbor General Hospital about three hours ago. He got shot in the shoulder and took some pain pills and went to sleep."

"Who else is in the house," QT demanded.

Jaybo said, "Nobody. My moms went to bingo at the casino."

QT taped both of their mouths up and had Nat pull into their driveway. He said, "Watch these idiots until we get back. If they try anything, shoot them."

Nat pointed the Uzi at Jaybo and Ceebo. They could see that the smile was gone and what they saw now was a mask of hate. QT and Goldie got out of the van and went to the front door. It was unlocked. Jaybo had told QT that Madd Mike was in the first room on the right side. The bedroom door was open and the TV was on. When QT peeked inside, Madd Mike was asleep on his stomach with his head turned in the opposite direction.

QT went over to him and put the Beretta to his head. He smacked him awake and told him not to move. Goldie cut on the light and handcuffed him. For a minute, Madd Mike thought he was dreaming; this couldn't be happening to him. QT didn't know where he lived, or else he would have been there long ago. Reality set in when QT put the duct tape over his mouth and snatched him up to a sitting position. Madd Mike moaned, hurting from the gun shot wound to his shoulder.

QT looked him in the eyes and said, "You had to know that I would come and find you. I know you didn't think you could hurt my family and live to talk about it. Look at you, you still living at yo mama's house and you think you can fuck wit me." He snatched him to his feet. "The only reason I didn't smoke yo bitch ass here is becuz we got to talk. I need to know who that bitch is that you had set my lil brother up. Other than that, yo mama would find you bitch ass right here stankin."

Outside when the van door opened and Madd Mike saw his two younger brothers inside, he knew it was a wrap. He knew that not only was he going to die, he had also brought the death penalty down on his brothers.

As the van pulled out of the driveway and rolled to its destination, Madd Mike thought to himself, What was the fuck I thinking trying to open a spot up in the Fays knowing that it was claimed by the G-Code Mobb? I should have took what I had coming and moved on. At least me and my brothers would be alive another day.

His brothers looked at him as if to say, do something, get us out of this shit, but Mike couldn't even look them in the eye. That's when the brothers realized that they were at the point of no return. This would be their last ride, living and breathing. Tears ran down both of their faces. Right then and there, they knew they wasn't Gangstas and they weren't cut out for this shit.

QT gave Nat the directions to the warehouse as she drove. They got there at 1 a.m. Nat pulled around to the back, and when the door was opened, she drove in. Lil Man, Big Bam, Crip Crazy, and Boxer were all there anxiously waiting, ready for whatever. Nat parked the van, got out, and opened the side door. QT kicked Jaybo, Ceebo, and Madd Mike out of the van.

Big Bam walked up to Madd Mike and ripped the duct tape off of his mouth. "Cuz, have you lost yo muthafuckin mind? Nigga, you ain't no Gangsta, that's why yo bitch ass got booted out the hood. You thank you can go against us?"

Crip Crazy said, "Nigga, I been knowing you all yo life. Yo ain't shit, ain't never been shit, and ain't goin to be shit." He back-handed Madd Mike like a bitch.

QT said, "Hang all of them from those chains that's hangin from the ceiling."

Once their hands were above their heads and cuffed to the chains, QT spoke. "You know what, Mike? I ain't going to torture yo brothers becuz they just got caught up for having a wannabe reject piece of shit for a brother. So I'm going to get them out the way quick." He looked at Lil Man.

Lil Man pulled a 9mm out of his waistband. It had a silencer on it. He walked up to Jaybo and shot him twice in the head, as Boxer did the same to Ceebo. QT pulled the tape off of Mike's mouth and said,

"Now tell me who that bitch is and I promise you, you won't have to suffer. It will be quick and painless."

Mike cried out, "You didn't have to kill my brothers, they had nothing to do with this."

"You were going to try to kill me, right?" QT said. "That's why I had to kill yo brothers so they couldn't have any get back at me or my family. But in reality, you killed them becuz yo actions set everything that has happened in motion. Now, enough of the bullshit. Where is the bitch?"

Mike tried to get QT or anyone to talk as long as he could becuz he knew once he told them where Keisha was, it was a done deal for him. He looked from face to face hoping somebody would say something but nobody did. Finally, he looked at QT and said, "Keisha's in a room at the Embassy Suites in Norwalk. Room 136. She's supposed to leave tomorrow for Vegas."

QT looked at his watch. It was 2:15 a.m. He pulled out both of his Berettas and handed one to Nat. Everybody pulled out their straps as well. QT pointed the Beretta at Madd Mike and said, "This is for Rocc."

The bullet hit Madd Mike in his mouth, crushing his front teeth. Once he fired, everybody else fired as well. Madd Mike was history.

"Me and Nat will go handle Keisha. Put them muthafuckas in the back of the van, take it down past the 91 Freeway on Alameda and burn it. Burn it good." He tossed Boxer the handcuff key, and he told Goldie to meet him on Tucker in an hour. He told everyone else he would see them at the hospital later that day.

QT and Nat got in one of the throw-away cars and QT drove to Norwalk. When they got there and were walking up to the room, Nat turned and said, "This bitch is mine, baby. Let me do her punk ass."

At room 136, QT kicked in the door. They ran straight to the bedroom. Keisha was in the process of trying to get off of the nigga's dick that she was sitting on. QT instantly shot him twice, once in the head and once through the heart. Keisha began to scream.

Nat hit her upside the head with her Beretta. "Shut the fuck up, you scandalous ass bitch."

Keisha knew who Nat and QT were so she knew why they were

there. As tears streamed down Keisha's face, Nat told her, "I just wanted to make sure you know why you dead, bitch. This is for Rocc." Nat blasted Keisha four times, twice in the face and twice into her chest.

They walked out of the room and were on Tucker Street within twenty minutes. Goldie's car was parked in the driveway but he was sitting on the porch talking on the phone. He was telling Monica about Rocc getting shot and that he would be home soon. As QT pulled up, he hung up and met them in the driveway.

QT gave Goldie the Berettas. "Get rid of these."

Goldie took the straps and the keys to the throw-away car. He gave QT the keys to his car. QT told him he would see him later at the hospital. Goldie got in the throw-away and pulled off. QT and Nat got in Goldie's car and headed home. Nat laid her head in QT's lap as he drove. It had been a long tiring day but the business had been handled and for now their family was safe. When they got home, Nat gave QT the Uzi. He laid it on the dresser in the bedroom then they took a hot bath together.

As they were sitting in the tub, QT said, "I want you to start keeping a strap with you at all times. It's not becuz I think someone is going to fuck wit you, it's just always better to be prepared."

Nat turned and softly kissed QT. "Whatever you say, baby. You my king."

QT kissed her back. "Yes, I am and you are my queen."

Later that day they arrived at the hospital to find everyone there. QT and Nat walked over to G-Moms and Lisa and gave them each a hug.

G-Moms said, "There hasn't been any change for the better or for the worse, he's the same."

QT pulled his mom to the side and told her, "There's no unfinished business. Everything has been handled. All of them are just a memory."

G-Moms said, "Yo brother called this morning. He wants you to come and see him as soon as possible."

QT already knew that was coming. He had already planned to go see Gangsta that weekend. QT told his homies to go back to whatever it was they did from day to day. Nat, Lisa, Moms, and Gangsta's wife Tonya would stay at the hospital with Rocc. The homies could drop in from time to time to sit and talk to Rocc.

Nat and QT went in to see him. QT took his hand said, "Don't trip, Crip, it's all good, we took care of that nigga and that bitch. They pushin up daisies. All you got to do is get well so we can get you a wifey."

Then Nat said, "We love you, Rocc, and we need you back here with us. You are the brother I never had but always wanted. When you stop playin with us and come on out of this, we will be right here waiting for you."

They went back to the waiting room. QT kissed Nat and told her he would be back later if she needed him. He was going to the shop. QT really didn't want to leave but he couldn't stand being there and not being able to do anything to help Rocc. He also couldn't stand to see him that way.

When QT got to the shop he went straight to his office. About an hour later the phone rang. He picked it up and said, "Imagine This, Quinten speaking."

A soft, sweet voice said, "This is Destiny. I'm sorry about what happened to your brother."

"Thanks."

There was silence for a few seconds, and Destiny said, "There is something I need to discuss with you, it's very important. I didn't just want to pop up, that's why I'm calling first to see if it's okay to stop by. I'm only a couple of blocks away."

QT said, "Yeah, it's cool, come on by."

When Destiny got there, the manager Paul escorted her to QT's office. QT told him he was expecting her. Paul left and closed the door. Destiny was looking professional with a skirt suit and heels on, and as beautiful as ever. He stood up and she walked over to him with real concern on her face. She hugged him and said, "I'm truly sorry about Rocc."

She smelled so good—it was like QT was in a rose garden. She broke the embrace and he said, "I saw you at my wedding, you wedding crasher."

"I just wanted to see it for myself since I couldn't be the one. I can see that you and Natalie are in love, and as long as you are happy, I'm happy for you," she said. "But I didn't come here to discuss that. I came to tell you that the task force with the Compton PD, FBI, DEA, ATF, and the IRS, will be formed and in operation within the next two weeks. I have transferred to Compton PD to be on the task force. I can tell you now that you are one of the names on their list to take down. All of your phones will probably be tapped within the next three weeks."

"Why are you telling me all of this and why would you risk your career for me?"

Destiny got on her knees in front of QT, pulled his sweats down and slowly stroked his dick. She looked him straight in the eye and said, "I'm in love with you and I'll do anything for you. Anything." She took him in her mouth and sucked him to orgasm. He came in her mouth and she swallowed every drop. When she finished, she stood up, picked up her purse and went in to QT's bathroom to brush her teeth.

While she was in there, QT thought, I have got to keep her on my line. She's really going to be useful and I do like her.

Destiny walked out of the bathroom and said, "Whenever I have info for you I will page you from a pay phone and just leave 69-69 on your pager. That way, if they decide to clone your pager they will think it's a female calling you for sex. Go to a pay phone and call me at this number." She handed him a slip of paper. "Memorize it. It's my personal cell phone. Remember—always call me from a pay phone and never the same one twice."

She hugged him and this time, QT gripped both of her ass cheeks in his hands. This time, he kissed her slowly. She felt good in his arms. He wanted to fuck her but he thought about Nat and figured for now a blow job was good enough. He broke their embrace and told her, "You trying to get me in trouble. I don't have any condoms. I threw them away the day I got married."

Destiny smiled and said, "Next time I'll have some."

She kissed QT on the neck and licked her tongue up to his ear. As she walked out of his office, QT thought, damn, I must be the luckiest nigga alive. He didn't tell Nat about Destiny becuz he knew that once Nat saw her she would know off the top that he had fucked her. So he kept Destiny to himself.

That Friday, QT and Nat drove to Represa, California, to see Gangsta in Folsom. Nat's visiting form hadn't been approved so she stayed at the room while QT went to see his brother. QT waited about fifteen minutes before Gangsta finally came out. They shook hands and embraced.

They sat down and Gangsta asked, "Cuz, what's going on out there, and what's up with that nigga that shot Rocc?"

QT ran everything down for Gangsta, even how Nat handled her business, and then he told him about Destiny.

Gangsta said, "All that's to the good and definitely keep Nat and Destiny on yo team. I talked to my lawyer a few days ago and he said once he file the motions, he say I should be able to get the manslaughter, and even if I get the max, I'll only have four years left."

QT said, "That's all good. I can't wait for you to touch down."

"So how is Rocc really doing? Don't sugar coat shit for me, give it to me raw."

"He's in a coma but he strong. I know he goin to pull through this shit."

"He will pull through. He probably laying there now, dreaming about some pussy."

They both started laughing. Gangsta said, "Now on a serious note, word is it's some niggas out there that's on some straight Gangsta shit kidnapping and killing niggas wit loot. They hitting niggas at random. They even kidnapped a few bitches too. They ain't letting nobody live so all the 'give us the money and we'll let whoever go' is bullshit. You, Nat, and the homies better be on yo Ps and Qs, and tell Nat never come home the same way. What you need to do is find out who these niggas are, just in case. That way, if they do get one of ours we got something to bargain with, and we can hit they ass hard."

QT said, "I'm on it like yesterday."

"So how's the businesses going? Moms told me you opened up two of them."

QT smiled and said, "They going good, real good, all thanks to Nat."

"Next time you come she should be approved and I'll finally get to meet my sister-in-law."

"She can't wait to meet you. She was really disappointed that she couldn't see you today. Anyway, how was the fam-bam (family visit)?"

"Nigga, you know it was all good shit. I can't wait till the next one—that shit is five months away. But once I get this time off, I can transfer closer to home where a nigga can fuck damn near every sixy days. That's love," Gangsta said.

They kicked it and talked until the visit was over. They embraced and shook hands and Gangsta walked back through the door to loneliness, frustration, and madness.

On the way home, QT informed Nat about the niggas that was going around kidnapping, robbing, and killing. He told her to be extra careful and don't take nothing for granted, to stay strapped, and be aware of any and all smooth-talking niggas trying to get at her.

When they got home Saturday night, Nat cooked dinner for them. They made love and went to sleep. Santana and Blocc slept at the foot of the bed.

The next morning, QT called a meeting at his pad with the G-Code Mobb. He told them everything that Gangsta had told him about the jackers. He told them about the info that he got from his source that worked at the Compton Police Station.

QT said, "Tonight is the last time that we are going to be meeting together for awhile unless it's really an emergency. From now on, Goldie is going to handle all the dope so whenever you need to reup, get at Goldie. Don't use nothing but pay phones and when you on a pay phone make sure you got somebody watchin yo back. Always use our code when paging anyone in the Mobb, that way we know to call back ASAP. Stay out of Compton as much as possible until this heat blows over. They can't stay on us forever, especially when they ain't coming up with nothing. I haven't said nothing, but I've been sending a couple of homies OT (out of town) to Seattle. They been making a killing too. Birds are going for $16,500 out here, but out there they going for $28,000 easy, and it ain't no waiting they just get there, dump the birds whole and they on their way back."

"The best thing to do is for each one of us to get a state, that way there will be less risk. No phone contact or nothing. Once they leave we don't want to hear from them until they come back, and then they still can't come straight to us. If they ever call before they get back, we know something ain't right. If they get jacked, it ain't shit to send a couple of homies down there to put some work in and come back home."

Everybody agreed to work on getting a state to serve. After the meeting and everyone had left, Nat told QT, "Baby, you are truly one of a kind and I love you so much."

"I love you too, Nat. You make my heart beat for you."

Chapter 7: Operation Take Down

Monday morning at 9 a.m. the task force was assembled at an empty building in downtown Compton. Special agent White of the DEA was to head the task force. There were a total of eleven of them in the room: 3 DEA, 2 ATF, 2 FBI, 2 IRS and 2 from the Compton PD, which consisted of Destiny Stevens and Mike Foster. Foster had been working on the force for sixteen years, mainly with the gang unit.

"We all know why we are here," Agent White began. "Today is the first day of the end of this gang. We don't know who all the members are but we do know that they are originally Santana Blocc Crips. They were started by Gangsta, who's in Folsom serving a life sentence, so we don't have to worry about him. Gangsta's younger brother, QT," he said as he passed out photographs, "is the head of this organization now. QT's younger brother, Rocc, is also a part of this crew but, fortunately, he's in MLK in a coma. He was gunned down last week at the house of one Keisha Thomas. She was murdered the same night in a hotel room, along with a man named David Jones. I think he was just in the wrong place at the wrong time. There were also three bodies found on Alameda in a burned van. DNA tests show they were brothers. The oldest had had a beef with Rocc. That's the short and the long of it; there hasn't been any witnesses come forward. Now, what we have to do is find all the members of this organization and bring them down. Check their tax returns...brothers, sisters, mothers, whatever."

"I want QT under surveillance, and anyone he comes in contact will be checked out. Also, QT just got married. His wife owns three fast food franchises and has $900,000 in the bank. She seems to be clean, but we will see. She also made a loan to QT for $600,000 before they were married. He started up two tire and rim shops, called Imagine This. One is in Inglewood and the other in West L.A. I'm already in the process of getting phone taps on QT's mother's house, his house, his cell phone, and his two shops."

"Stevens and Foster, I need you to hit the streets and put pressure on the street pushers in that neighborhood. Somebody is bound to give us something of good use. Davis and Jones of the DEA will keep an eye on QT. We know that these guys have guns so see if we can come up with a murder weapon. I don't have to tell you this is a big case. It could make all of our careers better. We will meet here every morning, Monday to Friday, for a briefing."

A block over at the Compton Police Station, Beckman and Ross sat in their office sipping coffee and eating donuts. "It's really going to be hard to get QT's black ass now," Beckman said. "The task force is going to be all over his ass."

"I know," Ross said. "If that dumb asshole hadn't of went and gotten himself killed, maybe we could have busted QT's black ass."

"What we need to do is find the gun that killed him or the other three that were found in the burned out van."

"Yeah, those dumb fucks don't get rid of guns, and that will be to our advantage."

Two months later the task force had not gotten any closer to QT or his crew. Some of the lower level homies that were slangin in the hood had been busted, but QT quickly bailed them out of jail. Everyone had stayed solid but even if they hadn't they still couldn't have given up QT because they had never dealt with him.

Rocc was still in a coma. G-Moms, Lisa, Nat, Monica, Tonya, QT, Goldie and other members from Santana Blocc still went to see and sit with Rocc on a daily basis.

Nat and Monica had gotten even closer since Monica moved in with Goldie. They even started going to the shooting range together. Nat taught Monica how to load and shoot a pistol.

All of the G-Code Mobb had found a state to start sending kilos of cocaine to. The money was coming back so fast that QT had Goldie buying two hundred kilos instead of the regular 100 kilos. All of the info that the feds had was pertaining to instate California sales of cocaine—only they didn't know about the out of state sales.

It was 11 a.m. on a Saturday morning and QT was dressed and in the den playing with Santana and Blocc. When Nat came downstairs she was surprised to see him home because usually he would be at one of the shops on a Saturday morning. Nat had on a Fila sweat suit with tennis shoes to match. Her hair was pulled in a ponytail and she had her Louis Vuitton purse in her hand.

"What's up, baby?" she asked. "Why aren't you at the shop?"

QT smiled and said, "Because I want to do something different today. Come on, roll wit me today. I got something for you."

Nat was curious as to what QT had up his sleeve. First they went to breakfast at Roscoe's Chicken and Waffles. Then Nat was really wondering what was up when they pulled up in front of the spot on Tucker Street. A smile crossed her face when she looked in the driveway and saw the 63 Chevy that QT had won for her sitting there freshly washed and waxed and looking like new. Nat had thought QT had forgot all about her wanting to learn how to drive a Low Rider and hitting the switches.

"Today is your day, baby. Come on, let's roll."

QT got in the driver's seat and as he drove he schooled Nat on different things such as the best height for the car to be while driving, to never let the car all the way up in the front and back while on the freeway or going fast because it would be uncontrollable. QT took her to a big empty lot and showed her how to drive it and also how to hit the switches. Just up and down. It would take time for her to learn how to hop a Low Rider. They stayed at the empty lot three hours. QT told her that he would bring her every Saturday until she was ready to roll on her own. Then they would hit the Shaw again but only she would be behind him driving the 63 on her own.

QT drove the 63 back to the spot and put it in the backyard. He dropped Nat off at home to get her car. Nat and Monica were going to the Fox Hills Mall to shop and QT went to his second shop in

Inglewood. Business had been good at both shops and they were making money.

He didn't procrastinate on trying to find out who the niggas were that was doing all the jacking and killing. Through his sources and money, he found out who the whole crew was. There were five of them and they were all Bloods from the east side in the 20s. The leader was a nigga named Boss-T who had done eight years in the state pen for robbing restaurants. He had been out nineteen months. Then there was Nacho, Ed Dog, and G-Rob, they all had a reputation for jacking and gang bangin. The last one was a nigga called Nutt. Nutt and Boss-T were the most dangerous, and they were killers. QT got all the info on all of them including their families and baby mommas. All of the G-Code Mobb had all of this info as well. QT was ready; he hoped the niggas didn't come his way but if they did QT wasn't taking any prisoners, he was playing for keeps becuz he knew these niggas would as well.

QT left the second shop and went to the one in west L.A. He was in his office and was going through his desk when he came across Tasha's phone number. He thought about it for a minute then said to himself, fuck it. He had a burn-out cell phone that he changed every seven days so he knew the feds didn't have it tapped. He dialed Tasha's number.

When she answered, he asked, "What's up, sexy?"

She instantly knew that it was QT. She hadn't talked to him since the last time that they had sex. She had seen him plenty of times but he hadn't seen her. It had been over three months and she still hadn't been with another man. She only wanted QT; she fantasized about being with him all the time.

"Oh daddy! I don't believe it's you but I know it is. I know that sexy voice anywhere. Oh, I have been missing you."

"Calm down, baby. Where are you?"

"I'm in Baldwin Hills on my way home. Why?"

"Come by the shop where I last saw you. I'll be in my office."

"I'm on my way," she said.

Tasha couldn't believe her ears as she hung up. She had waited what seemed like forever to get that call. She didn't understand the hold that QT had on her. She had never fallen for a man the way she fell for QT. Usually niggas hounded and sweated her as they still did. Tasha knew that on a scale from 1 to 10, she was at least a 9, plus some niggas even felt like she was a 12. But to QT, it seemed like she was just some cool regular broad—at least that's what Tasha thought he was thinking. Tasha knew that QT's wife was good looking but she felt she could stand up beside any female and hold her own. As she drove to the shop, she hoped that they would make love. It had been awhile for her and just thinking about QT made her wet.

QT didn't know why he called Tasha. Everything was going right with him and Nat. He loved her but there was something about Tasha's sexy black freaky ass. QT called the manager and told him he was expecting a female so when she got there just to tell her to come on to his office.

She arrived about thirty-five minutes later. She looked beautiful as usual. It was September in California so the weather was still warm. She had on a sundress that stopped above her knees, and was wearing some high heels. Her long silky black hair hung down her back and over her shoulders. Her skin was dark and smooth with a glow to it.

QT stood up and said, "What's up, baby? How you been doing?"

She came in and closed the door. "I'm miserable becuz I don't have you." She walked up to QT, hugged him, and didn't want to let him go. She took his hands and put them on her ass. It was nice and firm, and it felt good too. She could feel QT getting hard. She broke her hold on him, went to her knees, and quickly slid him into her mouth. The head was fantastic. Before QT could cum, Tasha stood up, pulled down her panties and said, "Fuck me, daddy, please."

He told her, "I don't have any condoms."

Tasha smiled and pulled out a fresh box of Magnums that hadn't been opened. She took one out and gave it to QT. He put it on and Tasha bent over the couch. Her pussy was dripping wet. QT pushed his dick into Tasha all at once. She screamed out and instantly started cumming. QT was long stroking her with two fingers in her ass. She was wet but the pussy was still tight and hot. He pulled out of her pussy, took the condom off and pushed his dick in her ass. She started hollering and saying, "Daddy, oh, daddy, fuck it. This is yo ass, daddy. I told you everything is yours. Oh, I missed this dick. Oh, I missed it, please, daddy, don't make me wait this long again. Oh, it yours, it's yours."

QT was really turned on by her hollering. He was long stroking her ass on the brink of cumming, and when he came, Tasha came with him. She felt his hot cum shooting in her ass and she was cumming at the same time. She collapsed, her legs shaking uncontrollably. It took her fifteen minutes to get herself together. She joined QT in the shower and began to cry. He held her and asked, "What's wrong, baby?"

Through tears, she replied, "I love you so much. You don't understand—I really love you. I will do anything for you. I haven't been with anyone. Niggas get at me all day everyday but I turn them all down because they are not you."

QT just held her. He didn't want to lie to her and give her false hope becuz even though he messed around every now and then, he loved Nat and would never leave her for any woman.

Tasha broke their embrace. She stepped out of the shower and came back with another condom. She smiled and said, "It might be awhile before you call me again." She took him into her mouth. When he was fully hard, she put the condom on him. She stood up, put her hands around QT's neck as he picked her up and she wrapped her legs around his waist. QT slid her down on his dick. As he fucked her, she proclaimed her love for him in his ear. After he came they finished showering, dried each other off and got dressed.

It was an hour from closing time at the shop. QT told her that he had feelings for her but he didn't want to mislead her; he loved his wife and wasn't going to leave her.

Tasha said, "I feel where you are coming from. That's one of the reasons I love you because you keep it real and you let me make the choice of being here for you, knowing I can never have you fully to myself. Just call me whenever you need me, no matter what time it is, or where I need to come to." She embraced QT, kissed him softly on the lips, and walked out of his office.

When QT left the shop he got an emergency page from Goldie. He went to the phone booth in front of Ralph's grocery store and called Goldie who was also at a phone booth. Goldie answered on the first ring.

"Yo, QT, the homies just got back from Seattle. They got jacked for ten birds. Lil Mike got blasted but he going to be all right. He still in the hospital out there."

"Send some of the homies down there, just two of them gunners. Also, send one of the homies that gets money for us out there with them to show them who's who," QT said. "Fuck the work, it's gone. Just tell the homies to send a good message. I want a body count. I want them niggas to know we ain't to be fucked with."

"Will do."

They hung up and QT went to his car. He wasn't trippin the ten birds—he was mad becuz them square-ass, wannabe-ass niggas had the balls to disrespect his crew which meant they disrespected him as well. Since QT knew the feds was on him that limited who he could fuck with. He didn't want to go fuck with a lot of other niggas from L.A. and Watts that he usually fucked with becuz they all were in the game. He didn't want to be the reason that the feds got on them. So he only fucked with them at a club, on Crenshaw or at the skating rink.

QT decided to go to the hospital to visit Rocc. On the drive over, he had an idea. He called Tasha on his cell phone. When she answered he said, "What's up, girl?"

"Today gots to be my lucky day—two calls from you in one day."

"Where are you?"

"I'm getting my hair redone."

"Can you take off work for about three days?"

"I told you I can and will do anything for you."

"Okay, check this out. I need you to take a drive to Seattle for me. The car will have some guns in it but that's all. Park the car at the airport, leave the key under the floor mat and catch a flight back home."

Tasha said, "When do I leave?"

QT said, "Tomorrow. My homeboy will call you to pick the car up later tonight."

"Call me when I get back, please."

"Okay, baby, drive the speed limit, be safe, and if anything goes wrong, my homeboy is going to give you a number to call. No matter what, never talk to the police, no matter what they say."

Tasha said, "You may not know this but I'm a street bitch. I know the first and most important rule of the streets and that's never snitch."

QT smiled and said, "Have a nice trip."

When he got to the hospital, he paged Goldie from the phone in the hospital. Goldie called back within ten minutes. QT told Goldie to have the homies fly to Seattle. He gave Goldie Tasha's phone number and told him to call her and give her one of the throw-away cars with the gun stash in it. He added, "Put one Ak-47 with two clips and two Glocks in the stash. Also, give Tasha ten thousand dollars. Also, send Lil Ken and Moonie with E-Bone. Tell them to stay undercover, find out where the niggas handle their business, make sure there's no prints on the guns and throw them in the first gutter they get to. They go straight to the airport and catch a flight home. Leave the car in long term parking. When they get there, the car will be in long term parking with the keys under the floor mat."

When QT went in Rocc's room, his moms was sitting next to him and holding his hand. QT kissed his moms on the forehead and sat down next to her. "How long have you been here?" he asked.

"Since this morning. Lisa was here too, but I told her to go on home and get some rest."

"How is he doing? What are the doctors saying?"

"He's still strong but there hasn't been any change in his condition. The doctors say that he could come out of it any day, or it could be years, or never."

QT said, "I know my brother. He will come out of it—this is just his way of making us sweat."

Nat, Tonya, and Monica walked into the room and all kissed Rocc on the forehead.

"See, mama," QT said. "Look at all the attention he's getting. He's loving this. He's like a kid in a candy store."

G-Moms smiled and said, "Boy, be quiet. Let him enjoy himself as long as he comes back to us. I miss my baby. He would still come by for breakfast every morning. I used to tell him, 'Boy, all the women you got, you don't got nobody to cook for you.'" Tears were in her eyes. "Rocc, would just smile, kiss me on the cheek, and say, 'can't none of them cook like you, ma.'" She started crying openly.

QT embraced her and said, "Everything is going to be all right. Rocc will pull through this and he'll be right back at yo house every morning with a spoon and fork in his hands."

Goldie called Tasha once he had everything set up. He told her to have someone drop her off in the McDonald's parking lot on Long Beach Boulevard and that there would be a brand new tan Buick Regal with lightly tinted windows there for her. The driver's side door would be unlocked and the keys would be under the floor mat. He also told her there would be something in the glove box for her.

Tasha followed all the directions and when she got there and looked in the glove box, she couldn't believe her eyes. She went home and counted the money: it was $10,000. She had been working hard saving her money to buy herself a house, now this would put her where she needed to be. She could have easily hooked up with a nigga with money who could have given her what she needed, but she didn't want any strings attached. Tasha took one thousand dollars out for the trip, put up the rest, then she took a long hot bath. She packed what she needed and fell asleep thinking about QT and hoping one day—one day—he would be hers.

Goldie hooked up with E-Bone, Lil Ken, and Moonie and gave them the rundown, telling them they would be on a flight in two days for Seattle. He gave all three of them fake IDs and round-trip plane tickets. He told them to dress like squares and once they got to the airport to act like they were not together and didn't know each other.

Just go and take care of business, he told them. Leave the car in long term parking with the keys under the floor mat, and fly back home. "The main thang is to make sure you make a statement with what you do," he said.

After QT and Nat got home, he told her, "It's still early. It's only 8:45. Come on and roll wit me."

Nat didn't question QT, she just got her purse and followed him out the door. She didn't know where they were going but she smiled when they turned into the Santa Monica pier. QT parked and they went straight to the game room where they played Ms Pac-Man and Centipede. Nat won at Ms Pac-Man and QT won at Centipede. They took a photo together and had it put on a calendar, then they went down to the beach and walked together hand in hand. As they were headed back to the car, QT noticed three fools following them.

Before he could say anything, Nat said, "Baby, don't look back but three niggas have been following us since we left the boardwalk."

"I peeped them out. I see you on yo Ps and Qs. That's a good thang."

"I got my strap in my purse."

"Mine is in my shoulder holster," he said. "As soon as we get to the car and they get within ten feet of us, we draw down on these muthafuckas."

Just as they got to the car, two of the niggas headed to QT's side of the car and the other headed towards Nat's side. QT and Nat turned and drew down on them. "You take one more step muthafucka, and it will be you last."

QT and Nat had caught them off guard. They were strapped as well and had planned on robbing them and taking QT's Benz to get away in. They had spotted the big diamond ring on Nat's finger and the Rolex watches that they wore and decided to rob them.

QT walked up to the two on his side and pointed his strap at the face of the one closest to him. Nat had her strap pointed at the face of the third one. One of the niggas tried to play it off by saying, "Yo, what's up with pulling a gun on us? We don't know you. We are just going to our car."

"Cuz, you think I was born yesterday? I spotted you dumb ass niggas when I was playing games in the Arcade. I used to be a jacker and I was way smoother than y'all idiots." QT put them on the car hood and searched them all. He took two pistols from them—9mm Llamas. "The only reason why you niggas ain't dead yet is becuz I'm in a good mood and tonight is ya'll lucky night. Now get the fuck out of here before I change my mind."

They took off walking fast, constantly looking over their shoulders to get away from QT.

QT and Nat got into the Benz and drove out of the parking lot. They got on the 10 Freeway heading east. QT handed the straps to Nat and told her to wipe their prints off them and throw them down the side of the freeway. When they got home, Nat cooked them some tacos. They made love after dinner, and fell asleep.

The DEA had been watching QT at his shops every day. The phones were tapped as well but QT knew all of this because Destiny had kept him updated on everything she knew. The feds were getting impatient because they didn't have anything to connect QT to illegal activities. They wondered where QT kept the cocaine, who his supplier was, and how was he moving it. They started thinking that the drugs were at the shops because of the steady flow of traffic at the shops and because trucks were constantly delivering big boxes—supposedly containing rims.

At the next briefing, Special Agents Davis and Jones of the DEA briefed all the other members of the task force on what they believed about QT and the likelihood of drugs at the shops. The decision was made to get a search warrant for both shops. They would serve the warrant and search both places at the same time. The raids were to take place in forty-eight hours, as soon as QT arrived at one of the shops. Destiny immediately paged QT and left her code: 69 69.

QT was sitting at his shop frustrated because he hadn't been able to kick it with his homies because of the feds. He knew that the feds could only be on him so long before they would have to turn their attention on someone else if they didn't come up with something on him to justify continuing the investigation.

QT called Destiny's personal phone from his new burn-out phone that he had got the day before. She answered on the first ring. "Hey, daddy, what's up?"

"You paged me, so you tell me what's up."

"I hope that your shops are clean because they are going to be raided on Thursday as soon as you arrive at one of them."

"Don't worry, my shops are as clean as the Board of Health. I would never bring nothing dirty to my shops. I ain't no fool."

"I figured that you wouldn't," Destiny said. "I just wanted to let you know so you would be prepared for all that bullshit."

"Good looking out, baby. By the way, what are you wearing?"

"Are you flirting with me? Don't start something you can't finish."

"What color panties do you have on?"

"I don't have any on, big daddy." In a teasing way, she then hung up the phone.

QT laughed and thought to himself, I got to go hit that sweet tight ass. Nat had been visiting her mother and father on a regular basis so QT decided that the next time Nat left to visit them, he would call Destiny and see if she really wasn't wearing any panties.

Thursday morning, five minutes after QT got to his shop in Inglewood, the task force hit. He was sitting behind his desk, smoking on a Lemac (Camel) when agents rushed into his office and pointed their guns at him. Special Agent White walked in behind them and handed QT a search warrant.

QT read the warrant, sat it on his desk, and continued smoking his cigarette. Between tokes he looked up at Agent White and said, "I don't use or sell drugs. I am a businessman."

"Yeah, I know your kind," White said. "This shit ain't nothing but a front. You are nothing but a street punk who thinks he's slick. I deal with scum like you all day everyday. You ain't no different."

QT looked at Agent White and said, "Just make sure yo boys put my shit back the way they found it and don't take all day. Time is money."

Agent White turned and told Agent Davis, "Make sure you go through everything."

Three hours later, when the search was over and nothing had been found at either shop, Agent White was red in the face. On their way out, QT said, "Next time, get a reliable informant not a dummy that will say anything."

Agent Davis turned and headed towards QT but White grabbed him by the arm. "He's not worth throwing away your badge over. It might take a little time but we will get his ass."

Destiny had gone to the raid at the other shop because she didn't want to see QT in the presence of her co-workers. She didn't want to reveal anything through facial expressions unexpectedly.

Agent White, as well as all the other agents, was frustrated. Back at the task force office, he addressed the others in the briefing room. "Since we started this investigation, we haven't been able to find out who is part of this organization, nor have we been able to connect QT to anything or anyone. All he does is go to work and spend time with his wife, his mother, and sister and brother in the hospital. Shit, we haven't even caught this asshole cheating on his wife. I know that we are not wrong about this guy because too many people in the streets have given us reports on him. Plus, I know he's dirty, so where do we go from here?"

Agent White looked at Destiny and asked, "When you were with L.A.P.D., all you worked was undercover narcotics. I've gone over your record and it's very impressive. What I need you to do is go undercover. You are a very beautiful young woman. Go to his shop and get his attention. The only people that know you're a cop is your mother and father—besides the little assholes that you and Foster have sweated. QT doesn't really associate with anyone so I think you are perfect for this assignment. I already have some false identification, a condo, and a new convertible 850 Beamer that we took off a dope dealer in San Diego. Get close to him and then let him know that you are transporting cocaine out of state. We well even provide some for you to have at your condo for him to see by mistake. Once he knows you are in the game, he may bite. Then we will have him. You won't have to worry about wearing a wire until he bites, then we'll have his ass. But we will give you a cell phone that will be bugged."

After his speech, he waited for an answer from Destiny. She didn't want to seem eager or anxious to take the assignment so she took her time. Only when she saw Agent White getting impatient, did she reply. "Okay, I'm in."

Really, this was a dream come true for her because so many nights she had longed to be able to be with QT.

After the meeting, everything was put into motion. Destiny got the car, spending cash, the condo in Granada Hills, and new ID. Her new name would be Teresa Johnson. Once she was settled in, she paged QT and told him everything. All QT could do was laugh and she laughed with him. He told her that he would see her the next day when she brought her car into his shop to get some music installed.

QT hung up the phone and thought to himself, I really got to be careful. These assholes really want me bad. They got to know that she can't get close to me without me fucking her so if they are willing to let me fuck her, they want me bad.

He smiled and said out loud, "They just throwing the pussy at me and it is my duty to get some of that booty." He started laughing out loud as he drove home in his Porsche bumpin to Kurtis Blow's "If I Ruled the World."

Tasha had handled her business without problems and had been back for three days, but QT hadn't called her yet. He decided it was time. When she answered, he asked, "How was your trip?"

He could tell by the way she sounded that she was smiling. "Daddy, the trip was fine and I thought about you all the way there and back. For a minute, I thought you wasn't going to call me. Daddy, you didn't have to give me that money. I told you I will do anything for you."

QT said, "It was a present from me to you, besides you deserve the better things in life. Check yo mailbox when I get off the phone. I got to go. I'll call you soon."

When QT hung up the phone, Tasha ran out of her apartment to her mailbox. When she opened it she found an envelope with just TASHA written on it. It contained a deed to a condo located in Rancho Cucamonga, with the keys, and a note. It read: What's up, baby. The condo is yours. It's already furnished. You deserve it. I'll call you soon. QT.

Tears ran down her face — they were tears of joy. She didn't think that she could love QT any more than she already did but at that moment she felt something for him that was indescribable. It was a feeling she had never felt before.

Tasha lay awake all night tossing and turning. Not only had QT bought her a condo, it was in her name. She was up at 5 a.m. and dressed, ready to go out to see her new home.

When E-Bone, Lil Ken, and Moonie got to Seattle, they got the Regal, checked the stash to make sure the straps were there. Paper plates covered up the real license plates. They went and got a suite at the Hyatt hotel. They didn't want to be there any longer than necessary. E-Bone knew his way around Seattle because he was one of the homies that was slangin for QT there.

Lil Ken told E-Bone, "Cuz, go find out where them niggas are and come back and get us. We'll handle the rest."

E-Bone didn't find them that night but the next night he came back to the room excited. "Cuz, I found them bitch ass niggas. They moved to a new spot, that's why I couldn't find them last night. It's about ten or fifteen of them hanging out. That nigga that shot Lil Mike he supposed to be their leader. He's sitting in front of the spot in a new 500 Benz. The nigga calls his self Big Wayne."

When they got in the car to go handle the business, E-Bone continued: "We only been dealing with this nigga Big Wayne for about the last three times we come down here. The nigga seemed to be cool. He bought about five or six birds every time we dealed wit him. The last time he ordered ten and tried to go on some Gangsta shit. He shot Lil Mike becuz Lil Mike told him he was living on borrowed time."

They got to the spot and E-Bone drove by so Lil Ken and Moonie could see Big Wayne in the Benz, and also so they could see how they were going to approach the situation. Lil Ken and Moonie could see that these wannabe ass niggas was slippin, and it was evident that they thought everything was everything. Lil Ken and Moonie dressed in the car and put on all black.

E-Bone parked around the corner. The spot was two houses from the corner so it would be an easy hit. While E-Bone stayed in the car with the motor running, Lil Ken and Moonie decided to go through the two back yards on the opposite side of the street and walk out from the back and take out Big Wayne first.

Lil Ken had the AK-47 and Moonie had the two Glocks. They put their brownies (gloves) on, checked the weapons, and got out of the car. They hopped over the gate at the first house, and when they got to the back yard at the second house, they could see the Benz across the street. Big Wayne was sitting in the driver's seat smoking on a blunt with one of his homies. By the time Big Wayne or anyone else noticed, Moonie and Lil Ken were in the middle of the street three feet away from the Benz.

Lil Ken started unloading on the Benz first, then Moonie starting unloading on all the niggas in front of the spot. Big Wayne was dead after the first three shots from the AK-47. Niggas were screaming like bitches. Lil Ken unloaded the whole clip on the Benz then he reloaded and blasted the niggas on the ground that Moonie had hit.

When they were finished, eight niggas were laid out on the ground and two in the Benz. All dead. Ten in all. Lil Ken and Moonie ran and jumped in the Regal and dumped the straps in the first gutter they got to. They headed straight for the airport, changing their clothes on the way. At the airport lot, they snatched the paper plates off the license plates on the Regal, E-Bone wiped it down for finger-prints, and they caught the first thing smoking back to Cali.

The shooting was something that was beyond comprehension in Seattle. Nothing even close to that magnitude had ever happened in Seattle before. The story made the world news: nine dead and one in critical condition. Lil Mike made it back home the day before the shooting so there were no more homies out that way. As for the car, fuck it, the city could have it—it couldn't be traced back to anyone.

QT would have to find another OT spot. But the niggas out in the streets and in the game in Seattle, even though no one could prove it, knew them niggas from Cali put that work in. QT was at home when he saw the news about "Murders in Seattle." He smiled to himself and said out loud, "Don't ever test my Gangsta. My Gangsta is official."

QT had security cameras put in both of his shops so he could sit back in his office and watch everything that was going on, becuz there were a couple of shops like his that had been robbed. He wanted to be prepared in case robbers came into his shop where he was there. It was also to make sure that if he was in his office getting his dick sucked or fucking another woman, he would be able to see if Nat walked in. She only came to the shops every now and then because she also had businesses of her own to run. But at times, Nat did pop up unexpectedly.

QT was watching the screens when Destiny walked in. She talked to the manager for about five minutes, picked out a music system for her car, and gave the manager her keys. The manager called QT and told him a customer wanted to talk to him.

When Destiny walked into his office, QT got up from his desk to close and lock the door. Destiny was looking beautiful and she had her hair flat ironed and wore it parted in the middle. Her hair ran way down to the middle of her back and over her shoulders down to the middle of her stomach. She had on a two-piece skirt suit with a silk blouse and a pair of 4-inch high heel pumps. She carried a Donney & Burke purse.

He took Destiny in his arms and kissed her slowly. When he broke their embrace, he asked, "So how do yo boss think that you are supposed to get close enough to me for me to let you in on whatever it is that they think I'm doing?"

"I don't know what they really expect but what I do know is, if it wasn't you I wouldn't have taken this assignment," she said. "When I leave and file my report, I'm just going to tell them you asked me for my phone number and I gave you the number to the tapped phone, and that hopefully you will call soon."

"I'm going to make them sweat and not call the number for two weeks."

They both started laughing. Then Destiny slowly started taking her clothes off. QT just stood there and watched, admiring her beauty. When she was completely nude, she started undressing him. When QT was naked she guided him to the sofa, pushed him down and got between his legs. Slowly, she took her time licking and sucking on his inner thighs, putting his balls in her mouth and licking up and down the length of his manhood. She wanted to tease him for awhile before she took him into her mouth. After ten minutes of foreplay, she took QT into her mouth and slowly sucked him in and out. Before QT could cum she stopped. He pulled her on top of him, flipped her over on her back and slowly started licking and sucking on her breast. He made his way down to her inner thighs and decided to tease her just as she had teased him. All of Destiny's pubic hair was shaved off so QT kissed and licked her everywhere except where she really wanted to be licked. He licked real close to her clit and blew his warm breath on it. Destiny couldn't take all the teasing and said, "Oh, daddy, please, please daddy, lick it please."

In the middle of her pleading, QT put his lips on her clit and slowly began to suck and lick it softly. She started grinding her lower body against his face. As she moaned and squirmed, QT inserted two fingers into her pussy, he then he pulled one out and pushed it in her ass as he sucked on her clit. Destiny couldn't take it, it felt so good. She tried to push his head away saying, "Daddy, I'm cumming, please stop, please I can't take it."

QT didn't let up. He licked and sucked her clit even faster. When she climaxed, cum shot out like someone hitting the knob on a water fountain. Cum ran all down the crack of her asshole. He positioned himself to fuck her in the ass but Destiny said, "Wait, daddy, wait." She reached into her purse on the floor beside her and pulled out a box of Magnums. She said, "I told you I would be prepared next time. I need to feel you inside my pussy first." She gave him the box of condoms and he took one out and put it on.

He pushed his dick inside of her, slowly at first. She felt good, real good. Her pussy was hot and even though it was real wet she was still tight. He put her legs on his shoulders and positioned his arms under hers. He started to fuck her. In the position that they were in, she couldn't get loose, all she could do is take the dick and fuck him back. As QT started long stroking, Destiny was talking in his ear, saying, "Please, daddy, please slow down. Oh...daddy, oh daddy...you kill in this pussy...oh, you killin it...please, daddy...please."

QT said, "Who's pussy is this."

"Oh, oh, oh daddy. Oh, daddy, it yo pussy. Oh, it's yo pussy. Fuck you pussy, daddy, fuck you pussy...oh, it's yours."

QT was about to cum so he pulled out. He wanted to fuck her in the ass. He pulled the condom off and rammed his dick back into her pussy to get it lubricated. He pulled out of her and slowly pushed his dick into her ass. He had to let her legs down so that she could relax her ass. Once he got the head in he slowly worked into her halfway. As he fucked Destiny in her ass, he rubbed her clit.

"Oh, daddy, I love you, I love you...this yo ass, daddy, only yours, please cum in my ass."

He stroked her ass harder and harder. It didn't take long before he was cummin in her ass. Destiny held QT tight and started bucking with him as they came together. She was holding onto QT and didn't want to let go. Five minutes later, she was still holding him and telling him how much she loved him.

Afterwards, Destiny wrapped her hair up and they took a shower together. She got on her knees and sucked QT until he came in her mouth. When they got out of the shower, they dried each other off.

As Destiny was brushing her teeth, QT stood and watched her, admiring her beauty. He thought to himself, I'm living the real American dream. It don't get no better than this. This is the kind of shit niggas dream about.

When Destiny's car was finished, the manager called QT in his office to let him know. QT walked her to where her car was parked.

She tested the sound system and loved it. After she paid the manager, she got in her new Beamer, cut the music up, and put in Alexander O'Neal's "Never Knew Love Like This." As she pulled off, QT walked out to the sidewalk and watched her push up Venice Boulevard. He only did it because he knew that he was being watched by the DEA from somewhere.

When QT came out, Agents Davis and Jones had smiles on their faces. They were parked down the street on the opposite side, sitting in a van with tinted windows. Jones said, "Look at him. He's taken the bait. It's just a matter of time before we get his ass."

"Shit," Davis said, "if Stevens offered me some play she would have me too. I wouldn't mind fucking the shit out of her. She's beautiful, single, and I know she can suck a good dick."

Jones said, "Yeah, I bet that she is a good fuck and suck."

When Tasha found the condo that QT had bought for her, she was astonished. She couldn't believe it. It was beautiful; the living room was all white and glass, with white leather sofas, white carpet, glass tables and a glass grandfather clock. The two bedrooms were done in all blue—light blue walls with dark blue carpet and comforters. The beds were king-size and the frames were real oak wood. The fridge, stove, microwave, washer and dryer were all black. The den had blue leather furniture, a big screen TV and a Pioneer sound system. She walked into the garage, and fell to her knees. She saw the white Honda Accord and broke down crying. There was a note on the windshield.

She read: Surprise! Everything is yours and paid for.

The key was in the door. She opened the door and saw the pink slip to the car on the seat. When she read it, it was in her name. Tasha had nice stuff in her apartment but it wasn't as nice or expensive as the stuff that QT had bought for her. She rushed back to her apartment and got all of her clothes and toiletries and took them back to the condo. The condo had new dishes, pots, pans, and silverware.

Even the phone was turned on with the new number taped to it.

Once she moved all of her things to the condo, she got on the phone and started selling everything else to her friends. She already figured that QT moved her that far away for a reason so didn't tell any of her girlfriends what was going on. She just told them she had to sell her stuff but she was fine. It took her two days to sell all of the furniture in her old apartment.

Settling in at her condo, Tasha lay back in her big bed watching TV with a smile on her face. She wasn't stupid, she knew that she would have to do something for QT for all of this but she didn't care because she would have done whatever it was that he wanted for nothing. She loved QT and whenever he called, she would come running.

QT had to find another OT spot since going back to Seattle was out of the question. He called his cousin Too Cool in Louisiana. He knew that his cousin was a stand up nigga and he was also in the game. His operation was based out of the 9th Ward in New Orleans. QT told him to fly to L.A. so they could talk. He would have somebody at the airport to meet him.

Too Cool booked a flight that would arrive at LAX the next morning at nine. QT told him a female would be there to pick him up. He described her to Too Cool and told him her name was Tasha. QT then called her.

"Hello, Tasha speaking."

"What's up, baby? What are you up to?"

"Nothing, daddy. Just wondering when you were going to call. Daddy, I love everything—the condo, the car, the furniture, everything."

"I got to make sure my baby is right. Check this out: I need you to pick up my cousin from LAX tomorrow morning at 9 a.m. and bring him to my shop in Inglewood."

Tasha said, "No problem. What does he look like?"

QT described Too Cool to her and said, "You will really recognize him when you see his walk."

The next morning, Tasha was at the airport waiting for Too Cool's flight to arrive. QT had described him as being 5'10", 200 lbs, dark skinned, dark eyes, a Jheri curl in his hair, well dressed and having the coolest walk she had ever seen. She recognized him instantly and had to smile. He recognized her as well and he smiled with perfect white teeth. They greeted each other and Too Cool followed Tasha to her car while admiring her beauty and her nice fat ass.

They pulled up to the shop as if they were customers. Tasha told the manager to check out her music and put an amp in the trunk. QT met them in the work area and escorted them to his office. He hugged and kissed Tasha, then slapped her on the ass and told her he would get at her in a minute. She automatically knew what QT was saying. She walked out of the office to go look at rims in the shop.

QT and his cousin embraced and shook hands.

"Damn cuzzin," Too Cool said, "I was at the wedding; that ain't wifey. I see you still a playa for real."

QT said, "Yeah, that's my baby too, before yo freaky ass get any ideas."

They both laughed and QT said, "Have a seat and let's get down to business. First off, what are birds going for down yo way and how much are you getting them for?"

"They going for 28, but I get them for 24."

"I can give them to you for 18, but I need you to dump mine for 26. The other two is yours if that's how you want to do it, or you could sell them for the 26 and get all the clientele."

"So how am I going to get them to me?"

"Tasha will bring them to you and you only. I don't want her to deal with nobody but you. You make sure you take care of my baby."

"Nigga, we family. She yo girl then she's family too."

QT said, "She's going to drop the work off to you and get a room until you through. So how long do you think it will take you to get rid of fifty birds?"

"At 26, I can move them in two days."

QT thought for a minute. "Okay, look, I don't want to have her driving back and forth like that, so I'm going to hit you twice a month with a hundred birds each time. Tasha will drive the birds down to you and fly back. When you are finished she will fly back down and drive the money back. The stash I have in the car is foolproof."

Too Cool said, "I'm ready whenever you are. Let's get paid."

QT told Too Cool to go get Tasha and give him about fifteen minutes to talk to her. When she came in, QT sat her down and explained everything. He told her that she would be transporting cocaine and he wanted her to know up front what was up. What was so sweet about everything was that the car would be a rental. QT had the manager at the car rental spot on his payroll. He had already rented a Honda Accord and had the stash put in it. Whenever Tasha was to take a trip she would rent a Honda. The manager would make sure it was always available. The manager didn't know about the stash—he was just paid to keep that car ready. If Tasha was pulled over and the dope was found, all she would say was that she had just rented the car, she didn't know shit, and that she would call her lawyer.

Tasha listened to everything and when QT was finished, she said, "Just let me know when to roll and it's done."

QT called Too Cool back into his office and all three of them went over everything, even the details for when Tasha got to New Orleans. QT didn't want to be seen with his cousin so he told Tasha to take him to lunch, cook him dinner, and then take him to the airport for his flight which left at 10 p.m.

QT paged Goldie. When Goldie called back, QT told him to meet him at TGIF Friday's in the Marina. QT ran everything down to Goldie and told Goldie to handle everything. QT had already told Tasha there wouldn't be any phone calls; whenever he wanted her to take the trip, the Honda would be parked in front of her garage, with gas and travel money in the glove box. When it was time for her to go back to New Orleans and pick up the car and the money, she would get a page with all zeros. Then when she got back, she was to park the Honda in her garage, leave it unlocked, and put the keys under the floor mat. Then she was to get a room for that night.

After QT explained everything to Goldie, Goldie said, "Cuz, that's why you the man. You got this shit planned out to the T."

QT said, "Cuz, I miss being around the G-Code Mobb. I go in the hood and kick it wit the other homies becuz I got to go feed Blocc and give him water every two days, or I go over to mom's pad. But shit ain't the same."

Goldie said, "I know, I feel the same way. I was thinking about giving a Gangstas Ball at the Century Club. That way I can be at the door to let whoever I want to come in. VIP will be for the G-Code Mobb and other real niggas we fuck wit in the game."

"Shit, hook it up. I need to see my niggas. I talk to them on the phone but it ain't the same."

Goldie said, "I'm going to hook it up for three weeks from Saturday."

The two ate lunch and went their separate ways.

Two days later, Tasha woke up to find the Honda parked in front of her garage. Everything went as planned and when she went back to pick the money up a week later, the trip home went smooth. She parked the Honda in her garage and went and got a room after she paged Goldie and left her code.

The next morning when she got back to the condo, the Honda was gone. She parked her car in the garage and went into the house. In her bedroom, she found twenty stacks of bills on her dresser, each stack was one thousand dollars. There was a note that said: I'll be over tonight at 7 p.m. Cook me a good dinner.

There was no name on the note but she knew that it was QT.

Tasha put the money in a shoe box in her closet and lay on her bed thinking about him.

Tasha cooked a steak smothered in bell peppers, onions, and gravy, and made rice, macaroni and cheese, mustard greens, corn bread, and sweet potatoes. When QT got there, she had just got out of the bathtub and put on a sexy teddy and a silk house robe. Her hair was done and she smelled good enough to eat.

QT rang the door bell even though he had his own key. He had driven his Lumina because he didn't want to draw any attention to himself or Tasha. She opened the door with a big smile on her face. He walked in and hugged and kissed her.

"Daddy, you didn't have to give me all that money. I told you, for you, I'll do anything."

QT smiled and said, "You earned every dime of it. Every time you go, you will get twenty stacks. You need to get you a safety deposit box and start putting your money in it. Really, you need two at two different banks. I'm going to send you to my man so he can hook you up with two different sets of IDs with social security numbers, birth certificates, and all. With them, open two different bank accounts and two safety deposit boxes. Put a thousand in each bank account and then five hundred ever time you come off a trip, and put the rest in the two boxes. Don't keep the IDs here; make sure you have somewhere safe and secure to keep them."

Tasha listened to QT thinking to herself, I wish this nigga was mine all to myself. Ain't too many niggas left like this nigga; he's always looking out for me. I know this nigga don't need me...damn, I love him.

They sat down and ate dinner together. After dinner they had sex twice, watched a movie, then QT went home.

When he got home at 11:45 p.m. Nat wasn't there. She and Monica and two other girlfriends had gone to Hollywood to the Comedy Club. QT took a shower and then watched a movie with Santana and Blocc by his side. In four days, Tasha was due to take another trip. QT hoped everything continued to work out the way it was going becuz he had a smooth operation. At the rate things were going now, he would retire in a year and have enough money put up for Gangsta when he came home so he wouldn't have to get back in the game. He also thought about buying him and Nat a house since the house he was living in was Gangsta's. He loved the house but he didn't know if Gangsta would want it once he came home. He mentally added that to his list of things to talk about with his brother the next time he went to visit him.

Nat got home around twelve thirty. QT was still up. She walked in the bedroom and he was lying in bed smoking on a Lemac and listening to Anita Baker's "Angel." Nat smiled becuz she knew that that was the song played at their wedding. She went over to the bed, bent over and kissed QT, her tongue exploring his mouth.

All QT had on was some silk boxers. He pulled Nat on top of him and she slowly kissed and licked her way down to his manhood. She pulled his boxers off and took him into her mouth. Even though QT was tired from his escapade with Tasha, Nat always turned him on. He made love to Nat hoping that he got her pregnant. He hadn't talked to Nat about it yet but he would soon.

QT finally called Destiny sixteen days after she had come to his shop and given him the tapped phone number. He knew to call her Teresa, her false name, so when he phoned and she answered, he said, "Teresa, you sound more sexy on the phone than you do in person. Don't let me find out you are a phone sex operator."

They both laughed and she replied, "I don't think that job could pay my bills."

They talked for about an hour with QT playing it off asking all the questions that the feds thought he would ask. The whole time the feds were listening in and smiling from ear to ear. Before QT hung up the phone, he asked Teresa if he could take her to lunch the next day. She told him she would be out of town the next day but as soon as she got back she would call him at the office. QT told her that would be fine and hung up.

The feds were very please, especially because of how Teresa slid in the part about being out of town because they knew if thing progressed, QT would eventually ask her why she was going out of town. That conversation could lead to who knows what, they thought.

Goldie hooked up the Gangstas Ball at the Century Club. Everybody and they mamas wanted to go but only the niggas and bitches that QT and Goldie wanted in was in. Even Too Cool flew in with a couple of his boys. Too Cool got suites at the Hyatt Hotel by LAX. The night of the Ball, that's all the talk was about all over Compton,

L.A., Watts, and Long Beach. Niggas was pulling up in Benzes, Porsches, Lamborghinis, Beamers—you name it, niggas was in it.

Everyone was dressed to impress with all the accessories. QT had the VIP room. All his crew and their women were there chilling, drinking Cristal and smoking chronic. QT hooked Too Cool and his boys up with some fine gold diggin hoes. The Ball was packed and they had to stop letting people in. QT spotted Tasha and Destiny in the crowd sitting at different tables. For a few hours, QT and his homies chilled, talked, and enjoyed each other's company.

Finally, QT said, "Let's get this muthafuckin Ball to rolling."

He grabbed Nat by the hand and said, "Come on, beautiful, let's show these muthafuckas how to dance." As QT lead the way, everyone else that was in VIP followed him.

Cherell's "Saturday Love" was booming from the sound system. Everyone was getting their groove on and having a good time. QT and Nat danced to four songs in a row. Finally, Nat told QT she was going back to the VIP room to relax. QT went to the bar and had bottles of Cristal delivered to Tasha and Destiny.

A loud mouth nigga that was usually cool had had a little too much to drink and asked Tasha to dance. She refused and he went off calling her bitch and ho. QT peeped out the scene and went over to Tasha's table. The fool's name was Boscoe; he was a playa in the game but he wasn't a gang member. QT walked up and tapped him on the shoulder. Boscoe sped around, knocking QT's hand off his shoulder. QT instantly reacted and grabbed Boscoe by his shirt and swept him off his feet.

There were ten homies inside the Ball that were strapped and they were there only to make sure QT and the other homies were secure. Boscoe had three of his boys with him but as soon as they tried to react they found Glocks in their faces.

When Boscoe got up off the floor, QT said, "Baby's a special guest of mine. You can either apologize to her and we can keep on partying or we can get into some Gangsta shit."

Boscoe knew of QT's reputation and he also knew that he didn't want to start any shit with QT. Just the way QT's homies had blended in and drew down on his boys showed Boscoe that it was a fight he didn't want. He was drunk but he wasn't stupid.

He looked at Tasha and said, "I apologize, baby. That's my bad. Any friend of QT's is a friend of mine."

QT put his arm around Boscoe, walked him to the bar and bought him a bottle of Cristal to show him there were no hard feelings.

Boscoe looked at QT and said, "You a classy nigga. Shit could have went different and I know I would have been the one to lose. Good looking out."

They shook hands and QT walked off. He told Lil Ken to keep an eye on Tasha and Destiny and if anybody sweated them, to let them know that they were his special guests.

When QT got back to VIP, Nat asked him what happened and QT told her that everything was cool. "Just a nigga too drunk and mad becuz a female wouldn't dance with him."

After the Ball ended, QT had two of his homies escort Tasha and Nat to their cars. Once outside, all the G-Code Mobb and Too Cool went their separate ways as if they didn't know each other. QT was escorted to his car by three of his lil homies.

As he and Nat drove off, the jacking crew of Boss-T, Nutt, Ed Dog, Nacho, and G-Rob, followed QT in a van with tinted windows. Boss-T, the driver of the van, told the others, "I know we can get at least a meal ticket (a million dollars) from this nigga and that's cash that ain't counting jewelry."

Nutt said, "I want to fuck his bitch before we smoke his ass. I want that crab (Crip) ass nigga to watch while I fuck the shit out of her."

The others laughed and agreed they wanted to fuck Nat as well. Boss-T had been watching QT at both of his shops. He tried to follow QT home but QT always went a different route through different neighborhoods and always lost them in traffic. They figured QT would be slippin tonight after the Ball. They figured QT would be drunk and high but what they didn't know was that neither QT nor Nat drank or got high.

QT kept looking in his rearview mirror. At first he thought it wasn't nothing but after hitting a few corners he knew he was being followed.

"Baby, we got company," he said.

Nat looked in the rearview mirror and said, "You think it's the police?"

"Naw, they don't need to follow me they know where we live plus it's late for them to be on me like this."

"So what do you want to do?"

"I could easily out run them but I want to send these niggas a message to let them know I ain't no joke."

Nat had already retrieved a Glock from her purse. QT had a 9mm on his lap. He said, "You been going to that shooting range two times a week, let's see if it has been paying off." He rolled down the window on her side of the car. "As soon as I turn at the next corner I'm going to slow down. As soon as the van hits the corner, light that bitch up."

QT turned and slowed the car, and when the van hit the corner, Nat was leaning out of the window with the Glock in her hand. She unloaded and the first shot hit the passenger in the shoulder, the second one skinned the driver in the neck, and the rest of the shots went into the van. After she emptied the Glock, QT handed her his Beretta.

The niggas in the van panicked. They really weren't expecting what was happening to them. They were used to being the aggressors and not the victims. When the van hit the corner and Boss-T and Nutt saw Nat leaning out the window with a strap, Boss-T yelled, "What the fuck is this?" He hit the brakes and was trying to back the van up but it was too late; bullets started flying through the windshield.

Nutt hollered, "Blood, I'm hit! The bitch shot me!"

All they could do was try and duck the bullets to keep from getting shot.

When QT handed Nat the Beretta, he told her to hold on and he floored the Benz. "Yeah, baby, that's how to blast on whoever them bitches was!"

Once they got home, QT paged Goldie and when Goldie called QT back on the burn-out phone, QT told him what had gone down and told him to watch his back and also to call the other homies in the G-Code Mobb and let them know what's up.

He hung up and went over to Nat. He said, "From now on, I'm going to have Lil Ken and Moonie go with you wherever you go for awhile."

Nat started to say something but QT raised his hands and she fell quiet.

"Let me finish. They are not going to be with you in your car or anything like that, they are just going to follow you wherever you go and watch yo back. They are not going to interfere with whatever you do. Even when niggas try to holla at you, as long as they can accept rejection respectfully and keep movin, the homies will stay in the background. Look, I don't know who those muthafuckas were that was following us so I got to make sure you safe."

"And what about you? Who is going to watch yo back?"

"I'm going to have Keebo wit me. I'll have him meet me at the shop every morning," he said. "I'm going to have to tell Lil Ken and Moonie where we live but it's all good, they good niggas and they are loyal and respectful, and they will die before they let anything happen to you."

Nat said, "I trust you and if you think this is best for now, then I'm all for it."

The next morning QT called Keebo and told him to meet him at the shop. He called Lil Ken and Moonie and gave them directions to his house and told them to be there in an hour and ride together. All the other members of the Mobb were calling QT on the burn-out phone asking him about what happened. He told them him and Nat was cool but to put their sources' ears to the streets and see what they could come up with.

Lil Ken and Moonie got to QT's house and they were amazed at the size of it and the contents inside. When they were invited in, the first thing they saw was Santana and Blocc. The pit bulls were right by QT's side, ready to attack. They growled at QT's homies because they had never seen them or smelled their scents before. QT told them to sit down and be quiet and they obeyed instantly.

Lil Ken said, "Cuz, that's what I'm talking about. I gots to have my dogs like this."

Moonie said, "Well, you need some new dogs cuz them mutha-fuckas you got is mutts. They will open the door and help a nigga rob yo ass."

They all laughed. Lil Ken said, "Cuz, you ain't right."

QT had them sit down and he told them what went down the night before and he told them what he wanted them to do for Nat and how to do it. Then he told them to never tell anyone where he lived under any circumstances. He instructed them to be there every morning before Nat left the house and to make sure she got in the house safely every night.

Nat came downstairs and said, "The first thing we got to do is go to the mall and get ya'll some different gear. I be going places that if anyone saw ya'll around dressed like that they would instantly call the police and we don't need that."

They both looked down at their khaki suits and Chuck Taylors.

QT went to the den and when he came back he tossed both of them a stack of fifties and hundreds. Each stake was $10,000. Nat picked up her purse, kissed QT, and told Lil Ken and Moonie to follow her to the mall.

QT stopped both of them, looking from one to the other straight in the eyes, and said, "Take care of my baby at all costs."

They both nodded and at the same time and said, "Death cefore dishonor."

When Nat got to the mall she took Lil Ken and Moonie to the men's store and had them get seven pair of slacks each, plus seven dress shirts with ties to match, seven pair of dress socks and two different pair of dress shoes. She had them change into one of the outfits. When they looked in the mirror they actually liked the look. The only thing was, they didn't tuck their shirts in because of their straps. When they got to the register, Nat told them it was on her. She pulled out her platinum credit card and paid for everything.

As they walked through the mall, Nat told them, "Dressing like this will get you another class of woman."

They both smiled and Lil Ken said, "I got too many women as it is."

Nat said, "It's not all about quantity; it's all about quality."

QT arrived at the shop and Keebo was there, posted up like he was expecting some drama. QT ran everything down to Keebo who pulled up his shirt exposing two Glocks, one on each side of his waistband. "Cuz, I got you. Whatever it takes," he said.

QT told the workers at the shop that Keebo was his cousin and whenever he was at the shop, Keebo would be there as well. He told them, "Keebo wants to learn the business so if he asks any of you anything, take yo time and explain it to him."

QT went to his office and called Teresa on the tapped phone. When she answered he said, "I thought you were going to call me when you got back? I was surprised to see you last night at the club."

"I thought I would surprise you," Teresa replied. "And thanks for the bottle of Cristal."

"A woman as beautiful as you deserves the best."

"You wouldn't be flirting with me, would you?"

"It's a possibility."

"You are a very mysterious man. I have been inquiring around about you. All the women seem to love you and even the niggas that don't like you respect you."

QT said, "Well, that seems to be a good thang for me. So when can I take you to lunch, dinner, or something? I want to see you."

Teresa asked, "How about if I cook you dinner?"

"I hope that you can cook. I don't want no take out."

"Get a pencil and take down my address and we will see when you get here."

She gave QT her address and told him dinner would be at 7 p.m. sharp.

Boss-T and Nutt were still at the hospital getting sweated by the police. They told the police that someone in a blue Camaro just drove past them and the passenger leaned out the window and opened fire. They didn't know who the guys were and they didn't get the license plate number. After Nat blasted on the van, Boss-T had driven to the hospital. Him and Nutt got out and he told G-Rob to go put the van up and to come back and pick them up in a few hours.

After the police left, Boss-T and Nutt were side by side in beds waiting to be discharged. Boss-T said, "That bitch was really trying to smoke our ass. We underestimated QT and his bitch, but that won't happen again."

Nutt said, "I can't wait to get a hold of that bitch. At first, I was just going to fuck her, then put a bullet in her head. But now I'm going to torture that bitch. I want to hear that bitch scream and beg."

Boss-T said, "Both of them muthafuckas is breathing borrowed air. The main thang is making sure we get paid in the process."

The nurse came into the room and told them all they had to do was sign the release papers and they could leave.

When they got to the lobby, G-Rob and Nacho were there waiting. Once they were all in the van, Boss-T said, "We got to find out where that nigga lives. More than likely we will catch his bitch slippin before we will catch QT slippin. All we got to do is snatch the nigga's bitch if we can't find out where they live. We will get the money, fuck the bitch, then let Nutt torture the hoe."

They all laughed and started talking about how they would fuck Nat.

Chapter 8: Rocc

QT and Goldie were at the hospital in Rocc's room and Goldie was telling QT that he was thinking about marrying Monica.

Before QT could answer, Rocc said, "Cuz, I thought you was a playa."

QT and Goldie turned at the same time. Rocc had awakened five minutes prior and was looking and listening in to QT and Goldie's conversation. They were turned away from him so they hadn't noticed when his eyes opened.

QT said, "Cuz, I knew you would pull out of that shit. Goldie, go get the doctor."

Rocc said, "Cuz, I need some water."

QT poured him some water and helped him drink, then sat down beside Rocc anxious to talk to him.

The doctor came back with Goldie and he told QT and Goldie to wait outside while he examined Rocc. QT immediately called his moms and told her about Rocc then he called Nat and told her. QT was supposed to hook up with Destiny for dinner but he called her and told her about Rocc and that he would have to reschedule. She said she understood and asked him to call her when he got a chance.

QT's moms, Lisa, Nat, Moonie, Lil Ken, Tonya and Monica were all at the hospital within thirty minutes. G-moms told the others in the waiting room, "I knew my baby was coming back to me. I prayed every night and every day. Now my prayers have been answered."

QT hugged his mother as tears of joy ran down her face. QT and Nat pulled her to the side and told her about kidnappings that had been happening and what had happened with him and Nat after the Gangstas Ball. Nat told her that Lisa and she could move into her house in La Dera because she no longer lived there and moms could rent her house out.

At first, G-moms didn't want to go along with it, then she thought about Lisa and also how Rocc always came over for breakfast. After a little thought, G-moms agreed to move. QT told her he would hire some professional movers to move her since he didn't want people knowing where she lived.

The doctor finally came out of Rocc's room to the waiting room. He told G-moms, "He's going to be fine. Everything looks good. I just have to have a few tests run on him but I think he will be fine."

In twos, they all went in to see Rocc. When Lil Ken and Moonie went in, a smile came on Rocc's face. He was tired and could barely talk but he managed to say, "I ain't been gone that long. What's up? Ya'll niggas done went GQ on a nigga." He was talking about the way they were dressed.

Lil Ken said, "Cuz, you know this is Santana Blocc Crip for life. It's a reason we got this shit on. I'll tell you about it when you get out of here."

Moonie pulled his shirt up to show Rocc his two Glocks. "Ain't too much changed. We still strapped and will blast a muthafucka."

Within a week, Rocc was released from the hospital. G-moms was already living in La Dera. She wasn't for Rocc living at his own house—at least not until he was one hundred per cent well. So when he was released, G-moms brought him home to stay with her and Lisa. QT gave him a welcome home party and dinner with family and the G-Code Mobb.

Everything was running smooth and everyone was making money. QT and Nat's businesses were doing well. Rocc was home and Goldie had proposed to Monica. She accepted and the wedding was set for July.

But as Murphy's Law goes, if anything can go wrong it will.

QT made another dinner date with Destiny, a.k.a. Teresa. When QT got to Destiny's condo in Granada Hills, she was waiting for him outside her front door. She told him she wasn't sure but she thought the condo might be wired with cameras and for sound. She also reminded QT to call her Teresa.

They went inside the condo where Teresa showed QT around, then she told him to go in the den while she prepared dinner. As he sat on the sofa thinking to himself, he realized that if he hadn't known that Destiny was police, he would know once he came to her condo; there were no photos of herself or her family anywhere. The second thing was the way she dressed and the car she drove didn't add up to the way the condo was decorated. It looked like it was finished by a male with no taste.

Teresa brought the food to the den and they ate together. She had cooked smothered chicken with onions and bell peppers over rice, corn, cabbage, corn bread, and for dessert she made a peach cobbler.

QT figured that if the condo was bugged, the task force was watching and listening so he decided to play with them. He asked, "So, Teresa, why are you out of town so much?"

"I have business in Texas that I have to take care of."

"And what kind of business is that?"

"I have a shipping company here and in Texas. I go to Texas twice a month to make sure everything is in order and running well."

QT said, "So what does you company ship?"

Teresa said, "Whatever the different companies I deal with wants shipped." She knew what QT was up to. She had made up the story about owning two shipping companies because she knew that if her boss or anyone else was listening, they would be very pleased to think that she was baiting QT.

Destiny was right about both things. The condo was bugged and there were hidden mini-cameras installed in every room except the bathroom. Special Agents White, Davis, and Jones were watching and listening in to the conversation at that very moment.

Agent White said, "She's smarter than I thought. We are going to have to set up a fake shipping company just in case QT decides he wants to use Agent Stevens to ship his drugs across the country."

Davis said, "If she plays her cards right, we will be able to nail this piece of shit to the wall."

QT was a little disappointed because he had planned to fuck the hell out of Destiny. It had been awhile since he had fucked her but now because of the bugging and the video cams, he would have to meet her somewhere else when he wanted to have sex with her. QT bit on purpose and said, "I might want to use your shipping company to ship some tires and rims to customers in a couple of different states."

Teresa said, "That's no problem. Just let me know where and when and it's done."

Since QT knew he couldn't fuck or get any head after dinner was over, he left about an hour later. He told Teresa he would call later but he also would let her know when he needed to use her company. He played it off and kissed on the cheek, but he did get two hands full of ass. He gripped her ass, pulled her close to him, and whispered in her ear, "You know I need some of this good hot pussy."

Before she could say anything he kissed her on the forehead and walked out of the condo.

"Oh, shit. Look how he just gripped her ass," Agent Jones said. "I wish I could get a nice feel of that sexy ass." Jones said it out loud but all of them were thinking the same thing.

Agent White said, "Let's go. We have to get that dummy shipping company set up so when QT does want to use it, hopefully he will be shipping cocaine in those boxes instead of rims and tires."

Nat and Monica wanted to pick up a couple of pairs of shoes at the mall, so Lil Ken and Moonie followed them in Lil Ken's new Camaro. It had been a month since the incident with Nat and QT after the Gangstas Ball. Nothing had happened since then, but QT still insisted that his homies continue to follow Nat everywhere she went.

As the two women walked through the mall, Lil Ken and Moonie casually followed them but not so that anyone would notice. When Nat and Monica were in line at the food court, Lil Ken and Moonie were four people behind them.

Also present and sitting at a table eating Philly Cheese Steak sandwiches and fries were Boss-T and his crew. They had come to the mall to buy some Timbs and also to see if they could come up on a lick in the process.

As Nat and Monica walked past their table, Nutt almost choked on his sandwich. The two women sat five tables away.

After watching them sit down, Nutt said, "Blood, that's that bitch! The one that blasted on us. I can't believe this shit. It must be our lucky day."

Lil Ken and Moonie took a table directly behind Boss-T and his crew. As they sat down, Lil Ken heard Nutt saying, "We got to get that bitch…fuck it, both of them. I know she ain't hangin wit no broke bitch."

They all saw Lil Ken and Moonie when they sat down but by looking at them and what they were wearing, they chalked them up as just being some square busters.

Lil Ken could tell by the way they kept looking at Nat and Monica that they were talking about them. He put Moonie up on what he heard, and then he went into the men's room and called Nat on her cell phone.

"Nat, this is Lil Ken. When you get a chance, look to your right casually. The five niggas at the fourth table from you are talking shit about snatching you and Monica up. When you finish eating, go to your car. Me and Moonie will already be waiting for you. These niggas ain't going to try shit inside the mall but as soon as you get to your car, you and Monica just duck behind the car. Me and Moonie are going to blast these bitches. I think these are the same niggas that you blasted on."

When Nat got off the phone, she told Monica what was up. Both of them were strapped as well; they carried 9mms in their purses. Nat casually looked their way and instantly she could tell that they were up to something. Lil Ken and Moonie had already gone so Nat and Monica picked up their bags and headed for the underground parking lot.

When they got to the lot, they didn't see Lil Ken or Moonie but they knew they were there. Nat said, "I hope you got that nine in yo hands becuz we are going to blast these bitch ass niggas."

Monica had never shot at anyone let alone actually shot anyone before, but she had been going to the shooting range with Nat twice a week so she knew how to shoot. She said, "It's either us or them and I show ain't ready to leave. Fuck um, it is what it is."

Boss-T and his crew slowly walked behind Nat and Monica, trying to bob and weave so they couldn't be seen. Boss said, "As soon as we get in the parking lot, we split up and run up on them bitches, guns drawn, so they know we ain't for no bullshit. G-Rob, you go get the van."

Lil Ken was to the right of Nat's car and Moonie was to the left. Both of them had two Glocks with extra clips. They saw Nat and Monica as they came out of the door and entered the parking garage. About seven seconds later, Boss-T and his crew were out the door and behind them. Moonie stepped from behind a Blazer when he saw them pulling out their straps. He started blasting. The first two shots hit Nacho in the chest and he went down instantly.

As soon as Nat heard the first shot, she and Monica ducked down and ran between cars until they got to her Benz. They crouched behind the car with straps drawn.

Boss-T and his crew were totally taken off guard as they scrambled trying to get behind cars.

Nutt said, "Blood, what the fuck is going on?"

Boss-T hollered, "It's a fuckin set up."

Ed-Dog was two cars away from Nat and Monica. Their attention was focused on the door so they didn't see him creeping up on them.

Lil Ken saw him and crept up behind Ed-Dog.

"You fuckin with the wrong muthafuckas!" he said. Before Ed-Dog could turn around, Lil Ken blasted him twice in the back of his head.

People were running and screaming all over the lot at the sound of the gun fire. When G-Rob heard the shooting, he hurriedly drove the van to where he saw Boss-T and Nutt ducking behind a car. As he pulled up, they quickly jumped in the van.

When Nat saw the van she knew it was the same one that had followed her and QT that night, even though it was painted a different color. Nat hadn't fired a shot but when she saw them leaving, she raised her Beretta and unloaded it. Bullets hit the van like it was target practice. Lil Ken, Moonie, Nat and even Monica were blasting on it.

Boss-T told G-Rob, "Punch this bitch. Let's get the fuck out of here."

G-Rob hit the gas and the van took off. "Where's Nacho and Ed-Dog?"

Nutt said, "Blood, they dead. Dem muthafuckas set us up. On my momma and all the dead homies, dem muthafuckas goin to pay for this shit. That's on everything I love."

Boss-T didn't say nothing, he just sat there thinking about how he could get that bitch. The bitch was smart; she wasn't the average bitch that just hooked up wit a baller. QT and his bitch was smart but it wasn't over by a long shot. This shit was personal now. Fuck the money, both of them had to die—QT and his bitch.

Lil Ken ran to Nat and said, "Let's go. We got to get the fuck out of here. Culver City P.D. will be here in a minute."

They jumped in separate cars and took off. Lil Ken told Moonie, "We got two of them niggas fo show. I know QT will be able to find out who these niggas are now."

Nat had already called QT and told him to come home. That's all she had to say; he knew that it was important. Actually, he was already on his way home from Destiny's house.

When he got home, Lil Ken and Moonie were in the den and Nat was upstairs. He went straight up and found the dogs were with Nat. She told him what went down and that it was the same van. She told him that she thought two of them had been killed.

QT went back down and got Lil Ken and Moonie's versions of what happened. He then called Goldie and told him to put the word out that he wanted to know who had gotten blasted at the mall and where were they from. QT knew it wouldn't take long becuz the shooting was already on the news. The newscaster said that two African-American men had been shot and killed and that both were found with guns. It was suspected to be gang-related.

QT told Lil Ken and Moonie to take their straps and give them to Goldie and he would give them new ones.

"Lay low for a couple of days," QT said. "I'll call you at the end of the week. Also, paint yo car just in case." He knew the Camaro was new and didn't have any license plates on it yet. "Just kick it in the hood and don't tell nobody shit. Nat is going to stay at the pad for a few days."

Lil Ken said, "Whoever dem niggas were, they were slobs (Bloods). Two of them had red shoestrings in their shoes, and red belts too."

After Lil Ken and Moonie left, QT started thinking and it hit him: there had been five of them, and they were Bloods—that sounded like the nigga Boss-T and his jackin crew. QT called Goldie and told him to check on that becuz Goldie was from 43st Gangsta Crips in L.A. and Boss-T and his crew was from the 20s Bloods—they were 43st Gangsta's rival enemy. If it was them, Goldie would know by the next day. QT had to find out which two it was that was killed and make arrangements to smoke the other three.

QT knew as well that for sure, now it had become personal. He knew that they would want to get some get back so he had to get them before they had the chance to get him. He knew that he had the advantage becuz he had money resources and if it was them, he already had the info on them and their baby mamas, their hang-outs, and where their immediate families lived. QT knew that Boss-T and Nutt were the real killas of the crew, so they would have to be the first to go if neither one of them was one of the deceased.

A couple of days later, Goldie called QT.

"Holla," QT said when he answered the phone.

"Cuz, I checked with some of the bitches I know from the 20s and it was them niggas that got smoked at the mall. It was Nacho and Ed-Dog that got smoked."

QT said, "Okay, we already know where these niggas be at so get Moonie, Lil Ken, and Keebo and find out if them muthafuckas are at any of the spots we got intel on and smoke they ass. We got to end this shit as soon as possible."

"Don't trip, Crip, if any of the niggas are around, they will be history," Goldie said.

Goldie hit all the spots that he knew about with Lil Ken, Keebo, and Moonie. They went to Boss-T and Nutt's spots first since they were the most dangerous. After hitting all three of their spots for three days in a row, they finally spotted G-Rob standing on his baby mama's porch holding his son.

It was already dark so Goldie parked the van a couple of houses down and on the opposite side of the street from were G-Rob was. Goldie, Lil Ken, Moonie, and Keebo all had on red baseball caps and red sweatshirts since they were in Blood neighborhood, so if anyone saw them they wouldn't look suspicious. As they sat in the van and waited, Goldie said, "I got this nigga. Ya'll just watch my back. I been at this nigga for awhile anyway. Word is, he smoked my homie T-Ray a couple of years ago."

Lil Ken asked, "So how you going to do this?"

"When he comes out of the house and goes to get in his car, I'm going to be waiting on the side of the house. I'm going to catch him off guard and blast his ass."

About 9 p.m., Goldie got out of the van and walked straight

across the street to the gate at the side of the house. It was the perfect spot; there was a fence and some large bushes separating where Goldie was hiding from the next door neighbor's house. The neighbors wouldn't be able to look out of the windows at the side of the house and see him.

Goldie had a Mac-10 in his right hand and a 9mm Beretta in his waistband. He knew G-Rob and G-Rob knew him. They had grown up together from elementary school. They chose different gangs and that turned two dudes who had been friends into enemies. Goldie tied a red bandana around his face. But then as he thought about his homie T-Ray and of Nat and QT, he snatched the bandana off his face. He wanted G-Rob to see who it was that was putting him to rest.

At 10 p.m., the front door opened. Goldie crept to the corner of the house so he could see who was coming out. Just as he peeked around the corner, he saw G-Rob close the door and walk down the steps with a smile on his face. He seemed like he didn't have a worry in the world.

G-Rob stepped off the porch and was halfway to the gate when Goldie came out from the side of the house. He was about fifteen feet away. Goldie pointed the Mac-10 and was ready to fire. G-Rob sensed something behind him and turned around. When he saw Goldie, his smile quickly vanished. He knew that it was over. His time was up. But he also wasn't going to go without a fight.

G-Rob reached for the Glock in his waistband but it was a little too late. As Goldie squeezed the trigger, the first ten bullets from the fully automatic Mac-10 ripped through G-Rob's chest, neck and face. It was over in seconds and G-Rob was dead before he hit the ground.

Goldie was out of the gate and in the van within six seconds of the shooting. As soon as he jumped in, Moonie hit the gas and the van roared off into the night.

After they got back to Compton safely, Goldie called QT and told him G-Rob went to see Nacho and Ed-Dog. QT hung up the phone and said aloud but to himself, "Three down, two to go."

Boss-T and Nutt heard about G-Rob's death about fifteen minutes after he was killed. As they sat in Boss-T's car down the street from G-Rob's baby mama's house, Boss-T said, "We got to get on and lay low for a while. This shit ain't happen by coincidence. QT is on to who we are, and if he knew where to find G-Rob, he knows where to find us. That nigga got money and resources. We got to get out of town until shit cools off and that nigga put his guard down. Then we can come back and smoke his ass."

Nutt said, "I got family in Texas. We can go down there and kick it for about six months. By then, the nigga should be slippin."

Boss-T said, "Yeah, we can do that. I still got about $150,000 left. Shit, we might be able to hit a lick or two while we are down in Texas. Them country niggas got loot."

"I know. Shit, most of dem niggas don't even spend the money. We got to stay away from all the spots we normally kick it at. We can leave after the homies' funerals. Believe me, Blood, dat nigga goin to pay for the homies' deaths if I got to find out where his mama lives and smoke her ass."

Boss-T said, "Blood, fuck that crab (Crip) ass nigga. I'm down for whatever. He goin to wish he never fucked with us."

He started up the car and drove off passing G-Rob's baby mama's house. G-Rob was still lying on the ground with a sheet covering his body. They had lost three homies and neither Nutt nor Boss-T planned on being next. They had a plan, it hadn't been fully planned all the way out yet—but they had a good idea of how they wanted to proceed.

Rocc gained his strength back and was back kicking it in the Fays. He also moved from his mom's house in La Dera back to his house in Cerritos. The money was coming in fast and all of the G-Code Mobb's pockets were fat. It had been a month since Boss-T's homies had been buried. Boss-T and Nutt had disappeared. QT and everyone else that knew and had love for Rocc were looking out for Boss-T and Nutt. Eventually, QT found out they were somewhere in Texas. So now the plan was to find out where and go down there and end it for good. But before that could be handled, something else came up.

Lil Man, one of the G-Code generals who had Golden Street sewed up, had been getting into it with the Mexicans from T-flats (Tortilla Flats) because a couple of them moved over there and when they saw all the money that was coming through, they tried to open up shop. First, they were in violation because they were in Santana Blocc Crip neighborhood. And second, because the dope spots had already been established by someone else. They just couldn't open shop fucking with someone else's clientele. Lil Man sent a few of the homies to blast their spot and shut it down. In the process, two of their homies got blasted. They immediately packed up and moved but everyone knew it wasn't over. There would be retaliation. It was just a matter of when.

Chapter 9: Gang War

QT heard about Lil Man getting into it with the T-Flats again. The first time QT heard about it was at a meeting at his house. He called Goldie and told him to make sure all the lil homies in the hood had straps. QT knew that they had the advantage because Santana Blocc had Mexicans from the hood. That would give them a better chance at making hits on the T-Flats. SBC also had Mexican home girls as well. A pretty face, a nice ass, and a smile could damn near have anybody slippin.

The retaliation didn't take long. Three weeks after the T-Flats were shot, Lil Man and one of his lil homies, Primo Pete, were walking to Lil Man's car in front of one of his spots on Golden Street at around 12:30 a.m. (All of the G-Code Mobb only came to the city between 11 p.m. and 4 a.m. because they knew the task force was off during those hours.) As Lil Man and Primo Pete were standing and talking, Lil Man observed a car coming down the streets with four heads in it and the windows rolled down.

He immediately pulled out his two Glocks and said, "Check out this car coming our way. The windows are all down."

Primo Pete said, "That looks like that fool Smiley's car from T-Flats." He pulled out the Uzi he was packing as he and Lil Man backed up to get some good cover at the side of the apartment building.

Smiley, Loco, Wedo, and Joker were in the car. They were all from T-Flats and they were on a mission to smoke a Santana or anything black that lived in the Santana neighborhood.

Smiley, who was driving, said, "Look. There goes two of those *miyatays* standing by that car."

Joker said, "Yeah, let's smoke they ass."

No one saw Lil Man and Primo Pete standing next to the car or pull out their straps. As soon as the car was fifteen feet away, Lil Man surprised them and opened fire. Primo Pete followed suit with his Uzi.

The T-Flats were so shocked that they didn't get a chance to get a shot off. All they could do was duck and try to avoid being hit. Smiley floored the gas and as the car sped by, all anyone could hear were bullets hitting the car.

When the car was out of sight, Lil Man and Primo Pete jumped in Lil Man's car and drove off in the opposite direction.

"That will teach dem muthafuckas about coming through here trying to catch a nigga slippin," Lil Man said.

Primo Pete said, "Fuck dem bitches. This is the Blocc and the Blocc don't stop."

When Smiley hit the corner he said, "Damn, them muthafuckas were waiting on us. Is everyone all right?"

Loco, who was riding in the front seat, said, "I'm hit in the arm and leg, homes."

Joker said, "I'm cool. I ain't hit." But when he looked over at Wedo, he saw Wedo's head was lying to the side on the back seat and facing out the window. His eyes were open but he was dead. There was blood running out of wounds in his head and neck. Joker started crying and hollering, "Wedo's dead. They killed Wedo. They fuckin killed Wedo!"

All four of them were around the same age and had grown up together from elementary school. This would be the beginning of a gang war that would never end. Santana Blocc and T-Flats were now sworn enemies.

The next day, QT called Goldie and told him to call all the members of the G-Code Mobb and tell them he was calling a meeting at 12:30 a.m. at the Sizzler in Lakewood. When QT got off the phone, he told Nat what was going on.

She asked, "Baby, what are you going to do?"

"I'm not worried about them fucking with us or the G-Code Mobb because we are too mobile. All they will do is go in the hood trying to catch somebody slippin, and if they can't they will shoot anybody that's black, whether they are gangbangers or not, because they are stupid like that."

"Why would they just shoot innocent people?"

QT said, "Becuz to them, instead of it being a gang war they make it a race war."

"That's stupid."

"I know it is but that's the way they roll."

When QT got to the Sizzler, it was 12:45 a.m. Everybody was already seated at a large table in the back of the restaurant. QT's seat was left empty. He walked up and took his seat at the head of the table and signaled for the waitress so they could order.

QT opened the meeting by saying, "Shit in the hood is going to get real funky. It's a good thing that all of us are doing business OT (out of town) so regardless of how bad shit goes we are still going to be making money. We know for a fact that it's going to get worse before it gets better. They have suffered the first casualty so they are going to really be trying to catch one of the homies slippin. We really don't have to worry about it because we don't live in the hood. But for the homies that do live in the hood, we have to make sure that they all have straps and they are aware of what's going on."

Rocc said, "Everybody already know what's going on. They just have to stay on their P's and Q's so they don't get caught slippin."

Boxer said, "We just have to make sure those fools know that we ain't to be fucked with. We got to blast them fools at random. The homies in the hood have to take it to those fools and when they try to come back blastin, the homies have to be ready for them. That way, they will know that it's always going to be a chance that they will get smoked in the process of trying to smoke the homies."

The waitress started delivering the food so QT changed the subject to Crenshaw and Low Riding until everyone was served.

Once the waitress left, Big Bam said, "Look, Cuz, I know that niggas are going to die from both sides becuz that's the way it goes but what we have to do is limit the loss of real homies in this war. We know that when it comes down to it, they will shoot base heads and anything else that's black. While they are doing that, we need to be steady, hitting them hard where it hurts. In other words, we need to be consistent at blasting niggas that are members of the T-Flats."

QT looked at Boxer and said, "I want you to have the S.A. home girls hook up with a couple of those fools and find out who's who, where they kick it, where they live, what stores they go to to get liquor. That way, we will have a big advantage when we want to put work in on those fools."

Crip Crazy said, "Me and Lil Man will school the homies in the hood. We will also make sure that if they need some more heat (guns), they'll have them."

QT said, "Everybody here at this table has a crew of homies becuz all of you run a different part of the hood, so it's up to each one of you to make sure that your part of the hood is secure. Lil Ken and Moonie will continue to watch Nat's back and Keebo will post up with me when I'm at the shops. Remember to stay out of the hood during the day and don't be out in the open when you're in the hood."

They finished eating and they all went their separate ways. Before he left, QT pulled Goldie to the side and told him, "Get at all the homies that we do business with and put them up on the game."

Goldie said, "I got everything covered. I'll get at them as soon as I get back to the Blocc."

Lil T-Bone walked out of his baby's mama's house on Spring Street. He lived a block over on McDivitt Street so he always walked to and from her house to his because it was a short walk and it was in his neighborhood. Lil T-Bone's brother, Big T-Bone, was an OG from Santana Blocc Crips. He was locked up in the L.A. County Jail

for being an ex-felon in possession of a firearm and a parole violation. He was in the 4800, the Crip module in the County Jail. The
Crips had been causing so much trouble beating, robbing, gang-
bangin, and raping fools on the mainline that they were put all
together in a module of their own to keep the jail population safe.
The 4800 wasn't big enough to hold all the Crips in the jail so OSS
(Operation Safe Streets), the Sheriff's gang unit, put the most violent
and known Crips in 4800. Big T-Bone was known so he was sent
straight to 4800 as soon as he was processed.

As Lil T-Bone walked home, he was thinking about his son who
was a year old. He had called Lil T-Bone "dada" for the first time. Lil
T-Bone was happy and proud at the same time. He was so caught up
in his thoughts that he didn't notice a blue four-door Caprice Classic
slowly coming up behind him. Lil T-Bone had a strap in his waistband but it wouldn't do him any good tonight because he was
definitely slippin.

While QT and the G-Code Mobb were having their meeting,
Smiley, Loco, and Joker were in a G-Ride (stolen car) riding through
the Blocc looking for someone to take revenge on for Wedo's
murder.

Smiley said, "Homes, I ain't going home until we smoke one of
these black muthafuckas. This is for Wedo, R.I.P. (rest in peace)."

Loco said, "We got to show these fools we ain't no joke. They
can't just smoke one of our homies and thank it's all over. We goin to
make these fools hurt just like we been hurting."

When Smiley turned down Spring Street he immediately spotted
Lil T-Bone walking on the right side of the street. They could tell he
was a Crip by the way he was dressed.

"Look! There go one of them niggas right there," Smiley said and
pointed.

Loco said, "Pull up on that fool. As soon as we get to him, me and
Joker are going to blast his black ass."

When the Caprice pulled up on Lil T-Bone, it was too late for him to do anything. When he turned to see who it was, all he saw were the barrels of two guns sticking out of the windows of the car. The first shot hit him in the chest. He tried to turn and run but ten more bullets hit him in the back, neck, and legs. As he fell to the ground, his last thoughts were of his son smiling and calling him dada.

Lil T-Bone's baby mama heard the shots and instantly knew it was Lil T-Bone—he hadn't been gone from her house five minutes. As she ran out the front door she saw the Caprice take off speeding up the street. She started running and screaming Lil T-Bone's name as tears streamed down her face. When she got to him, he was lying on his stomach in a puddle of blood. She turned him over, screaming and crying for help, and held him in her arms. It was too late. Lil T-Bone was gone and his son would never get to know his father.

Smiley, Joker, and Loco went back to their hood and were laughing and telling their homies how they had blasted on a Santana. They were drinking and smoking weed and PCP.

Smiley said, "Now the homie can rest in peace."

Joker said, "Them muthafuckas don't want to see us. I know they didn't think we was going to let that shit slide."

Their big homie Spanky said, "This shit is just beginning. I hope ya'll don't think it's over. Them niggas over there got money, and money is power, so I advise ya'll not to be slippin."

Smiley said, "Fuck them niggas. We can handle them. They ain't shit."

Spanky looked at Smiley. "Okay, big shot. When the shit hit the fan—and it will—come get at us." Spanky and eight other OGs from the T-Flats walked away.

Right before QT pulled into his driveway, he got the call telling him about Lil T-Bone. QT and Big T-Bone were tight. He knew that Big T-Bone was in the County Jail so he would have to go see him later that day. Big T-Bone was going to take it hard because Lil T-

Bone was his only brother and he loved him. When he went to jail he had asked QT to watch out for him. QT had kept Lil T-Bone off the streets by giving him a job at his shop, and also gave him extra money to take care of his baby boy so he wouldn't have to be out in the streets trying to sell dope. QT had love for Lil T-Bone.

He found Nat asleep so he took a shower and went to bed. As he lay there and thought about his next move, he knew that there was no turning back now. QT had love for all his homies just because they were from the Blocc but this was different. This was more on a personal level. He fell asleep thinking about Big T-Bone.

That morning, QT told Nat about Lil T-Bone and that he had to go see his brother in jail. He called Goldie and told him to call all the members of the G-Code Mobb and tell them to tell all the homies to chill until after Lil T-Bone's funeral.

QT went to see Big T-Bone on the early visit at noon. When he got there, the line was already kind of long but he didn't care. He had to see the homie. There were so many females there to see their men that it seemed like it was a long line for a ladies night at a club. QT knew a lot of them in line. Most of the ones he didn't know wanted to get to know him but females was the last thing on his mind.

When he got up to the counter, the sheriff deputy looked at him, and at his jewelry, and asked him if he was on probation or parole.

"Naw, I ain't on nothing. I work for a living and pay my taxes."

The deputy took his ID and ran a check on him anyway. It can back clean and the deputy handed QT his ID back. He went back to sit down and waited. It took about thirty minutes.

When Big T-Bone's name was called, QT went to the counter to pick up the pass and when he got to the window, Big T-Bone was already sitting there. Big T-Bone was 6' 2", dark skinned, dark eyes, bald head, big chest, and was very muscular. He had been in and out of jail since he was eleven years old and was now twenty-eight.

QT could tell he had already heard the bad news. He could see the sadness in his eyes and they were red as if he had been crying. QT sat down, the phones came on two minutes later. Both of them knew that certain things couldn't be said because the phone conversations were recorded.

"I'm sorry, homie, I did all that I could to keep him safe."

"It ain't yo fault, cuz. He told me everything that you were doing for him and I appreciate it. I beat the gun charge but I still have to do a violation. I know that I got a year coming. I will be out in eight more months."

"Don't worry about nothing, homie. I got everything covered, everything. I'll pay so you are able to come to the funeral. Hook everything up and I will give the money to your moms."

Tears were running down Big T-Bone's face. "Good lookin out, homie." Then he looked QT straight in the eyes and said, "I'm hurting. My family is hurting."

"I'm hurting too, homie, a lot of people are hurting. Don't sweat nothing. I got it, you know how we do it."

Big T-Bone knew that QT was talking about taking care of the fools that smoked Lil T-Bone.

After his visit to the County Jail, QT went to his shop in west L.A. About thirty minutes after he arrived, Destiny walked in his office. She closed the door and locked it behind her. "I heard about that youngster that got killed early this morning on Spring Street. What's going on?"

Even though QT knew that Destiny was in love with him and was on his team, he wasn't going to let her know anything, especially about the hood. He already had her thinking that he didn't indulge in the gangbang activities in the hood, that all he did was sell dope.

"I don't know what that was about. It probably was some Crip and Blood shit. I stay away from the gang shit. I know them and grew up with most of them but I'm about the money."

Destiny said, "Compton P.D. is enforcing a policy now which is whenever they see a gang member, or a suspected gang member, they pull them over and search him for weapons, no matter if he's walking or driving."

QT said, "It don't affect me becuz I rarely go to Compton."

"Enough of that," she said and changed the subject. "Why haven't I seen you lately? You know that I miss you, daddy."

She walked up to QT, got on her knees, took his pants and boxers down and guided his manhood into her mouth.

He was hard instantly. Destiny's mouth felt so good, she sucked him until he came in her mouth. She swallowed all of his sperm and kept sucking him until he was dry.

She got up and went to the bathroom and brushed her teeth while QT pulled his boxers and pants up, fixed his clothes, and sat back down behind his desk. He had missed Destiny and was thinking about going in the bathroom and fucking her when she walked out smiling—and butt naked holding a condom in her hand.

"I know you didn't think I was finished with you," she said.

She walked around the desk as QT stood up. She helped him take his pants and boxers completely off this time. QT was hard the moment he saw Destiny's naked body. She got back down on her knees, took QT in her mouth teasing him, then she put the condom on him. She went over to the sofa and bent over, spreading her legs.

QT could see the wetness seeping out of her pussy. He walked up behind her, opened her pussy lips with his hands and slowly guided his manhood inside of her. It felt so hot and good that he was moaning right along with her. She was tight and QT slowly started stroking her until he had made his way into her fully. As he stroked her, Destiny moaned and said, "Oh yes, oh yes, oh I missed you, daddy. Oh, I love you and this dick. Fuck me, baby, fuck me."

This turned QT on even more. He quickened his pace and when he pushed a finger into her asshole, she started bucking like a horse.

"Oh oh oh! I'm cumming, daddy, I'm cumming!"

QT pulled his dick out of her pussy, pulled the condom off and slammed his dick back into her pussy as hard as he could. Then he pulled out and pushed it into her asshole. She couldn't take it; she collapsed on her stomach, moaning, her legs shaking. QT continued to fuck her in her ass. When he was about to cum he reached under her and pushed two fingers in her pussy. When he came in her ass, she exploded and came with him. She couldn't move when he pulled out of her. She balled up like a baby, legs shaking, and repeated over and over, "Oh, I love you, oh daddy, I love you."

QT went and got in the shower. In a few minutes she joined him. As she soaped his body up, she said, "QT, I'm in love with you. I know that you're not going to leave your wife and I can't have you to myself but I do need you in my life."

He pulled her close and held her in his arms. "I will always be here for you," he said. "You are my baby and I love you too."

Slowly, they began to kiss. As the water ran over their faces, tears ran down her face as she wished she was married to QT. She loved him with all her heart. If she couldn't have him for herself, she would settle for what she had. She loved him and she would do anything to protect him.

Afterwards, as they got dressed, Destiny said, "Agent White has set up a shipping company for me hoping you will try to send some drugs to other states through my company."

QT smiled and said, "I do have some rims and tires I need to send out of state. I might as well use your company at a hell of a discount since you like me. In reality, it will be at their expense."

They both started laughing.

QT said, "I know that they are still watching my shop, so when you leave they will probably want to know why you were here so long. So you call White and tell him that I came at you and want to send some rims and tires out of town through your company. I know he will think that it's going to be drugs and that he'll finally will have something to arrest me on."

"We can only investigate you for so long," Destiny said. "The judge already has said he is not going to renew the phone taps because it's been six months and we haven't come up with anything. After getting nothing through the shipping company, we may be forced to break this investigation off."

After Destiny left QT she called Agent White and filled him in on QT's request to use her shipping company to ship rims and tires to other states. White called all the agents working on QT's case to the office for a meeting.

Once they were assembled, Agent White told them, "I think this may be it. We may be finally able to take this asshole down. He has to be shipping drugs. Why else would he decide to use Detective Stevens' shipping company? He has been using UPS so why change now? This could be our big break. I don't want any mistakes. It's scheduled to go down in two weeks. So until then, just keep doing what you are doing."

Destiny and her partner Foster left, Special Agent White and the DEA agents stayed in the room.

White said, "In the beginning, I thought Detective Stevens was going to fall for QT but he's not even interested in her. I've had her followed...she's only seen him a couple of times and he's only called her phone twice. From the phone conversation, she does flirt but she was told to do that. I know that he will be calling her phone more often now since he wants to use her to send drugs across the country."

QT paid for Lil T-Bone's funeral and also for Big T-Bone to come to it as well. The funeral was packed; all the Santana Blocc Crips were there as well as other Crips from different Crip sets in Compton. All the Santanas wore black. The funeral was truly a sad one. Big T-Bone was escorted in by two deputies. When they saw all the gang members in the church one could see they were getting nervous.

QT went up and embraced Big T-Bone. He looked at the deputies and said, "Don't worry about nothing. Ya'll's safe. Thanks for bringing my homie to say bye to his brother."

Lil T-Bone was loved by everyone in the hood. The females and males alike all shed tears for the homie. Lil T-Bone's mother and his baby's mama had to be carried out of the church they were so upset. There was a whole lot of hurt and pain in that church.

When Big T-Bone went to view Lil T-Bone for the last time, QT went with him. The brother broke down; he couldn't handle seeing his lil brother like that. Tears were running down QT's face as well. QT and Big Bam took Big T-Bone by his arms and escorted him out of the church with the deputies right behind them.

QT whispered in Big T-Bone's ear, "Don't worry about nothing. We won't be the only ones hurting. We got this covered. You know how we do it." He said goodbye but he didn't go to the cemetery with the others because he didn't want to see his lil homie put in the ground.

It was already established that the night of the funeral was going to be pay back night—that night and every night after that for seven days. QT didn't have to roll but he wanted to because of the love he had for Big and Lil T-Bone.

That night, around 9 p.m., QT, Lil Man, and Crip Crazy got in a G-Ride and headed to where the T-Flats hang out. T-Flat neighborhood was in Fruit Town where the Fruit Town Pirus were located. Crip Crazy drove with QT riding up front and Lil Man in the back. They were in a 4-door Cutlass. The windows were tinted which is why they chose the Cutlass to roll in. As they drove through Fruit Town, they saw plenty of Bloods slippin, but tonight it wasn't about Bloods, it was about T-Flats.

After driving around for fifteen minutes, they went down a street and saw about ten to fifteen T-Flats partying in a front yard drinking and getting high.

QT instructed Crip Crazy, "Park the car and keep it running— we'll ce back in a tic-or-a-toc."

QT had two 9mm Berettas with two extra clips, and Lil Man had a .45 mag and a Uzi. They were dressed in all black. As they walked to their destination, QT said, "Make sure you save some bullets for the ride to the hood."

"I got two extra clips, we all good," Lil Man replied.

"We got to make a statement tonight. We got to let these fools know what's up with the Blocc."

The T-Flats were so busy partying and getting high that they didn't notice the two figures in dark clothing creeping along the side of the cars on the opposite side of the street. Smiley, Loco, and Joker were all there. Smiley was in the house trying to fuck one of his home girls. Loco and Joker were in the front yard partying and yelling out their neighborhood.

When QT saw and heard them, he decided to blast on them first.

By the time anyone saw QT and Lil Man, it was too late. They were directly across the street from where the T-Flats were, and were already crossing the street. QT's first shot hit Loco in the neck; two more went in his chest. Joker tried to pull his gun out of his waistband but he was a second too slow. QT shot him in the head and he was dead before he hit the ground.

Lil Man unloaded; he shot two T-Flats in the head and sprayed four more with the Uzi.

As they turned to run, QT wanted them to know who did the shooting. He yelled, "Fuck T-Flats! This Santana Blocc Crip, muthafucka!"

When Smiley heard the shots he was butt naked fucking one of his home girls. By the time he got to the front yard, four of his homies were dead and five more had been shot. When he saw Loco and Joker lying on the ground not moving, he knew they were dead. He started to cry uncontrollably.

One of his homies that had run when the shooting started and made it inside the house had come back out and was saying, "The muthafuckas yelled out, 'Santana Blocc Crip.'"

Smiley fell to his knees holding Joker in his arms and asking God out loud, "Why Joker, why Loco, why?"

When QT and Lil Man got back to the car, as soon as they got in Crip Crazy took off. They made it to the hood safely. QT gave the guns to Goldie to get rid of. Crip Crazy took the G-Ride on Alameda and set it on fire.

QT went home and took a shower. Afterwards, he cut on the TV to catch the eleven o'clock news. When it came on, the broadcaster way saying, "We have breaking news…In Compton, four men were killed and five wounded, three of them in critical condition, in a gang-related shooting."

That was all QT wanted to hear. He cut the TV off and went to bed. Nat called and told him she was on her way home from her parents' house.

The next day, Big T-Bone was in the day room watching TV.

When the news came on, he saw the broadcast about the shooting and where it happened. Instantly, he knew that QT had handled his business. He looked up as if he was looking to the sky and said to his lil brother, "Now you can rest in peace."

Nobody knew that QT, Lil Man, and Crip Crazy had done the shooting except for Goldie. The homies knew that someone was supposed to put work in but if it wasn't them that was designated, they didn't know who it was. They only knew it had been a homie.

Goldie broke down all the guns and took them to QT's boat at the marina. He took the boat out on the ocean and threw the dismantled guns overboard.

All the homies were told to stay off the streets during the daytime. The dope spots were still open because the homies from the Blocc were safe inside, but the homies that sold dope on the street had to close shop until it got dark.

As planned, the homies hit the T-Flats every night for a week. The T-Flats came back but the homies were waiting for them. During those seven days, over twenty T-Flats were shot. Five of them died. Four Santanas got shot but they all survived. Four base heads were killed too even though they had nothing to do with the war. They had been shot by T-Flats because they were black.

Big Spanky called a meeting for all the T-Flats to attend and about one hundred and fifty of them showed up. The first thing Spanky did was look at Smiley and tell him, "So, you can handle them, they ain't shit? Tell that to the homies that ain't here no more and to the homies that's laid up in the hospital. I told you lil muthafuckas in the beginning, don't try to open up a dope spot in somebody else's hood, but you niggas is money hungry and disrespectful."

"It's on now and we are all involved," he told all the T-Flats. "We can't change the past. We got to make this shit right—the homies didn't die for nothing. I found out the main niggas from over there, with the money, say-so, and the power, don't live nowhere near Santana hood. I don't know how we are going to be able to get to them but I did find out that one of them, name QT, got a tire and rim shop in Inglewood. So for now, the main focus is to smoke his ass. I know he should be slippin at his shop, being that it's nowhere near Compton or his enemies."

Smiley spoke up and said, "Let me smoke his ass. I owe that to the homies."

Spanky said, "Okay, you got that, but Chewy is going to roll with you to watch you back."

QT called Destiny on the bugged phone the feds had given to her. When she answered, he played it off and said, "What's up, Teresa?"

"Hi, QT. What's on your mind?"

"You are on my mind. What are you up to? Do you want to go to dinner or catch a movie with me?"

"Yeah, we can go to dinner. I haven't eaten yet."

"Do you want me to come get you, or do you want to meet me in the Marina at Friday's?"

"I'll meet you at Friday's in an hour," she said and hung up.

White, who had been listening in, immediately phoned Destiny and told her to take a mini tape recorder and tape the conversation over dinner. She immediately paged QT and left her code. When he called her back on her real cell phone, she told him what Agent White wanted her to do and QT said okay.

When she got to the restaurant, QT already had a table. She told him when she was cutting the tape on. As they ate dinner, QT told her that he would be shipping his goods through her company in two days. He told her that he would be dropping everything off himself. Destiny said that she would be there to handle his shipments personally. Then QT started getting sexual with Destiny, telling her how beautiful she was and how he would love to make love to her. She told QT that, while she liked him, he was married and she couldn't have sex with a married man. QT told her to just think about it and if she changed her mind to give him a call.

After dinner, he walked her to her car. Destiny cut the tape off and said, "More than likely, Agent White has someone watching me, so I'll just give you a hug and a kiss on the cheek."

She hugged and kissed QT, got in her car, and drove off.

Across the lot, DEA Agents Davis and Jones sat in their car watching Destiny. Davis said, "I would pay to get some of that pussy."

Agent Jones said, "So would I. If we can't get this asshole this time, Detective Stevens may have to give up some of that good pussy in order for us to get him."

"That's the only time that I would wish that I was QT, and that's to get some of that good pussy."

"I second that."

The next day when Destiny played the tape for Agent White and the rest of the task force, White told her, "He's trying to get close to you so that he can use you to send his drugs state to state. This time tomorrow, we should have all we need to bust his ass."

When QT pulled in front of his shop in Inglewood, it was already open. Keebo was there and waiting for him at the front door.

QT had Keebo wearing the store's uniform to throw off anyone who came to the shop for the wrong reasons. Keebo worked behind the counter writing out orders and collecting the money. He packed a .45 auto in his waist band and he had his 9mm in his car outside. The .45 auto had been bought by Nat for the shop only. That way, if Keebo had to shoot anybody at the shop, he would be covered.

QT was in his office on the phone ordering stock when he looked up at the surveillance monitors and saw Smiley and Chewy walk in looking suspicious. He hung up the phone and zoomed in on the pair with the camera. There was something about them ... they were out of place. Sure he had young Mexicans come to his shop many times but there was something about these two that alarmed him. QT switched to the camera monitoring the parking lot at the rear of the building and saw a 2-door Cutlass. QT didn't know the Cutlass was the car that they were in until he saw one of them go back to it. QT's anger started to rise; he was on the verge of going downstairs and blasting both of them. He had to calm himself down and think. He wasn't in the streets, he was at his place of business.

He called Keebo on the phone and told him, "Cuz, you peep those two Mexican fools down there?"

Keebo answered, "Yeah, I was on them as soon as they came in the shop. I think those fools are T-Flats. I can tell that they are strapped. What do you want me to do? It's your call."

"For now, just watch them. I'll watch them from up here as well."

He hung up the phone, laid his 9mm on the top of his desk and watched their every move on the monitors.

Neither Smiley nor Chewy knew what QT looked like so Smiley went up to the counter and asked Keebo if he could speak to the owner. Keebo told him the owner wasn't in, that he was on vacation and wouldn't be back for two weeks. He asked Smiley if there was something he could help him with. Smiley said no and that he would come back when the owner was there. The two left the shop, got in the Cutlass and drove off.

Keebo went up to QT's office and told him what was said. QT called Boxer and told him to bring Shy Girl, Lil One and Bambi up to the shop as soon as possible.

Once they got there, QT showed them the video of Smiley and Chewy. After he showed them the video, he said, "I need ya'll to roll over in T-Flat hood and act like ya'll are looking for some weed to buy. All three of ya'll are fine so I know that those fools are going to try and get at ya'll. Boxer, do you still have that spot in Paramount?"

Boxer said, "Yeah, I ain't kicked it there in a while but I still have it."

QT said, "Let the home girls stay there until we get these fools. I want ya'll to hook up with three of them fools from T-Flats, find out who's who, where they live and especially find out who these two fools are on this tape and where they live. Give all the info to Boxer and he will take care of ya'll."

When they left, QT sat back in his chair and thought about the situation. He knew that all three of his home girls were fine and they were one hundred per cent down for the hood. He also knew that a fine bitch could be the demise of almost any nigga. By the home girls living in Paramount, and saying they didn't gang bang, QT knew that it was only a matter of time before the trap would be set. QT had a plan, the Fruit Town Pirus were also getting into it with the T-Flats so when this hit was made he would make sure the homies wore red bandanas on their faces. That way it would take some of the heat from F-Troop (Compton P.D.) off of the Blocc.

Chapter 10: The Trap

When QT got home, Nat already had dinner cooked. She made their plates and they sat at the table and ate together. After they finished, Nat sat on QT's lap and slowly kissed him, sliding her tongue in and out of his mouth.

QT said, "I love you, Nat. You are truly one of a kind."

She looked him in the eyes and said, "I love you too with all my heart."

He could tell that she had something on her mind. "Tell me, baby, what's going on?"

Nat smiled and said, "I'm pregnant. We are going to have a baby."

QT was so happy he picked Nat up and started to dance with her in his arms. He said, "Oh shit, oh shit, that's great news! It's about time. I'm going to be a daddy."

He carried Nat into the den, laid her down on the sofa and made long slow love to her.

The next morning when Nat woke up, QT made breakfast and brought it to her on a tray.

"Breakfast in bed," she said with a smile. "I should have gotten pregnant a long time ago."

"Your wish is my command."

Nat looked at QT and said, "Baby, we got more than enough money saved up. We got legit businesses that continue to make money and now we are going to have a child. Nobody can do what you do forever without getting caught or getting caught up in some bullshit. I love you and I'm down with you for whatever. I just want you to think about us and our future."

"I have been thinking about us and our future," he replied. "As you know, Gangsta beat his appeal and he will be out in ten months.

I want to make sure that he doesn't have to do what I'm doing when he touches down. Just give me until Gangsta touches down, ten more months, and I'm out of the game, out of the hood, and out of everything that's not legal."

Nat kissed QT. "I'm down with you, baby. If that's how you want to do it, then let's do it."

Awhile later when Lil Ken and Moonie got to the pad to get Nat, QT pulled them to the side and told them Nat was pregnant. He said to make sure she stayed safe and if they saw her working too hard to let him know. They congratulated QT and told him not to worry about nothing, that they would guard Nat with their lives.

It was around 5 p.m. when Bambi, Shy Girl, and Lil One got into Bambi's Honda Accord and headed to T-Flats neighborhood. Bambi was 5' 10", 110 lbs, blonde hair, brown eyes, thin waist, nice hips and ass with 36-inch breasts. Shy Girl was 5' 6", long brown hair, brown eyes, big ass, thin waist, and big breasted. And Lil One was about 4' 8", 100 lbs, blonde hair, green eyes, nice round ass, thin waist, and 36-inch breasts. They were all attractive, that's why QT picked them.

On the way to T-Flat's hood, Bambi said, "Don't forget, we don't want to seem anxious to hook up with these clowns. Since we all live together, only one of us will give up the phone number."

All of them had grown up in the Blocc, and all of them fucked with brothas. They had been kickin it with brothas since they started fucking. They didn't like Mexican dudes. They had all tried dating Mexicans but they didn't do it for them. They had Mexican homies from the Blocc, but those all had black females they were fucking with.

The three girls knew the street where the T-Flats sold their weed so Bambi turned down it and pulled up on three T-Flats that were standing out front. They could see that there were more T-Flats in the house and in the back yard.

When T-Flats saw the three females in the car, more of them came out of the house and the back yard to see if they could get some action. Smiley was one of the first ones to the car. All the mijas recognized him immediately. He went to the driver's side to talk to Bambi.

"What's up, baby? What ya'll need?"

Bambi said, "We need an ounce of some good green weed."

"Don't worry about nothing. I got that, all day, every day. Where are ya'll from?"

Bambi said, "We aren't from anywhere. We live in Paramount."

Smiley said, "You got a number so I can call you? Maybe we could hook up and go out or something."

Bambi wrote her phone number down and said, "I'm Bambi, that's Lil One, and that's Shy Girl."

"I'm Smiley," he said, then he introduced his homies that were around the car. Chewy was one of the homies he introduced. Lil One was talking to him.

They talked for about fifteen minutes and bought the weed. When they drove away, Lil One said, "Girl, this is going to be like taking candy from a baby."

Shy Girl agreed. "Yeah, those fools ain't nothing but cock hounds and by us living in Paramount and not being affiliated with no gangs, their guards are really going to be down. All they are going to be thinking about is trying to get some of this pussy."

They called Boxer and gave him the rundown, then went to the spot in Paramount to kick it, get high, and wait for Smiley to call.

Phase One of the trap had gone off smoothly.

QT was in the truck with Keebo on his way to Destiny's shipping company. Keebo didn't know what was up. He just thought they were going to ship some rims and tires off; he didn't know Destiny was really a detective. All he knew was that she came to see QT and she had a shipping company. He suspected that QT had fucked her but he didn't know for sure. What he did know is he wished he could fuck her fine ass.

When they got to Destiny's company, she had them pull around to the back of the building. Her workers unloaded the rims and tires. In reality, all of the "workers" were DEA and FBI agents. It was a set-up and everything was being recorded and filmed.

After everything was unloaded and QT filled out the paperwork, he paid Destiny and told her he would call her later that evening. When he left, the feds separated each order by state and started opening the boxes thinking they would find drugs.

Special Agent White was so anxious he was there helping to open the boxes. But once they'd gone through the entire shipment and found nothing, White was furious. He didn't understand it; he just knew that QT would be trying to send drugs through the shipment.

Destiny's partner, Detective Foster said, "Maybe he's legit and not selling drugs. It's been over eight months since we've been on him and we haven't even got a phone call that sounded suspicious."

Agent White could hardly contain his anger. "No, no, no. I can't believe no shit like that. I've been on this job fifteen years — I know this asshole is a drug dealer. Either he has stopped because he knows we're on him, or someone is feeding him information."

Everyone was quiet and caught up in their own thoughts. They were thinking that Agent White just didn't want to admit to defeat.

Agent White finally said, "Okay. We will go to our original plan. Detective Stevens, you will call QT and invite him to dinner, but only this time, you'll have ten kilos of cocaine in your bedroom. I don't care how you do it—get him in your bedroom. Leave the closet halfway open so that he can see it. You then go to the bathroom and leave QT in your room. I'm sure he will look around. When he sees the coke, hopefully he will bite and we can take it from there. If this doesn't work, the investigation is over and we will have to go to the next suspect. There are too many snitches in the streets that have been telling us about QT selling drugs for him to be clean."

In his fifteen years on the job, White had never run across anyone as clever as QT and he had never been as frustrated trying to bust someone.

"All right," he said. "Let's get these rims and tires packed and shipped or else QT will know that Detective Stevens isn't who she says she is."

Destiny paged QT and left her code. When he called back she answered him on the first ring. She told him what Agent White's plan was and that after this, if nothing went down, they would have to drop the investigation on him.

He listened to what she had to say, then told her he was going to call her right back on the phone that was tapped.

When she's answered that phone, QT asked, "What's up, Teresa baby?"

"I was just thinking about you," Destiny replied.

"I hope you were having freaky thoughts."

"That's for me to know and you to find out."

"Is that right? I do need to find out. Before you make me forget I wanted to thank you for shipping that stuff for me today."

"That was business. I ain't turning no money down. Anyway, I was going to call you to ask you to dinner Thursday night. I'm cooking at my house."

QT said, "You got a date. I'll be there around seven."

"I'll see you then."

Destiny hung up the phone knowing her conversation had been listened to by someone on the task force.

The war between the T-Flats and Santana Blocc was still raging on as they went back and forth shooting each other. When Smiley told Spanky that QT was on a two week vacation, Spanky said, "Okay, that will give us time to prepare for his demise. But meanwhile, we have to continue to blast those muthafuckas and let them know that we in it to win it."

Smiley called Bambi to try to hook up with her but she told him that her and her home girls were going over to her sister's house in Cerritos for a bachelorette party. She told Smiley to call her the next day and they could hook up.

QT went to his shop in west L.A. He didn't want to go back to the one in Inglewood until after his home girls had given Boxer the information he needed so he could handle his business and get the T-Flats off his back.

He was in his office going over some paperwork when Tasha walked in, looking as sexy and good as ever. It had been awhile since QT had spent any time with her. Tasha had been taking cocaine to Louisiana and picking the money up for QT. It was running like clock work.

Tasha had accumulated a total of $350,000 plus the condo and the car that QT bought her. All of that was cool and she enjoyed it all but she would give it all up to be with QT. She was in love with him and she didn't want to be with any other man.

She closed the door behind her. "I hope that I'm not in violation for popping up here. I just had to see you. It's been forty-five days exactly."

She had on a skirt suit and some 4-inch high heel pumps. Her hair was in a ponytail hanging down the middle of her back, and just looking at her smooth chocolate skin gave QT a hard dick.

He smiled and said, "I missed you too, baby. It's just been a lot of bullshit going on and I haven't had time to get with you, but I could have called. Naw baby, you not in violation this time. I understand where you are coming from."

Tasha walked up to QT and kissed him slowly. She held him tight, tight like she didn't ever want to let him go. QT put his hands on her nice big ass and squeezed it hard enough for her to moan. She could feel his manhood pressing against her stomach.

QT pulled her skirt up and slid his hand down in her panties. Tasha opened her legs and QT slowly rubbed on her clit. As she moaned, he inserted a finger inside of her. Tasha was hot and wet and felt good. QT pulled his hand out of her panties and put his finger in her mouth so she could taste herself.

She started to undress, doing a strip tease. As QT watched her, he was undressing as well. Once they were naked, he just admired her beauty for a few minutes. Then he laid Tasha on her back on the sofa and slowly started kissing Tasha in her mouth. He made his way down to her shoulders, breasts, and stomach, then to her inner thighs. She was so excited she tried to guide QT's head to her pussy.

He gently knocked her hand off of his head and slowly made his way to her clitoris where he slowly started to lick and suck. Tasha couldn't handle it; her legs were shaking and she started cumming. QT went down between her pussy lips and pushed his tongue inside of her. He started sucking and licking all around the inside of her pussy. Tasha couldn't take it; it was feeling too good. She tried to push QT's head away but he didn't budge.

As he was licking her pussy and clit, he pushed his finger in and out of her ass. Suddenly, he stopped and positioned himself and guided his dick inside of her. Tasha had been moaning and telling QT how much she loved and missed him since he first started kissing and licking on her. But once he entered her, she was out of control.

QT always loved fucking Tasha because she was so tight and hot. As he started stroking, she said, "Yes, daddy, yes! Oh, this is yo pussy. Fuck yo pussy, daddy, oh oh oh, please, daddy, please."

QT was so caught up he had forgot that he hadn't put on a condom until Tasha said, "Daddy, I'm about to cum. Please cum with me, please, daddy."

He came back to his senses and pulled out of her, then pushed his dick in her ass. After about six or seven strokes, he was ready to cum. When Tasha started cumming, QT came in her ass. QT just laid there in her ass as she held him tight and shook under him. After a few minutes, they got up and went to shower.

As Tasha lathered QT up and cleaned him, she said, "Daddy, you know that I will do anything for you no matter what it is. I love you, QT. You are the only man that I have ever loved and that's for real." She went down on her knees and took QT in her mouth and licked and sucked on him until he came.

After they got out of the shower, she brushed her teeth, got dressed, and QT ordered some pizza and buffalo wings. They ate and talked for a couple of hours. Before Tasha left, QT told her that he would be by her place to see her soon.

When Tasha was gone, QT thought to himself, I got the three baddest females around and all of them love me. I got to be the luckiest nigga alive.

Bambi set up a date with Smiley and told him to bring Chewy for Lil One and a homie for Shy Girl. Then she called Boxer and told him what was up. Boxer called QT and asked him if he wanted Boxer and a couple more homies to smoke Smiley and him homies when they got to the spot. QT told Boxer to kick back—they needed to get more info on the T-Flats, shit like where they lived and where the niggas that was running the T-Flats lived. QT knew that without the head, the body was useless. He wanted to hit the heads, and then he wouldn't have anything to worry about.

Smiley, Chewy, and their homie Chino came to the spot where Bambi and her home girls lived. Bambi could tell that they were kind of leery at first but after smoking some week and some drink, they loosened up. They thought they were getting some pussy but Bambi, Lil One, and Shy Girl told them they could kick it, hug, and kiss, but there wasn't no fucking going down, not this soon anyway. Bambi made it clear to Smiley that she wasn't a hoe or a one night stand.

Smiley and his homies stayed until two in the morning then went home. On the way home, Smiley said, "Damn, homes. I'm feeling Bambi and the cool thang is, she ain't got no kids."

Chewy and Chino agreed and said they felt the same way about Shy Girl and Lil One.

The next day Bambi called Boxer and gave him the run down and told him that all three of them had been strapped. Boxer said cool, and to keep him informed. The next six days, either Bambi or the other two was hanging out with Smiley and his homies in T-Flat hood, or Smiley and his homies were chilling at their spot.

The second week is when they found out where Smiley, Chewy, and Chino lived. They also met Spanky and found out that he was running the T-Flats. Three days into the second week, by accident, they found out where Spanky lived. Bambi and Lil One went to pick up Smiley and Chewy and in the process saw Spanky coming out of a house with a female.

Bambi said, "There go yo homie Spanky."

Smiley said, "Yeah, that's his wife with him. They been together since junior high school."

Lil One said, "That's a nice house. Shit, I need a house like that."

"I feel you on that. I want a house like that too," Smiley said. "I helped Spanky move in that house. Ya'll should see the inside of that bitch. It's tight."

So there it was: Smiley had unknowingly signed Spanky's death warrant.

Later that night, Bambi called Boxer and they met on Willow Street. She got in the car with him and showed him where Spanky, Smiley, Chewy and Chino lived. Boxer wrote everything down so he wouldn't forget. He called QT and put him up on everything.

QT said, "I will take care of Spanky. I want you and a couple of the homies to take care of the rest of them once they leave the home girls' house and are back in Compton, that way the home girls won't be sweated. Tell the home girls once them niggas leave to pack they shit and go home. Give each one of them ten grand and I will give it back to you."

QT called Goldie and told him he needed to get at him, to meet him in Lakewood at the Sizzler at 12:30 a.m. QT wanted Agent White to sweat so he kept putting the dinner date with Destiny off. He would meet with her after he handled his business with the T-Flats. He had to meet Goldie and plan how they would take Spanky out.

Goldie and QT pulled up at the same time. They shook hands, embraced, and went inside. After they ordered, QT said, "The home girls found out where the fool lives that's callin shots on the T-Flats. When we make the hit I want it to seem like the Bloods did it, since the T-Flats and the FTPs are at it as well. Boxer and a couple of homies are going to smoke the fools that's fuckin with Lil One, Shy Girl, and Bambi. Make sure you get a red bandana becuz we are going to blast that fool tonight."

Goldie said, "I'm ready to roll whenever you are."

"Get one of the vans with tinted windows and pick me up at the spot on Tucker Street around nine tonight. I'll already have the straps with me."

They ate and talked about Goldie's wedding. Goldie and Monica were to be married in a few months.

Goldie said, "I'll be glad when all of this shit is over. I got about ten tickets (ten million) saved. I own my house, I got toys, and a good woman. I was thinking about settling down once Gangsta touches down."

"Me and Nat talked about this too and I was thinking the same thing. We've had a hell of a run. Don't nothing last forever. Besides that, you know Nat is pregnant."

"I know, congratulations. Monica told me. It's about time you stop shootin blanks."

QT said, "Look who's talkin, you older than me and you don't have any kids."

"That's why I want to get out of the game becuz when me and Monica do have kids, I won't have to take no more chances doing illegal shit. I can just enjoy life and my family."

"We all should have enough money to get out the game. We are going to have a meeting with the other members of the G-Code Mobb and see what's on their minds. I got to go meet Boxer so he can show me where Spanky lives."

Goldie said, "Let's roll. I'll follow you. I need to see the layout as well."

When they got to Boxer's spot, they got into his car and he took them to where Spanky lived.

QT said, "The hit is going down tonight so make sure the home girls have those other T-Flats over at their spot."

Boxer said, "Bambi told me that when they leave the spot they always come down Rosecrans to Fruit Town."

"That's cool. Make sure you don't hit them until they are over the bridge and back in Compton," QT said. "Hit them hard. I don't want nobody living when it's over. Make sure ya'll have red bandanas around ya'll's faces. Also, make sure someone sees ya'll so they can report seeing the red bandanas to F-Troop. When you burn the car up, leave the guns in it, and make sure you wipe the guns down and that there are no bullets in the clips."

Boxer dropped QT and Goldie off at their cars and they all went their separate ways. Boxer called Bambi and told her to make sure that Smiley and his homies came over to the spot that night and to make sure that they got drunk and high.

When QT got home and opened his front door, Santana and Blocc were sitting side by side waiting for him. He got on his knees and played with both of them for a while. "Good boys, don't let nobody in here that don't belong."

He went upstairs and took a shower, and then he got into bed with Nat.

QT stayed home all day just chilling. Nat wasn't feeling well so she stayed home as well. They kicked it and watched old black movies like *The Mack*, *Cleopatra Jones*, *Superfly* and *Across 110th Street*. At 8 p.m., QT got dressed in all black. He got two 9mms and put a red bandana in his pocket. This wouldn't be the first time that they played like they were Bloods. In the past, in order to get close up on Bloods, they had went so far as to wear red sweat shirts and red khakis to throw the enemy off guard so they could get close enough to blast them. QT knew that once he smoked Spanky, and Boxer handled Smiley and his homies, when the word got around that Bloods had made the hits, all the focus would be on the Bloods.

QT pulled up to the spot and Goldie was already there. QT pulled his Lumina in the back yard. As soon as Crip saw QT, he ran to him. QT bent down and patted and rubbed him. Crip was always happy to see QT. Santana and Blocc were Gangsta's dogs and Crip was QT's. QT had already planned on buying a house for himself, Nat, and the baby because the house he lived in was Gangsta's as well. So when he got his new house he would take Crip with him.

Bambi had called Smiley earlier that day and told him that her and her home girls wanted to kick it with him and his homies that night at the apartment. She told Smiley that they had a surprise for them.

Smiley and his homies arrived at spot at eight-thirty. They partied with the females, smoking Chronic and drinking 8-Ball (Old English 800). Bambi, Shy Girl, and Lil One were dressed in skimpy shorts and halter tops.

Around ten, Smiley and his homies couldn't believe what they were seeing when the females got butt naked in front of them. Each one of the girls threw a condom to the one they was hooked up with. Smiley and his homies broke records for getting naked.

Bambi stopped them and said, "Before ya'll can get this pussy, you have to eat it."

That wasn't a problem for them; that was right up their alley.

As Smiley and his homies were eating pussy and fucking, Boxer, Lil Mike, and Scudder were parked in a dark blue 4-door Caprice Classic with tinted windows in the parking stalls of the apartment building.

On the west side of Compton, in Fruit Town, QT and Goldie were parked in a van two houses down from Spanky's house on the opposite side of the street. At eleven o'clock, Spanky and another OG from T-Flats, name Shadow, walked out of the house. They were on their way around the corner to the spot where all the homies were kickin it and getting high

QT said, "As soon as they get to us we are out the van and blastin they ass."

Spanky was preoccupied with talking to Shadow about one of the home girl's cousins that he had got at earlier that day and was supposed to hook up with that night. Spanky was strapped but Shadow wasn't.

As they walked past the van they didn't even notice it.

Quietly, Goldie and QT opened the van doors and got out. They were ten feet behind Spanky and Shadow before the two men heard footsteps and turned around.

Goldie and QT had red bandanas tied around their faces. Spanky tried to go for his gun but QT and Goldie already had their guns out and pointed at their victims. QT fired first. The shots hit Spanky in the chest and stomach.

Spanky fell to the ground. Goldie blasted Shadow with a fully automatic Uzi. Within a second, Shadow was hit with ten to fifteen bullets. He was dead before he hit the ground.

QT ran up to Spanky and shot him twice in the head. He and Goldie turned and ran to the van and slowly drove off making sure people that came running outside could see the red bandanas over their faces.

As QT drove he said, "Mission completed. I hope that Boxer's mission goes off just as smooth."

Spanky's homies were around the corner at the spot when they heard the shots. When they ran over to where Spanky and Shadow were lying on the sidewalk, Spanky's wife was on her knees crying and holding him in her arms. One of their home girls who lived in the house that the two men were killed in front of, went up to the homies. She was crying and told them she saw two niggas with red bandanas on their faces.

About twelve-thirty, after Smiley and his homies had had sex with Bambi, Shy Girl, and Lil One, Bambi told them they had to leave because her mother was coming by at 1:00 a.m. when she got off work from the hospital. Smiley and his homies wasn't mad; they had got the pussy.

They smoked a couple more blunts and told Bambi and her home girls they would get with them the next day.

Outside, Boxer was parked five cars down from Smiley. The windows were tinted so Smiley and his homies didn't glance twice at the Caprice. They were high off the Chronic anyway, and too busy talking about getting some pussy.

As they got in their car and drove up Rosecrans, they were happy that they got the pussy and started discussing switching up the females.

Smiley said, "We fucked them all in the same room and we saw all of them naked. I knew them bitches was freaks. I want to fuck all of them. I know they will go for it."

Chewy said, "Yeah, I wouldn't mind fucking Bambi's fine ass."

As they talked they didn't notice the Caprice pulling up on the side of them with the windows down.

Inside it, Boxer had an SKS semi-automatic, Lil Mike had a Uzi, and a 9mm. Scudder was driving. They all had red bandanas covering their faces.

By the time Smiley noticed the Caprice, it was too late. Boxer already had the SKS pointed out the window at him. Smiley tried to duck and hit the gas trying to get away but he wasn't faster than the bullets that exploded out of the SKS.

Boxer and Lil Mike unloaded on Smiley and his homies.

Smiley's car veered right and hit a pole.

Boxer said, "Pull over. We got to make sure them bitches are dead."

Scudder pulled over. Boxer and Lil Mike reloaded their straps, walked over to Smiley's car and unloaded. All three of them were riddled with bullets. They got back in the car as onlookers passed by.

The next morning on every news station, it was headline news: five killed in Compton in gang-related shootings.

After that, the T-Flats and the Fruit Town Pirus went to war, all out war. They shared the same neighborhood so that made things even worse. The Blocc had quieted down and everything was back to normal. QT's trap had worked.

Chapter 11: Out Smart 5-0

QT called Destiny three days later and asked her if the dinner date offer was still on the table. She said yes and that dinner would be ready that night at seven.

The agent that was monitoring her tapped phone immediately called Agent White and told him the date was on for that night.

Destiny had already told QT what the plan was so he knew what was up.

When he got to Destiny's condo, she was dressed in a seductive pair of short shorts and a halter top. The shorts were made of the same material that sweat suits were made of so it they clung to her body and showed off every curve on her. Her breasts were a size 38 so they were barely contained in the halter top.

Agent White had put audio and video in every room in Destiny's condo, except the bathroom. As the agents watched Destiny on the video monitors, they got horny and hated QT even more for being able to be that close to Destiny.

QT even got horny looking at Destiny when she greeted him. She hugged QT and kissed him on the cheek. He wanted to tease the agents that were watching so he cupped both of her ass cheeks and squeezed them.

Agent Davis said, "Oh my God. He grabbed her ass, that lucky son of a bitch."

She quickly pushed his hands away and said, "Aren't you moving a bit too fast?"

QT smiled and said, "I couldn't help myself. Your beauty has me hypnotized."

Destiny had to blush at that.

QT said, "So, Teresa...what have you hooked up for us this time?"

"Have a seat at the table and you will see."

"Just a minute, let me wash my hands first," he said and went to the bathroom. He knew there were no cameras or listening devices in there. He called out to Destiny and asked, "Teresa, do you have any hand soap?"

"Yes, under the sink."

"I don't see it. You may have to come get it for me."

As soon as Destiny got in the bathroom, QT pulled her to him and kissed her, wrapping his tongue around hers. He slid his hand down in her shorts and pushed a finger inside of her.

She moaned, broke away from him and said, "You are a bad, bad boy."

He smiled and tasted the finger that he had penetrated her with.

"You can do all of that later," she said and rushed out of the bathroom.

A minute later, QT got back to the table as Destiny laid out lobster, crab legs, Caesar salad, and rice pilaf on the table. She knew he didn't drink but she played it off and poured QT some dinner wine.

"I don't drink any kind of liquor but I do love orange juice," he said.

Destiny then poured QT a large glass of juice. As they ate, QT decided to talk about her. He asked her why she didn't have a man and she answered that she hadn't met a man who wasn't full of games. She said she wanted a man that would be with her and her only.

As the agents watched and listened, Agent Jones said out loud, "Shit, you looking for me. I swear, I will be faithful to you."

David added, "That goes for me too and you can have all my checks."

The rest of the agents present laughed but they were all feeling the same way. Destiny was a beautiful, sexy woman that any man would love to have as his.

After dinner, Destiny asked QT if he wanted to watch a movie. He said he didn't mind and she led him to her bedroom where she put the movie *King of New York* in.

QT said, "This is one of my favorite movies."

As they watched the movie, slowly but surely QT got closer and closer to her. He tried kissing her but she kept turning her head.

Agent White shouted at the monitor, "God dammit, let him kiss you! He's got to be able to trust you if he's going to bite on what we are trying to do."

Agent Davis said, "She's playing it by the book, the way she's supposed to."

"Fuck playing it by the book," White said. "A kiss ain't going to hurt nothing as long as she don't fuck him." He grabbed the phone and called her number. When she answered, he asked sharply, "Are you trying to fuck up everything we've set up?"

Destiny said no.

"Well kiss him, that's within the rules as long as you don't fuck him," White said and hung up.

Destiny wordless hung up and lay back on the bed with QT who asked, "Who was that? One of your freaks?"

She laughed. "No, that was mother telling me she had a nice man she wanted me to meet. I told her no."

This time when QT pulled her to him and tried to kiss her, she kissed him back.

As they lay on the bed kissing, QT started touching her breast and ass. Everyone was getting hot and horny watching them.

Destiny was getting hot as well; she had to catch herself. She broke their embrace and told QT she had to go to the bathroom.

QT got off the bed and started looking around the room. Her closet door was open halfway. He opened the door all the way and saw at least ten kilos of cocaine sitting inside a box with Destiny's shipping company's logo on it. QT didn't touch it. He knew the agents were watching him, so he went into some theatrics — he backed up, put both of his hands on his head and said, "Shit."

When Destiny walked back into the room QT grabbed her by the arm, pulled her over to the closet and asked, "What in the fuck is that?"

"You know what that is."

"What's it doing here?"

"That's another way I get my money; it's so sweet you wouldn't believe it. I just ship it through my company with no problems. Don't act like you don't know what's up. I checked up on you. Yo name is ringing in the streets and the word is you are a solid nigga. That's the only reason I let you come to my house and the only reason I fuck with you is because I know you are a solid nigga."

QT said, "Check this out, baby. I don't got a problem with how anybody makes their money. It ain't my business. But me, I'm legit. Yeah, I used to fuck around but I haven't fucked with that shit in over a year. I'm cool. I don't need the headache or the heat."

Destiny said, "We can get rich doing it the way I'm doing it. I can ship this shit anywhere in the U.S. with no problems. All I need is a solid connection where I can get a quantity of this shit. In a year, we will be so rich nobody will be able to fuck with us."

He looked at Destiny with a serious look on his face. "I don't need to be rich. I'm cool. I got two businesses and I'm legit. What I saw here tonight and what you have told me is between us. I will never repeat it to anyone," he said. "I got to go, baby. You be safe."

As QT turned to leave, Destiny tried one more time just so everyone watching and listening would have no reason to question her about anything. "Okay, well, can you at least hook me up with somebody that I can get a stead flow of this shit from?"

"If I did that I might as well get back in the game," QT said. "Sorry, baby, but I don't want nothing to do with that shit."

He walked out of Destiny's bedroom and out of her condo. As the night air hit him in the face, he thought: Shit, I should get a fucking Oscar for that performance I just put down.

All the agents sat there in silence. They couldn't believe what they were hearing. They all thought for sure that QT was still selling dope and they would finally be able to take him down.

Agent White shook his head and said, "Muthafuckin son of a bitch … wrap this shit up! This was our last shot. We don't have nothing to show the D.A. or take to the judge to be able to continue the wiretap or the investigation. There's still big fish to fry and all of them are not smart enough to get out of the game before we bust their ass."

Destiny got dressed and went home to her real house. She was happy — she knew that this was Agent White's last shot at QT in order to keep the investigation open. She loved QT and she didn't give a fuck what she had to do to keep him safe.

As QT drove home, Nat called him and told him she was spending the night at her parents' house.

Agent White called Destiny and told her she did a hell of a job and that the task force would be meeting the next morning at ten to discuss the next suspect they would be investigating. Destiny paged QT and left her code. He called her back on her real phone.

When she answered, she asked, "I was on my way home but I need to know if you can come out and play?"

QT laughed and asked, "When and where?"

"At the Hyatt by the airport. Now." She hung up the phone.

QT smiled and said to himself, Baby, you truly earned this fuckin you are about to get…

When he arrived, Destiny had already got them a room and was there taking a shower. She paged the room number into QT's pager. He got to the room and found the door cracked open. He went in and heard the water running. QT got naked and joined her in the shower.

They made love on and off for two hours. As Destiny lay in QT's arms, she told him, "Agent White called me and congratulated me on doing a good job. He also said we had a meeting tomorrow morning at ten to discuss the next suspect we're going after. You should still keep doing things the way you are now, just in case White tries to be sneaky and tries to back track on you without me knowing."

QT left Destiny at the Hyatt about 2 a.m. When he got home, he was tired but he took a shower anyway and went to bed.

Goldie and Monica had a big church wedding. Goldie asked QT to be his best man and Monica asked Nat to be her maid of honor.

The wedding was beautiful. Monica had on a beautiful white wedding dress. Her bridesmaids were dressed in purple and lavender dresses and the groomsmen were dressed in purple and lavender tuxedos.

The reception was held at the Marriot Hotel. It was a grand event, just like QT's was. After it was over, Goldie and Monica left for Paris for a two-week honeymoon.

Gangsta was coming home in five more months. There was a lot he wanted to talk to Gangsta about: all the shit that had been going down and what did Gangsta want to do once he came home. QT hadn't been to see him in about six months so he decided to take the drive to go see him. Nat was now six months pregnant so QT decided that she should stay home and rest. Destiny was working on another case so she couldn't go either.

QT called Tasha and she was only too happy to go with him. She would finally be able to spend some quality time with the man she loved. QT picked her up at her condo.

He wanted to be comfortable so he drove the Benz. They were on the 5 Freeway heading north to Folsom State Prison and QT had Alexander O'Neal's "Sunshine" bumping in the tape deck.

He turned the music down and said to Tasha, "I have something important that I want to talk to you about. I know that you love me and I love you too. My wife is about to give birth to our first child. You know that I love my wife and I'm not going to leave her. I know that you have a nice piece of money saved up. When my brother gets out in five more months, I'm getting out of the game and I want you to as well. Other niggas ain't going to look out for you the way I do. I don't want you to be putting your life on hold for me. I want you to be happy."

QT continued, "I know that there's somebody else out there that you can love and will love you. You are beautiful, smart, loyal, and respectful. Any nigga would be happy to have you as his woman."

Tasha looked at QT with tears in her eyes. "I know that there are some cool niggas out here. Niggas try to get at me every day. When they do, the first thing I do is compare them to you and you know what? There is no comparison because you are one of a kind,

QT. I would rather be the side woman of a real nigga than be with a nigga that I know doesn't even come close to the man you are. So until a nigga comes along that can compare to you, I'm going to be yours. I haven't fucked another nigga since the first time I made love to you. If I'm considering fucking another nigga, you will be the first to know. So for now, you are stuck with me, daddy."

Before QT could say anything, Tasha leaned over, undid his pants and zipper, pulled his dick out and slid it in her mouth. All QT could do is cut the music back up and moan as Tasha sucked him to an orgasm.

When they got to the hotel, QT called Nat to let her know he had made it there safe. They talked for about forty-five minutes. Tasha sat quietly watching TV until QT hung up the phone.

QT said, "I'm hungry. Let's go across the street to Denny's."

Tasha walked over to QT, slowly kissed him, and said, "I love you, daddy."

"I love you too, baby."

After they ate, they came back to the room and made love.

The next morning, QT got up early and put on his Fila BJ sweat suit, his Fila tennis shoes, and his pieces. He also wore a gold Presidential Rolex, two pinky diamond rings of three carats each, a gold rope with a medallion with the letters "QT" in diamonds, a gold and diamond bracelet, and two diamond stud earrings in his left ear that were two carats each.

Tasha looked at him and said, "Don't make me come down there and have to beat them bitches off of yo fine ass. Why are you wearing all that jewelry down to that prison?"

"To make them jealous, hatin-ass guards mad. Most of them ain't but shit redneck, hillbilly, trailer trash ass bitches anyway. I wear it with a smile just to see the looks on their faces. The jewelry I got on cost more than what one of these bitches will make working in thirty years."

Tasha said, "Daddy, you sure are bad when you want to be."

When QT pulled in the parking lot of the prison, it was still early and a little chilly outside. People were already in line waiting for visiting to start. Mostly everyone in line were females with their kids. The females were eying QT and whispering to each other like he wasn't even there. They couldn't tale their eyes off of him or his jewelry.

QT got to the front of the line to fill out the paperwork to see Gangsta. The CO behind the desk was a hater and tried to give QT a hard time. When QT gave him the paperwork, the corn-fed, redneck white boy said, "You are not on the visiting list so you can't come in."

"You need to check that again. I've been up here to see my brother over ten times. I know I'm on the list."

"Look here. I told you, you ain't on the list so you need to get out of here."

"Check this out, pal. I don't know who the fuck you think you talkin to like that. I ain't in jail so you need to check yoself. Matter of fact, call the lieutenant or the OD (Officer of the Day). You fuckin with the wrong one, pal."

Another officer stepped in and said, "It was a mistake. I found you, you are on the list."

QT knew they didn't want him talking to one of their superiors. He looked at the redneck and said, "When you get fired, look me up. I might have something for you."

QT went through the metal detector and then into the visiting room. Everyone behind him was smiling; some of them were laughing at the CO because at one time or another he had given all of them a hard time. Gangsta had told QT that if the officers tripped on him or was disrespectful, to check them because the most they could do is not let him in. Also, just the threat of wanting to talk to the OD or a lieutenant would bring them back to reality.

He went over to the vending machines and bought some sodas and ham and cheese sandwiches. He then found a table at the back of the room and sat down.

Fifteen minutes later, Gangsta entered and headed his way. His presence and his walk demanded attention. QT observed a few niggas checking their bitches for looking at Gangsta a few seconds too long. He laughed to himself. He stood up and shook Gangsta's hand and embraced him.

"Nigga, what you smiling so much about?" Gangsta asked.

"I was trippin off these niggas checkin they bitches about looking at you too long."

"You know, I bust more bitches by accident then the average nigga do on purpose."

QT laughed and said, "Cuz, you a fool."

He then started off by telling Gangsta about Boss-T and his crew. Then he told him about Destiny and how she helped him get the feds off his ass. QT told him about Tasha and how he had hooked up with their cousin Too Cool in Louisiana. Finally, he told him about the war with the T-Flats and Goldie's wedding.

"Damn, lil bro. You have been busy."

"I was taught by the best."

Gangsta said, "Don't even trip. I will be out of here in five or six more months, then you can chill and I will take over everything."

"That's really what I came down here to talk to you about," QT said. "I got fifteen million dollars put up for you. You don't have to get out and be doing what you were doing before you came here. Me and Goldie are getting out the game. When I get back home, I'm going to call a meeting with the other members and see where they stand. I'm going to go house shopping next week, so when you come home you can have yo house back."

Gangsta said, "Don't trip, cuz. That's yo house now. I was only living there two months before I got busted; you been there over three years. When I come home, me and Tonya will find us a house."

QT said, "Well, I got to at least give you the money for a new house since I didn't pay a dime for the one I'm in."

"We will talk about this when I come home. It ain't important now."

"That's cool but what's up on you getting out of the game? You got enough money to go legit and you know that the feds don't play fair. They lie and cheat more than we do. By the time you come home I will have seventeen and a half million dollars in cash for you. Look, big bro, we have beat these muthafuckas. Ain't no need in us taking unnecessary chances. My businesses are legit and they are making money and so are Nat's. Staying in the game would be plain stupid."

Gangsta said, "I'll think about everything you've said and I will let you know before I come home. Congratulations again on you and Nat having another Gangsta in the family."

"We don't know if it's a boy or a girl."

"No matter what it is, it will still be a Gangsta."

The visit went by fast. The CO up at the podium announced, "Visiting is now over. Clear the visiting room."

QT and Gangsta stood up and embraced. As they shook hands, QT said, "I'll be seeing you soon."

"Count on it."

Gangsta strolled out of the visiting room and QT watched him go. He hoped Gangsta would get out of the game but he knew his brother and in his heart he knew that Gangsta would stay in the game.

After Gangsta was searched and was heading back to his building he thought to himself, I know QT means well but for me, it ain't about the money. It's never been about the money. It's about the homies and the power. I love the homies and the Blocc, and the power that goes along with it. I'm a street nigga and I'm going to die a street nigga.

As QT walked out of the visiting processing room, he saw the redneck white boy CO. QT looked him straight in the eye, winked at him and smiled. The CO turned red in the face but there was nothing he could do. When QT got to his car, there were four different pieces of paper on his windshield that contained names and phone numbers. He smiled. He put the numbers in his pocket and thought to himself, Naw Gangsta, I bust more bitches by accident than the average nigga do on purpose.

He drove back to the hotel and as he pulled into the parking lot he took the numbers out of his pocket, balled them up and threw them away. He called Nat on his cell phone and told her he just left seeing Gangsta and that he was going to Denny's to get something to eat, then he would be on his way home.

When QT opened the door to his hotel room, Tasha was laid out on the bed butt naked with her legs open. QT's dick instantly started to rise. She got off the bed and crawled to QT. She pulled his sweats and boxers down and took him in her mouth.

Before he could cum, QT stopped Tasha and took his clothes off. He told her to get on the bed doggy-style. QT took a condom out of his wallet, put it on, and positioned himself behind Tasha. Her pussy was already wet so he slowly pushed his dick inside of her. He started slowly fucking her. QT loved to watch his dick go in and out of pussy doggy-style. That turned him on even more.

QT fucked Tasha until she came then he turned her over and tit fucked her until he came all over her breasts and face.

They took a shower together, went to eat, and then hit the road headed for home.

"It felt so good waking up this morning in your arms," Tasha said. "I wish that it could be like this every morning."

QT didn't say anything, he just kept driving. He knew that she was in love with him and he didn't want to say anything that might hurt her feelings. He put in the Isley Brothers and put it on "At Your Best." He sang along with the song and held Tasha's hand in his.

About five hours later, they pulled up to Tasha's condo. He walked her to her door, kissed her, and told her he would call her.

When he got home, Nat had cooked dinner for them. He was tired from the visiting, the fucking, and the long drive home. He got undressed and put on his silk pajamas.

After he ate dinner, he lay on his stomach on the bed while Nat sat on top of him and gave him a massage. She could tell that he was thinking about something.

"Do you want to talk about what's on your mind?" she asked.

"It's Gangsta. I don't think he's going to get out of the game. The power is nothing to me but I know he loves the power, the hood, and the homies. I love the hood and the homies too, but I ain't trying to do this shit forever. My obligation is to you and our kid now."

Nat said, "Baby, your brother is a grown man and he's going to do what he wants to. You and him have different priorities."

QT said, "Don't you see that as long as he's still in the game, Rocc will be in the game? They are my brothers and if anything happens to either one of them, that brings me back in the game. As long as they are in the game, I can't do what I want to do."

"As long as you stay out the game we will be just fine. If you have to pick yo guns back up because of something that happens to them, I'll understand and I'll be right by your side. When Gangsta comes home, just hand everything back over to him. He started everything so let him do his thang."

She lay down next to QT and held him in her arms. "I love you, QT, and whatever you decide to do, I'm with you one hundred per cent."

"I'm out once Gangsta comes home. I know how the feds operate. I was in it for the money. Now I got the money so there's no other reason for me to keep taking penitentiary chances when I got what I was after."

QT and Gangsta were different. QT loved his homies but he didn't kick it with them all the time the way Gangsta did. Gangsta would be in the hood with the homies from early in the morning until late at night. To QT, that was giving any potential snitch too much access and knowledge about him. Gangsta wasn't dumb or stupid by any means; he just loved and trusted his homies too much in QT's opinion.

Gangsta was ruthless and everyone knew it. If you crossed him, you'd better make sure that he never found out because he didn't believe in mercy. He would kill your whole family without blinking an eye. Niggas knew that QT was a killer but Gangsta was on another level. QT hoped that that knowledge would deter any of his homies and anybody else from crossing Gangsta.

The next day, QT called Goldie and told him to tell the G-Code Mobb he was calling a meeting at his house that evening.

By eleven o'clock, all the members of the G-Code Mobb were assembled around the Round Table at QT's house. Nat was over at QT's mom's house a few blocks away. Everyone was kicking it, talking, and bullshitting around until QT walked in the room. Santana and Blocc were with him, one on each side of him. He walked to the head of the Round Table and sat down. The dogs stayed at the doorway entrance and sat down watching everyone.

Goldie got up and turned the music off and called the meeting to order.

QT stood up and said, "All of you know that Gangsta will be home in five or six months. I called this meeting tonight to let you know that once Gangsta gets out, I'm getting out of the game. We had a good run together and everyone here should be a millionaire at least ten times over. The feds were on us real tough and the only reason we are still standing is becuz I had a man on my team that was on the task force. If it weren't for that, we would be in the feds' hands right now. I'm not trying to influence nobody here to do nothing they don't want to do. I'm just saying that I'm cool. Gangsta will still have the same hook up on the work and I'm going to tell him how I was running thangs. I don't know how he's going to run things, but I know however he does it, he's going to ce fair. He love you niggas. Basically, I called this meeting to let you know I'm out and to see what ya'll wanted to do. So I'm going around the table to each one of you to see if you are still in or if you are out."

QT started with Rocc, but he already knew the answer. "So Rocc, are you in or out?"

"If Gangsta's in, I'm in."

Next was Big Bam, who answered, "When Gangsta started this shit I was here. If he in, I'm in."

Beside him, Lil Man said, "Cuz, the hood is all I know. I'm in."

Goldie spoke next. "Cuz, I'm with QT. I'm out. I love all you niggas, but it's time for me to settle down and start a family."

Crip Crazy said, "I'm in. Me and Gangsta started Crippin in the sixth grade together. If Gangsta's in, I'm in."

Boxer said, "This is my family. I love all you niggas. I'm in."

So there it was. Everyone was in except for QT and Goldie.

"We will have another meeting when Gangsta comes home," QT said. "For now, everything will stay the same. Is there anything that needs to be brought to the table while we are here?"

Lil Man said, "Everything in the hood is cool. We haven't had any trouble from the T-Flats. They are too busy warring with the FTPs."

Boxer said, "Bitch asses Ross and Beckman has been in the hood sweating the homies trying to get some info on you. But you know the homies in the hood don't know shit about you, so them bitches are shit out of luck."

QT stood up and said, "All right, you niggas ce safe and still stay out the hood during the day. As long as you keep doing what you have been doing you should ce cool."

They all got up and QT walked them outside to their cars.

After they left, Goldie stood on the sidewalk with QT and said, "You tried, homie, but they are grown men and they made their choice. All we can do is hope for the best."

"I really worry about Rocc. I know that Gangsta is going to look out for him. I'm just worried about his getting loose. You know when you get loose you start to slip. All it takes is one slip and a nigga can be dead or in jail."

Goldie said, "I feel you, homie, but it ain't shit we can do. They don't want to get out becuz the hood is all they know. All of them got money and don't know what to do with it. But for me, it's a big ass world out here and I want to experience some of it. I can afford it, so why shouldn't I."

QT said, "Cuz, I'm tired of all the killing. I kill to ensure safety to me and the people I love. I will kill again at the drop of a hat if I have to. But when Gangsta gets out, I'm going to enjoy life as long as I can becuz sooner or later something is going to pull me back in."

They shook hands and embraced.

Goldie said, "Ya'll my family, if ya'll hurt, I hurt. I will always be just a phone call away."

As Goldie got in his car and drove off, QT stood on the sidewalk enjoying the night air. When he turned to walk back to the house, Santana and Blocc were sitting on the porch watching him. He told them, "Good boys, good boys. I know ya'll got my back."

Nat was just pulling into the driveway. He went to the car and opened the door to help her out. They went into the house and QT told her what happened at the meeting.

"Baby, all you can do is try to give them advice and hope that they listen," she said.

The next day, QT went to Tucker Street to check on the spot and feed Crip.

After he fed the dog he was in the driveway talking to a few of the homies when Ross and Beckman pulled up. The detectives got out of their car with guns drawn and told QT and the rest of the homies to get on the hood of their car. Beckman searched them as Ross watched.

When he got to QT, he said, "I heard your brother was getting out soon."

QT said, "Yeah, I guess the bullshit pigs that locked him up wasn't as smart as they thought they were."

By now there were about fifteen of QT's homies gathered around watching.

Beckman said, "He won't last long out here. He'll be back in jail. Or dead."

QT said, "Anybody can be touched. Anybody."

Beckman grabbed QT by the back of his head and tried to slam his face on the hood of the car. QT was too fast for that; he stepped to his right, did a quick spin and was behind Beckman.

Ross pointed his gun at QT. Meanwhile, five of the homies that had been standing on the sidelines pulled out their straps.

E-Bone said, "Don't get this shit twisted. We don't give a fuck about you just like you don't give a fuck about us. You ready to die, you redneck muthafucka?"

Beckman and Ross looked at the faces of the homies and knew they were serious.

QT looked at Beckman and said, "I told you anybody can be touched."

Beckman and Ross backed up to their car and got in. Beckman yelled back, "This ain't over, boy."

QT grabbed his dick and said, "I got yo boy hangin low."

When Ross pulled off their faces were as red as a beet.

QT told the homies, "Good lookin out. Them bitches will ce back with reinforcements. Now, everybody get off the streets."

QT got in his car and headed home. He called his lawyer and told him what happened.

The lawyer told QT to meet him at the police station and they would file a complaint. Since QT had been in his own yard minding his own business, the police didn't have any probable cause to fuck with him.

While Beckman and Ross went back to the hood with reinforcements looking for QT and his homies, QT and his lawyer were arriving at the Compton police station to fill out a complaint against the two detectives. QT and the lawyer talked to the Watch Commander and told him what had happened and what was said. The lawyer threatened to sue the Compton PD if Beckman and Ross continued to harass and threaten QT or his family.

The Watch Commander had the dispatcher call Ross and Beckman back to the station. When they got there, they were shocked to see QT and his lawyer in the office. The Watch Commander shook QT's hand, and his lawyer's hand, and told them there was no need for a lawsuit and that he would handle the situation personally.

As QT walked past Ross and Beckman, he smiled and winked at them. When the two detectives went in, the Watch Commander told them to stay the fuck away from QT and his family. QT's brother had filed a lawsuit against them and the department earlier that day since his sentence had been overturned with the claim that the two detectives had planted evidence on him.

Ross and Beckman walked out of the Watch Commander's office mad as hell. Not only had their set-up backfired on them, now they were targets of a lawsuit.

When they got back to the car, Beckman said, "We have to figure out a way to kill Gangsta's black ass. We can get QT later."

Ross agreed. "Yeah, it could be just another gang-related killing."

As QT drove home, he thought to himself, I got to smoke them white muthafuckas. Me and my family ain't safe as long as them bitches are around. I know that they will kill me or Gangsta whenever they got the chance.

QT had to think about this. This hit had to be done right and done before Gangsta came home. He knew that Nat had her own sources—sources who could find anyone that had a job and was legit. He knew that Beckman wasn't married and had no kids so he would be easy, but Ross was married so QT would have to hit Ross differently.

When Nat came home, QT gave her two names and told her he needed to know where the two men lived as soon as possible. Nat knew not to ask questions because if QT wanted her to know anything, he would tell her.

Next, QT went to his drug supplier who owned a transmission shop. It had been awhile since QT had been there because Goldie was handling that part of the business now.

When QT walked into his shop, Carlos was sitting behind the desk.

"What's up, Migo? Long time no see," QT said.

He stood up and shook QT's hand. "What brings you to this side of town?"

"What's up, Carlos, you missed me?"

Carlos laughed. "Yeah, I miss our talks."

"Gangsta will be home soon so he will be taking back over the organization."

"I heard that you were stepping down."

QT said, "Yeah, it's time for me to enjoy my money."

Carlos said, "I wish I could step down and enjoy my money, but as you know I'm in it for life."

QT changed the subject and said, "I came to you because I need a silencer that will fit a 9mm Beretta."

"Goldie is supposed to see me in a few days when he comes through," Carlos said. "Is it all right if I give it to him?"

"Yeah, that's cool."

They talked for another thirty minutes and shook hands, embraced, and QT left. He was glad that he wasn't like Carlos; locked in the game for life.

Two days later Nat had all the info that QT needed on Ross and Beckman. The next day Goldie dropped off the silencer.

"Cuz, what's up?" he asked. "You need me on this one or what?"

QT said, "Cuz, I got this. This is something I have to handle my-self."

Goldie said, "If you need me, just call me and I'm there."

The previous night, after Nat had given QT the information, he had driven by the homes where Beckman and Ross lived, checking everything out. Beckman lived in Downey in a two bedroom house. QT knew all he had to do was get in and wait for him to come home. They usually worked sixteen hour days so he planned to smoke Beckman, and then catch Ross early the next morning going to his car on his way to work. Neither of them nor the neighbors had dogs, so getting to them would be easy.

Ross lived in Lakewood with his wife. His kids were grown, one in college and the other one was a piece of shit that was just in the way. But neither of the kids lived at home.

QT decided to kill Beckman Thursday night and Ross on Friday morning. They worked from 6 a.m. to 10 p.m. so when Ross would leave to go to work it would be 5 a.m. and still dark and quiet. QT knew that killing two police was a death penalty sentence if he was caught, that's why he didn't want anybody to know what he was about to do. That way, everything was all on him, regardless of what happened.

QT told Nat that he had to go OT over night to take care of some business. Nat knew something was up but she didn't question him.

He had a 9mm Beretta, the silencer, and two extra clips with him. He got one of the throw-away cars and went to a motel. Tasha had gone by a couple of days before and rented a room there for him for a week. QT had the key so he parked and went straight to the room. It was 7:30 p.m. and already dark outside. He pulled a baseball cap down over his face so if anyone at the motel were looking out of their windows at that moment they wouldn't see his face. The motel was only a couple of minutes away from Beckman's house.

At nine, QT got in his car and drove a block from Beckman's, and parked in front of some apartments. He got out and walked towards the house, observing everything. The streets were deserted and quiet; it wasn't like his neighborhood where people were out walking the streets 24/7.

When he got to Beckman's house he turned and walked straight to the back yard like he lived there. As he surveyed the back of the house, he observed an open bedroom window. He put his gloves on, pushed the window open and climbed in. Once inside, he closed the window and sat in the corner in the dark with the Nina in his hands.

Beckman and Ross got off work at ten but they didn't leave the station until 10:30. Beckman made it home at 11:10 p.m. When the front door opened, QT was ready and alert.

The detective went straight to the kitchen and got a beer out of the fridge. He headed to the bedroom to undress and take a shower. When he cut the light on in the bedroom, QT stood up from the side of the bed with the Nina pointed at his face.

Beckman looked shocked.

"Put yo hands up, muthafucka, and drop that beer on the floor."

Beckman did what he was told. "What is this all about? I'm a fucking cop. You can't do this to me."

"You're a dirty piece of shit. I told you anybody can be touched." He looked Beckman squarely in the eyes. "This is for Gangsta, you dumb muthafucka."

He shot Beckman in the face, head, and neck. Then he walked over to where Beckman lay slumped on the floor. He stood over him and shot him twice in the heart. "Fuck you, you heartless muthafucka," QT said.

He reached down and picked up the spent cartridges and put them in his pocket. QT wasn't really worried about the shells from the Nina being found because he had loaded the clips with gloves on and he had wiped the bullets off even before that. He cut the TV on and watched TV until 12:30 a.m. then he eased out the back door, went down the street and got in his car.

"One down, one to go," he said out loud.

He went back to the motel room and set the alarm clock for 4 a.m. He lay down and tried to sleep but he couldn't.

QT made sure that he kept his gloves on so if he touched anything in the room his prints wouldn't be on it. Tasha had rented the room with a bunk ID that QT had got back from her and cut up so nothing could be traced back to her. QT was a thinker, that's what made him so dangerous.

At four when the alarm went off, QT was already up. He went to his car and drove to Ross's house, again parking a block away.

As he walked up to it he looked at the high bushes running down the side of the house. No one could see him from the neighbor's house. QT sat on the ground until he heard the front door open and close. Ross was walking to his car in the driveway.

Quietly, QT walked up behind him and said, "A."

Ross turned and saw QT. There was nothing but shock and fear in his eyes.

QT immediately shot Ross three times in the head, then twice in the heart, the same as he had done to Beckman. When it was done, he took off running. He slowed when he got to the car, and took his time as he got in and drove off.

Ross's body was found about thirty minutes later when his next door neighbor spotted it as he was leaving for work. By then, QT had parked the car on Alameda and set it on fire.

He got in his own car and went to the marina where he got on his boat and took it out to sea. He went out about ten miles from shore where he broke the Nina down and threw all the pieces in the ocean. He also threw the silencer overboard.

When he got home, it was 8:15 a.m. Nat was up cooking breakfast and watching the news. QT walked into the kitchen, hugged her, and asked, "How's my baby doing? Both of my babies?"

He kissed her slowly before she could respond. Just as he finished kissing her, breaking news came on. The newscaster said, "Two Compton police officers were killed in two different cities this morning. Detective Ross was gunned down in front of his home and Detective Beckman was found dead in his home. He also had died of gunshot wounds. The men were partners in the Compton Police Department. At this time, the police have found no witnesses. We will keep you updated on any new developments."

Nat remembered those were the names that she got the information on for QT. She wasn't going to say anything about it to him because she knew that if he didn't tell her, it was for her own good. Nat asked, "Do you want some breakfast, baby?"

"Yeah, I'm starving. I'm going to take a shower while you cook."

By the time he finished showering and came back downstairs, breakfast was waiting on the table. QT stayed home all day resting and relaxing. Nat's mother came and picked her up so they could go shopping. QT called Destiny on her real phone.

When Destiny answered, she said, "It's about time I hear from you. I haven't seen you in three weeks."

QT said, "You know Nat is pregnant. I just been at home taking care of her."

"See, I need a good man like you to take care of me."

"You know you still my baby too."

"Yeah, that's what I needed to hear," she said, then changed the subject. "Have you been watching the news?"

QT said, "Naw, I been busy today. I usually watch it at eleven since that's the last one and I can find out what's been going on all day."

Destiny said, "You know detectives Beckman and Ross? Both of them were murdered this morning."

QT played it off. "Where were they at? In Compton?"

"No, both of them were at home. The way they were murdered looks like a professional hit."

"I guess ain't nobody safe, not even at home."

"I got to go. We are about to do a raid. I'll page you later."

"All right, baby, you be safe."

He hung up the phone and said out loud, "A professional hit. Damn, am I that good."

When Nat got home QT had her make some chicken tacos and Spanish rice. They ate dinner and afterwards QT gave Nat a massage.

As QT was rubbing her feet, Nat said, "You are kind of good at this. I might have to put you on the payroll."

QT said, "If that's the case, I want a hundred dollars a minute."

Nat smiled and said, "You are worth every penny of it too."

Chapter 12: Going Back to Cali

Boss-T and Nutt did some scandalous shit in Texas and had to leave quickly. It was all on a count of because they had hooked up with a major dope dealer, name Tank.

Tank was 6' 6", 280 lbs, dark skinned, bald headed, and was known for his brutality. Tank had played football in college, that's where he got his nickname. But he was in car accident during his junior year, and tore his knee up ending his football career. Tank's older brother Dre was in the dope game and had half of Houston sewed up. Some niggas from Austin that Dre did business with ended up robbing and killing him. That's when Tank stepped up and took Dre's spot in Dre's organization. At first, all the other drug dealers who had been under Dre were skeptical about Tank and wanted to go their separate ways. That was until Tank tracked down the niggas that killed Dre and killed all four of them. Then he cut their heads off and left them on their mothers' front porches.

Tank called a meeting and told everyone that his brother Dre was the one who started the crew, known as the "Syndicate," and he was taking over and wasn't shit to going to change. Only one member of the Syndicate tried to buck and he ended up dead. After that, every-one else fell in line and followed suit. Dre had been dead for seven years so Tank was now 27 years old and had been running the Syndicate for that long.

Boss-T and Nutt took ten pounds of chronic with them when they left L.A. Some of it was to smoke and the rest was to sell. They were at a club in Houston with one of Nutt's cousins, name Fly. He was called Fly because he had big eyes and in the face he looked like a fly.

They were sitting at the back of the club smoking chronic when Tank and three of his boys walked up. On occasion, Fly bought dope from Tank and they knew each other. They were the same age and had grown up together. When Tank walked up, Fly stood up and shook his hand and embraced him. Fly introduced Boss-T and Nutt to Tank as his cousins from L.A.

Tank said, "What's that smelling like that? Damn, that shit smells potent."

Tank loved to smoke weed; that's all he did.

Fly said, "Here, check it out," and passed the blunt to Tank.

When he hit it he started coughing. "Man, where did this shit come from? This is the best weed I've ever had in my life."

"That's L.A. chronic," Fly said. "My cousins brought it with them from L.A."

Tank told them, "Fuck sitting down here. Come wit me up to VIP."

When they got to VIP, some of Tank's boys and their women were up there drinking and smoking dirt weed. Nut pulled another blunt out of his pocket and passed it to Tank. When Tank's people smelled the chronic, they all wanted to hit it. The finest woman that Nutt had ever seen walked up to Tank, took the blunt out of his hand and took a long toke. She tried to compose herself but the chronic was too strong. She started coughing so much someone had to give her a drink.

Tank laughed and said, "That's what yo weed head ass get; you always tryin to hog the weed."

Tank's woman was Tricia. She was 5' 7" with caramel colored skin, light brown eyes, long light brown hair, thin waist, big country heart shaped ass and 38-inch breasts. Every chance Nutt got he would steal a peak at her. He didn't want it to be obvious that he was attracted to her. Tricia caught Nutt staring at her a couple of times but she didn't say anything and played it off like she wasn't paying him any attention.

Nutt thought to himself: I got to have some of that good country pussy.

By Nutt being from L.A., he automatically thought that he had the game and the advantage over Tank. That was his first mistake.

After the club was over, Tank asked Nutt if he had any chronic that he wanted to sell. Nutt lied and said all they had was a half a pound but he would give him a couple of ounces. Tank told Fly to bring Nutt and Boss-T to his house later that day.

Boss-T heard Nutt lie and wondered about it. Why not sell Tank a few pounds of chronic?

Fly dropped them off at the spot they were renting. When they were alone, Boss-T said, "Blood, what the fuck are you up to? We could have sold all that fuckin weed to that country ass nigga for top dollar."

Nutt smiled and said, "Calm down. Don't trip, the chronic is our way to get in close with that nigga. Once we are in, we can jack that nigga and go back home with real fat pockets."

Boss-T said, "It's about time you started using your head."

The plan sounded good but Nutt's only thoughts were fucking Tricia anyway he could, even if he had to take it. He had one thing working in his favor and that was that she was a weed head.

Tricia was a sneaky and scandalous bitch. She fucked other niggas but she made sure none of them were from Houston. Tricia was a pure freak. She was only with Tank because of the money. And Tank was a big nigga but he had a small dick. The only way he made Tricia cum was by eating her pussy. Tricia also knew that Tank was a killa and he wouldn't stand for being played a fool of so she knew that she had to be careful.

She was very aware of the way Nutt was looking at her. Nutt was from Cali so that was a plus for her and he was nice looking. All she had to do was feel the nigga out to see what was really up. If everything was cool she would definitely fuck him.

What Nutt and Boss-T didn't know was that Tank was buying most of his dope from QT's cousin Too Cool who lived in Louisiana.

The next day, Fly brought Nutt and Boss-T to Tank's house. Tank had one of those big Southern homes that looked like the mansions in the slavery movies in the South. Tank had remodeled it into a six bedroom, four bath home, with a family room, game room, and a weight room. Tank also had an Olympic size swimming pool and two Jacuzzis, one on each end of the pool. He had a Benz, a Porsche, and a Lamborghini in the driveway.

All Boss-T and Nutt saw were dollar signs. Surely this would be their big come up.

Tank opened the door and gave them a tour of the house. They finally ended up in the basement which had been turned into a small club with a bar, dance floor, sound system, TVs and two pool tables.

Nutt gave Tank the two ounces and blazed up a blunt with him. A few minutes later, Tricia came downstairs wearing some tight sweat shorts with the halter top to match. Nutt could tell that she didn't have any panties on because the sweat shorts were so tight you could see her pussy lips through them. Nutt's dick started to get hard so he sat down at one of the tables in the basement.

Tank asked, "So how can I get about twenty pounds of dis weed?"

Nutt answered, "You would have to go to Cali to get it like that or someone would have to go for you."

Tank passed the blunt to Tricia and asked, "How much is a pound?"

Nut lied and said, "Sixty five hundred a pound but you could make a killing out here."

(A pound really cost $4500 and it could be less depending on how many were bought at one time.)

Money wasn't a thang to Tank because, before he took over, his brother Dre was rich and now he was sitting on about $30 million. That's a lot of money for a nigga who grew up dirt poor.

Tank took Fly to the side to talk to him. While they were talking Boss-T was checking out the spot. Tricia was hitting the blunt and Nutt was sitting down looking between her legs. His dick was rock hard. Tricia passed the blunt to Nutt and when he stood up she could see the big bulge in his pants.

Nutt hadn't been thinking when he stood up to take the blunt; he just reacted. But when he stood he realized his dick was bulging in his pants.

Tricia looked him in the eyes and down to his bulging dick. She winked at him and passed him the blunt. Nutt sat down before anyone else could see the front of his pants.

She thought to herself: Oh shit, he has a big dick. I got to feel that big muthafucka in my mouth.

As Nutt hit the blunt, he thought: I knew that bitch was a freak. I got to figure out a way to fuck the shit out of her.

When Tank and Fly finished talking, they walked back over to where Tricia and Nutt were.

Tank said, "If ya'll go to Cali and get me ten pounds, I will give you $8,500 a pound but Fly has to go with you because I don't really know ya'll."

Before Boss-T could say anything, Nutt said, "We will make three trips for you but after that we are cool because we are going back home in about six to eight months. After that, you can send Fly or whoever and we will keep it rolling to you."

Tank thought a minute and said, "That sounds good to me."

When Boss-T and Nutt got back to their spot, Boss-T said, "So how are we going to get this nigga?"

Nutt said, "That nigga's bitch is all on me. She was winking at me; the bitch wants to fuck me."

Boss-T said, "We got to play it off and get close to this nigga, then we will decide how to get him."

Over the next three weeks, Boss-T and Nutt were with Tank daily. They went out to the clubs with him, to the Rockets basketball games, and chilled at his pad. Tricia had secretly slid Nutt her cell phone number so they talked dirty to each other on the phone. Tank had to go out town for a day to meet with Too Cool to get some more dope. He told Boss-T and Nutt he would give them the money and a car with a stash spot, and when he came back they could go and get the chronic from Cali.

As soon as Tank left, Tricia called Nutt and told him to meet her in Austin at the Hilton Hotel. Nutt told Boss-T what was up and headed to Austin. Nutt couldn't believe it; he was finally going to fuck her fine ass.

She called him and told him what room she was in. When Nutt got to the room, the door was unlocked. Tricia was sitting on the bed butt ass naked with her legs crossed. As Nutt walked closer, she opened her legs. She was shaved bald. Her breasts were firm and sitting up by themselves. She was 23 years old and fine as wine. She could see Nutt's hard dick bulging through his pants so she quickly undid them and pushed them and his boxers to his ankles.

Nutt's dick sprang straight to her waiting lips. He had the biggest dick that Tricia had ever had the pleasure of sucking. She grabbed his dick with both hands and guided him into her mouth. He felt so good in her mouth. Nutt had the dick that she had always longed for. As she licked and sucked Nutt's dick, he held her by the back of her head and forced her to deep-throat him. She sucked him until he came in her mouth. She swallowed every drop and lay back on the bed and opened her legs.

He got between her legs and started licking and sucking her pussy. His tongue felt good inside Tricia's pussy.

She was moaning, saying, "Oh Cali, suck this pussy, Cali. Suck it, it's all yours."

Nutt then went to her asshole and spread her ass cheeks and started licking her ass. This was something that had never been done to Tricia before and she loved the feeling, especially when Nutt pushed his tongue inside her ass.

"Oh shit, oh shit, oh that feels so so good, don't stop, please, don't stop. I love it."

Nutt started licking Tricia from her asshole up to her clit where he stopped to slowly lick and suck on it. By now, Nutt's dick was hard again and he positioned himself over Tricia and pushed his dick into her hard and fast. Tricia screamed out loud as Nutt held her close to him and started pounding her pussy.

Tricia didn't know that she would enjoy the pain as much as she did. As the pain turned to pleasure, she was saying, "Fuck me, Cali. Fuck me, this is yo pussy, Cali, it's yo pussy."

Nutt pushed a finger into her asshole and she started cumming. "Bitch, whose pussy is this? Whose is it?"

Tricia said, "It's yours, Cali, it's yours. I swear it's yours."

Nut was about to cum but he wanted to fuck her in that big country ass. When he pulled out of her, her legs were shaking and she was breathing hard. Nutt got up and grabbed his pants and got out a tube of KY jelly. He lubricated his dick then did the same to her ass.

Tank had fucked her in the ass but it was nothing because he had a small dick. Nutt had an extra large dick so it scared Tricia but she was a freak and wanted to feel his big dick in her ass.

Nutt rolled her over on her stomach, got behind her and told her to relax. "It's going to hurt but once the head gets in and I start stroking you, it's going to start feeling good." He opened her ass cheeks and slowly pushed the head of his dick into her ass.

Tricia put her face into the pillow and screamed. It was hurting but it also turned her on. Once the head was in and he slowly started stroking her, it started to feel good, real good. She took the pillow from her face and slowly raised up into the doggy position.

As Nutt fucked her ass, he gripped both ass cheeks and started to spank her. "Whose ass is this, tell me, bitch, whose is it?"

"It's yours, Cali, it's yours."

"Bitch, call me daddy."

"Okay, daddy. It's yo ass, daddy, it's yo ass, yo pussy, yo mouth. It's all yours, oh…it's yours!"

As Nutt got ready to cum he started pounding her ass. The pain and pleasure felt so good to Tricia that she hollered out loud and tears of joy ran down her face. Tank had never came in her ass before; he always pulled out and came on her ass cheeks. When the hot cum shot out of Nutt's dick into her ass, the feeling was incredible to her. She started cumming and screaming. It was a wrap; she had to have this nigga and she didn't care what she had to do to get him.

Nutt already knew if a bitch sucked yo dick after pulling it out her asshole she would do anything you wanted her to do. It was called "the Mustard Jar." Nutt pulled his dick out of Tricia's ass, turned her over, got on top of her breast and pushed his dick in her mouth. She starting sucking Nutt's dick and sucked it until he came again.

Tricia had already told Nutt that Tank had a little dick and couldn't satisfy her so Nutt knew how he was going to get Tricia hooked on him. He knew she liked him so he knew once he fucked her it would be a wrap. But he hadn't planned on the fact that he would get hooked on her as well.

They fucked all day. As they lay in each other's arms, Tricia looked at him and said, "How are we going to do this? If Tank finds out about us, he's going to kill both of us."

Nutt said, "Don't worry about nothing. I'm going to figure something out."

He didn't want to start asking her questions about Tank's money—it was too soon for that. He just had to play his cards right and when it was time to make his move, he would take Tricia back to Cali with him.

They left the hotel at 10 p.m. that night and went their separate ways. Nutt had a big smile on his face because Fly had told him and Boss-T that Tank was a millionaire. Fly had also told them that Tank was a killa and that he had killed the niggas that killed his brother and how he had cut off their heads and put them on their mamas' porches. Nutt thought to himself: It's just a matter of time and I will have it all.

When he got back to the spot he told Boss-T everything.

Boss-T said, "That's why I don't trust bitches. I just fuck them and keep it movin. Most niggas' downfalls are because of a once-a-month bleeding bitch."

Nutt said, "You know we leaving for L.A. tomorrow. We will make a couple of trips for that nigga, get him to trust us, then we will get his ass and go back home."

Nutt didn't tell Boss-T that Tricia would be going with them.

Tank was back from his trip to Louisiana the next morning around eight. When he got there, Tricia was still in bed. She wasn't sleeping, she was just lying there watching TV. Tank walked over to her side of the bed, pulled his little dick out and Tricia proceeded to suck it until he came.

Tricia got up and hugged him. "I missed you, baby," she said, but thought to herself: Yo lil dick ass should have never come back.

Tank said, "I missed you too, baby. What did you do when I was gone?"

"I went over to my mama's house and kicked it wit my sista."

Tank walked out of the bedroom and went down to the basement. There was a secret room in the basement that no one knew about and if the police did come there, they would never find it. He had a big walk-in safe that held $20 million dollars. Tank had another $10 million in safety deposit boxes at different banks under different names with his photo on the IDs. The IDs were at his grandmother's house in Alabama.

The room also had ten different TV monitors because Tank had secret security cameras installed all through the house that ran 24/7. Tricia didn't know about them. The only time he checked them was when he had to leave town and Tricia was home by herself. So far, he had never found anything out of the ordinary when he re-ran the tapes from when he was gone. That was his mistake because if he would have viewed the tapes from when Nutt and Boss-T would come by to kick it and get high, he would have seen Tricia and Nutt secretly touching and feeling on each other.

Tank had two big gym bags with the 150 birds that he had got from Too Cool. He had wanted the whole 300 birds that Too Cool had but Too Cool had to keep them for himself to make sure his people was right. QT had been sending Too Cool 300 birds a month for the last six months instead of the regular 100. Tank had hooked up with Too Cool a year ago when QT was giving Too Cool 100 birds a month. Tank knew Too Cool through his brother Dre. Too Cool and Dre had met at a club in New Orleans during Mardi Gras over ten years ago and they had become tight. Dre introduced Too Cool to Tank and they had become tight as well. When QT started sending birds to Too Cool, Too Cool got at Tank and they hooked up.

He put the dope in the safe, locked it, and watched Tricia on the monitor for a while from the feed from the hidden camera in the bedroom. He went back upstairs, called Fly and told him to pick up Nutt and Boss-T and come by his pad. Tank opened the safe in his bedroom and took out $85,000 to give to Nutt and Boss-T to go get the chronic. There was about $1.5 million in the safe.

Tricia knew that Tank had money but she couldn't even imagine he had over $30 million. She knew about the money in the bedroom safe but that was all. Tank had given her the combination to it months ago. That was more money than she had ever seen in her life. She thought that was the extent of the money Tank had. She thought it was at least $3 million. Tank wasn't a dummy because whenever he handled his business he always told Tricia to leave for a couple of hours, or he told her not to come down in the basement.

When Fly, Nutt and Boss-T got to Tank's spot, he told Tricia not to come to the basement. Tank tossed Fly the bag containing the $85,000 and said, "When you get back call PJ and he will come pick up the car with the chronic in it. Don't bring it here." Tank didn't want them to think he was storing anything at his pad. He then tossed a set of car keys to Nutt. "That grey Fleetwood Brougham that's parked outside is the stash car. Fly already knows how the stash works."

He walked them back upstairs and out the front door. He tossed Boss-T a stack of $20s and said, "That's for gas."

Fly got in the Fleetwood and Boss-T and Nutt got back in the car they came in.

On the way back to their spot, Boss-T said, "I know we can get ten pounds of chronic for $4,000 a piece, so at $8,500 a pound, we will make $50,000. That's twenty-five for me and twenty-five for you."

"What about Fly?" Nutt asked.

"Tank is going to look out for that nigga."

Tank knew that he could have gotten the chronic cheaper but he didn't have a hook up in Cali. Tank didn't trust Boss-T or Nutt, that's why he sent Fly with them. He had already instructed Fly to find out who their hook up was, so that in the future, they would have a direct line. Tank knew that Too Cool was getting his dope from his cousin in Cali. That's why Tank had Too Cool call QT and asked him how much a pound of chronic in Cali went for. The only thing that Tank didn't do, that he should have, was to have Too Cool ask QT if he knew Boss-T and Nutt.

Boss-T, Nutt, and Fly made it to L.A. in a day and a half. They hooked up with the chronic connection and was out of L.A. within three hours. They wasn't even trippin off of Fly; they let him meet the chronic connection and didn't even stop to think twice about it.

In three days they were back in Houston with the chronic. Boss-T and Nutt were each $25,000 richer. Nutt had been secretly talking to Tricia on his cell phone during the trip. They couldn't wait for Tank to leave town again so they could hook back up.

When they got back, PJ came and picked up the car with the ten pounds of chronic in it. Over the next six months, they made three more trips to Cali to get more chronic. During that time, Tank went out of town a total of eight times. Every time he left, Tricia and Nutt hooked up in Austin.

Tricia was now telling Nutt that she was in love with him and wanted to move back to Cali with him. Nutt was also confessing his love for her. She also told Nutt about the safe in the bedroom and the money that she thought was in it. They made a plan to take the money and go to Cali together with Boss-T the next time Tank went out of town.

Even though Nutt was Fly's cousin, Fly told Tank that he didn't trust his cousin and that he felt they had a secret agenda. Fly also told Tank that his cousin was scandalous and a jacker. Fly didn't want to be caught up in a cross by Tank if Nutt and Boss-T did something scandalous. And he had already slid under the chronic connection in Cali. They had traded phone numbers so after Tank came back from his trip OT, Tank was going to cut all ties with Nutt and Boss-T.

The next time Tank went OT, Nutt went over to his house. Tricia was there alone and answered the door. She was already packed and had everything ready that she was taking—except the money. She wanted Nutt to do that himself.

As soon as Nutt closed the door, they started kissing and hugging each other. They made their way upstairs to Tank's bedroom. They got naked and fucked on the bed that Tank and Tricia shared. She sucked his dick and Nutt fucked her in all three of her holes. They didn't know that everything was being recorded.

When they finished fucking and sucking, Tricia opened the safe. It wasn't $3 million but it was close to it because Tank had been putting money in it for the last six months. It was $2.6 million, plus Tank had most of his jewelry in that safe. He had three Rolexes with different color faces; two of them gold and the other platinum. Tank also had diamond rings, bracelets, and chains.

They packed everything into a suitcase and left. Nutt had bought a new Tahoe truck with some of the money he made off the chronic. They put Tricia's luggage in the truck and headed for the freeway.

Boss-T was already packed and waiting for Nutt's call. Nutt called and told him everything was a go. Boss-T had bought himself a new Camaro. He met Nutt at the gas station by the entrance to the freeway.

As they were putting gas in their vehicles, Nutt said, "Blood, we came up. It's over two tickets ($2 million) in cash and I got us top of the line jewelry, Rolexes and all."

Boss-T said, "That's all good. Now let's get the fuck out of here before we have to smoke some of these country ass niggas."

They finished gassing up and hit the highway. As they rode, Nutt put in Zapp's "So Rough So Rough."

When Tank got home the next day, he was shocked when he saw his safe open and empty. The first thing he thought was somebody had kidnapped and robbed Tricia. Then he looked in her walk-in closet and saw that it was damn near empty. He ran down to the basement to his secret room and ran the tapes back.

He sat there quietly watching Nutt fuck his bitch and her suck his dick. He watched as they cleaned out his safe. Tears ran down his face but they were tears of anger. He had been disrespected to the fullest. Nutt even fucked Tricia in Tank's bed.

Tank knew that they were gone and more than likely on their way to Cali. Once he got hisself together, he called Too Cool and told him to call his cousin in Cali and ask him if he knew Nutt and Boss-T.

Too Cool called Tank back an hour later and told him his cousin had a ticket for Tank if he could get a hold of them niggas and hold them until he got there. Tank told Too-Cool that they had pulled a scandalous move and was more than likely on their way back to Cali. He told Too Cool he needed him to roll to Cali with him. This was personal; he would fill him in when he got to Houston. Too Cool said he would be there the next morning.

Tank didn't want anybody else to know his business so he just sat there in front of the monitor smoking chronic and watching the tape over and over. He was so mad he couldn't sleep. Finally, he went upstairs, broke the bed down piece by piece and threw it out the back door. He loved Tricia and gave her anything she asked for. He even bought her mama a house. He couldn't understand how she could do this to him. He did know one thing and that was that all three of them muthafuckas was dead; living on borrowed time.

When Too Cool drove up the next morning, Tank was sitting on the front porch with a blunt in his hand. His eyes were bloodshot red. Too Cool had never seen Tank like that before.

"Youngblood, what's wrong?"

Tank stood up, almost falling back down, and Too Cool had to catch him.

"Follow me. Let me show you."

Tank had taken the tape out of his secret room and put it in the VCR in the den. He cut the tape on and watched it with Too Cool for the fiftieth time.

Too Cool knew that Tank loved Tricia and this had to be killin him to watch it. When the tape was over, he asked, "What you want to do? You need some money?"

Tank said, "The money ain't shit; was crumbs to a nigga like me. That didn't even put a dent in my pockets. Dem muthafuckas disrespected me to the fullest. I want dem bitches dead. I want they heads."

Too Cool said, "We need to hook up with my cousin in Cali. Let me make a call."

He called QT and told him he needed to see him ASAP and he would be bringing one of his partners with him. QT told Too Cool to call him and let him know what time his flight would be arriving at

LAX.

Too Cool hung the phone up and said, "Book two tickets. He's waiting on us. Pack light. We can shop when we get there."

Tank took a shower, then called his travel agent and booked a flight for L.A. for two. He packed one bag and put the tape in his bag. He then called PJ and told him he would be out of town for a while so he needed him to run shit while he was gone. He told PJ to come stay at his house but he didn't want no niggas and bitches in his spot.

PJ was there within fifteen minutes. PJ was Tank's right hand man. Tank gave him the dope he had just got from Too Cool and told him to handle it. PJ dropped Tank and Too Cool off at the airport. Then Too Cool called QT and told him what time their flight was due to touch down at LAX.

Chapter 13: The Big Pay Back

As QT was picking up Too Cool and Tank from LAX, Boss-T and Nutt were on the 10 Freeway coming into L.A. They got two rooms at the Embassy Suites where they split up the money. Boss-T got a ticket and Nutt got a ticket. Nutt gave the rest to Tricia.

What Nutt didn't know was that Tricia had A-1 credit, credit cards, and $500,000 of her own in a bank account.

After they split the jewelry up between them, Nutt said, "We are going to take a shower and go to dinner."

Boss-T said, "I'm going to go get me a freak. You ain't the only one that's going to have some fun."

QT was waiting at the gate when Too-Cool and Tank walked off the plane. He had already put the word out that he was offering a $500,000 reward to anybody that knew the whereabouts of Boss-T and Nutt. QT and Too Cool embraced and shook hands.

Too Cool introduced Tank to QT and told him he was solid and he was the one buying most of the dope that was being sent to him.

QT shook Tank's hand and said, "My house is your house."

When they got in the car, QT asked, "So what is this all about?"

Tank started at the beginning and told QT everything. QT could tell by Tank's voice he was hurt, mad, and had murder on his mind.

When Tank was finished, QT said, "I ran them bitch ass niggas out of L.A. It was five of them until they tried to jack me. Now there's only two. Don't sweat it, we will find them low-down mutha-fuckas. I already put the word out on the streets I'm giving up half a ticket just for their whereabouts. A lot of muthafuckas out here are starving, somebody is going to give them up."

QT took them to his house. He had already told Nat that they would be staying with them. When QT opened the front door, Santana and Blocc were there ready to attack.

When Too Cool saw them he jumped back and that sent the two dogs into action. They started to charge until QT stepped up and said, "Stop it. Sit down, now."

Immediately they stopped and sat down.

Tank said, "I need to get me two just like them to take back to Texas wit me."

Too Cool said, "I feel sorry for the nigga that try to break in here."

QT said, "Come on in. They cool. They know you with me and not against me."

They walked in the house and neither Santana nor Blocc moved until they all had passed them. Then they slowly turned and brought up the rear.

Nat walked into the living room from the kitchen and hugged Too Cool. QT introduced her to Tank. She told them dinner would be ready in fifteen minutes and returned to the kitchen while QT showed them to their rooms downstairs. Both guest bedrooms had bathrooms and QT told them they could get refreshed before dinner if needed.

In the kitchen, Nat was cooking steak smothered in gravy with onions and bell peppers, home style potatoes, biscuits, corn, okra, and sweet potatoes. When the men sat down at the table, Nat said the grace.

As they ate, Too Cool said, "Girl, you sure you ain't from down south out here fakin like you from L.A.?"

"I'm from L.A. born and raised."

Tank said, "I love the food and I want ya'll to know that I really appreciate the hospitality."

QT said, "Any friend of Too Cool is a friend of ours."

QT had already told Nat that Nutt and Boss-T were more than likely on their way back to L.A. She had to really be on her Ps and Qs.

After dinner QT, Tank, and Too Cool went out to the back yard.

QT and Nat didn't get high but QT always kept some good chronic for company. He gave Too Cool an ounce and some blunts.

Too Cool said, "You show know how to make a nigga feel at home, cousin."

"This is the quiet before the storm."

Tank said, "I can't wait for the storm to come."

Too Cool and QT knew he meant what he was saying.

The next morning after breakfast, they got in QT's new Range Rover and headed to Compton. It had been over two months since the murders of Detectives Ross and Beckman and the police still didn't have any leads. When they got to the spot QT got out and told Too Cool to pull the Range Rover in the back when he opened the gate.

When QT opened the gate, Crip was standing directly in front of him. QT bent down and Crip ran to him. QT stood up and walked into the back yard and Crip followed him while Too Cool pulled the car into the back, got out, and closed the gate. QT told Crip to sit. Instantly he sat down.

As Tank and Too Cool walked towards QT, Tank asked, "How many of these do you have?"

"Just the three, for now," QT answered. "Crip, go in the house."

The dog went in the house without hesitation.

Tank and Too Cool started admiring all of QT's Low Riders.

"Can these thangs really jump off the ground?" Tank asked.

QT didn't say anything, he opened the door of his midnight blue 64, got the keys from under the front seat, opened the trunk, hooked the ground cables up, and started hitting the switches. Tank and Too Cool were amazed at the height that the foe was hopping.

When QT finished hopping the foe, Too Cool and Tank both said, "I got to have one of these!"

"Wait until Sunday when we go on Crenshaw. You really going to want one."

Goldie walked into the back yard and QT introduced him to Tank. He already knew Too Cool. They went into the house and sat down in the living room.

"I got everybody on the east side that I fuck wit looking for them niggas and all the muthafuckas they fuck wit looking for them too," Goldie said.

QT said, "We will have a line on they ass soon."

While Nutt went with Tricia to the mall, Boss-T made the mistake of going to his hood to kick it wit some of his homies. One of his older homies that had always been jealous of him but always played it off like they were tight, walked up to him, shook his hand and embraced him. His name was Maniac.

"What's up, Blood?" Maniac said. "Long time no see. Where you been, my nigga?"

Boss-T said, "Me and Nutt been in Texas trying to come up."

Maniac said, "Looking at them jewels, and the new car you pushing, you came up on something."

"Yeah, a nigga got a lil somethin…somethin."

Maniac had already heard about the money out on Boss-T and Nutt's whereabouts. He didn't put Boss-T up on it because he wanted to find out where they laid their heads so he could collect half a ticket. At one time, Maniac had money but now he was broke after taking losses and not knowing how to manage his money. The half a ticket would put him back in the game. He knew he had to play it cool and not just rush in and ask Boss-T where he was staying. Boss-T was a killa as well and he wasn't a dumb nigga. He had plenty of street sense and a fair amount of book sense as well.

Maniac said, "Come pick a nigga up sometime so we can kick it, get high, and fuck wit some bitches."

Boss-T said, "I got you, homie. I know where yo spot is. I'll roll through and scoop a nigga up. Right now, I got to roll. I got some business to take care of."

Boss-T embraced and shook Maniac's hand, got in his new Camaro, and pulled off. As Boss-T was driving off, Maniac thought to himself: Nigga, you goin to put me back in the game. I never liked yo ass anyway. It's just a matter of time.

Nutt and Tricia was at the mall just buying up shit. Together they had spent over $25,000. Nutt still had some money from the trips he made to L.A. for Tank, and the money he had when him and Boss-T first left L.A. to go to Texas.

Tricia wasn't a dummy by a long shot. She had learned a lot from Tank. Tank was the one who had set her up with A-1 credit, her credit cards, and the two beauty salons she owned that she left behind in Texas.

As they were sitting down in the food court to eat, Tricia said, "Baby, we got to get out of that hotel and buy us a house somewhere away from yo homies. I know that nigga Tank and right now, more than anything, his pride is hurt. He ain't just going to let this shit slide. He probably already out here looking for us. I got good credit and some money in the bank that will cover a down payment on a house or a nice condo."

Nutt sat quiet for a few minutes thinking. Then he said, "That sounds good. Tomorrow we can go looking for a spot in the valley away from L.A. Matter of fact, we will get us a room at a hotel out that way just to be on the safe side."

Tricia said, "That's cool. We have to be careful until this shit blows over. Tank ain't never been to L.A. so if he does come he ain't going to be here long. When he can't find us he will take his ass back to Texas."

They went back to the hotel and Nutt called Boss-T and told him they needed to talk.

When Boss-T got to Nutt's hotel room, Nut ran down his plan to him and told him he would be switching hotels the next day.

Boss-T said, "Blood, I'm cool. I ain't movin to no fuckin valley. I ain't no fuckin valley boy. Fuck that shit. I'm going to get me a spot in L.A., buy me some chronic, and open up a chronic spot to keep the cash flow movin."

"That's yo choice, Blood, but I choose to do shit my way just like you are going to do yo shit yo way. You be careful out here, Blood. If you need me you know ain't shit changed. I always got yo back."

"I know that, Blood, and I always got yo back as well.'

The next day Nutt and Tricia moved to a hotel in the valley and immediately started house hunting.

Boss-T decided to stay at the hotel that he was at until he found him a spot in L.A. He wasn't in a rush; he felt that he had time. He would take his time, find a cool spot in his hood, and put one of his lil homies in it to slang chronic for him. Then he would find him another cool spot and let his sister get it for him. She had good credit and a good job so her getting it wouldn't be a problem.

He thought to himself: Nutt, you just pussy-whipped, bringing that snake ass bitch all the way to Cali. If it was me, I would have took the money and the jewelry and shook that bitch. It's bad bitches everywhere.

QT had already put the word out to the homies that they were going to hit the Shaw that Sunday so when he got to the Blocc on Tucker Street, the homies were already there posted. Goldie had some of the base heads in the hood clean all of QT's Low Riders, and Goldie charged up all the batteries in the trunks for the hydraulics.

QT pulled into the back yard and parked his truck. He and Too Cool and Tank got out and went inside. The members of the G-Code Mobb were there. QT introduced Tank to them all; they had already met Too Cool.

Goldie went into the bedroom and came back out with three 9mm Berettas. He gave one to QT and handed the other two to Tank and Too Cool.

Tank said, "I love this. This some Gangsta shit."

QT said, "Whenever we roll, we stay strapped. All of us."

Everyone pulled up their shirts to show their straps.

Tank asked, "Who are all those niggas outside?"

QT told him, "They are the homies too. They are rolling with us."

Too Cool said, "When they roll, they roll hard."

QT said, "Tank, you and Too Cool rolling with me in the foe. Come on, let's get up out of here."

They all went outside, got in different cars that they were driving and headed for the Shaw. QT was in the lead car. He put in NWA's "Straight Out of Compton." QT let the top down on the foe, put his locs (dark glasses) on, and opened the glove box and gave Tank and Too Cool each a pair. Then he hit the switches in the foe to test them to make sure they were hot.

The foe shot up off the ground. Tank couldn't stop smiling. He said, "I gots to have one of these. This is some real Gangsta shit." He turned around and saw all the cars that were following them and he realized that QT was a real nigga — a nigga like him: a boss.

When they got to a traffic light and were turning left, Boxer and Goldie pulled up in front of the oncoming traffic and laid their cars in front of them, making a road block so QT and all the cars that followed could turn without breaking up the caravan. Tank and Too Cool watched and were amazed at how QT and his homies rolled.

As usual, when QT got to the Shaw he had to make his grand entrance. Crenshaw was packed on both sides, full of cars and people. QT put the *Bangin on Wax* tape in and put on "Study Dippin." There were about twenty Low Riders behind QT and four undercover cars with homies in them that had the big guns just in case they were needed. Slowly QT cruised up the Shaw aware that everyone was looking at them.

QT said, "I think ya'll better hold on becuz I'm going to swang this bitch to show these fools I can't be fucked with."

He stopped in the middle of the street just for theatrics. Then he pulled off slowly. He hit the switch on the ass of the foe, and on the second hit it was in the air off the ground. He then started hitting the switches for the front. The foe was going so high that all Too Cool and Tank could see was blue sky. It was like they were flying.

QT started hitting his switches and all his homies starting hitting theirs as well. It was a sight to see twenty cars hitting the switches at the same time. QT stopped hopping and let the front and back of the car up, then hit the back right corner switch down and the foe went on three wheels. All his homies did the same thang as they made the left U-turn into the Island on the left hand side of the street where all the Crips kicked it at.

Once the turn was made, QT laid the ass of the foe on the

ground, let the front up, turned the music up and cruised on down the Island. Everyone was giving him his props and acknowledging him.

Tank said, "I ain't never experienced no shit like this in my life. I love this shit."

Too Cool said, "This shit here is on another level."

QT pulled up to a lot that was for washing cars but it was now charging cars to park there. He pulled up and told the dude in the driveway that was collecting money, "All the cars behind me are with me."

The parking fee was ten dollars per car. QT handed the guy three hundred dollars and pulled on in the lot and parked. Once all his homies were in the lot and parked, QT, Tank, Too Cool, Goldie, and some more of his homies started walking around checkout out the cars and the bitches. Wherever there are Low Riders there are always going to be bitches. Most of the bitches knew who QT and his homies were and they were giving them plenty of play action.

Too Cool said, "I know we taking some of these honeys back to Compton."

QT said, "I'm cool on these bitches but I know the homies are going to take some of these hoes back to the city. If you see one you want, get at her. I'll drop ya'll off at a cool room."

QT watched Too Cool as he walked away. The nigga had the coolest walk that QT had ever seen. Tank was calling QT's name and pointing at a fine red bone broad that was sitting on the hood of a convertible Beamer.

"Who is baby right there? Is it cool if a nigga get at her? I don't want to be stepping on nobody's toes, especially if it's somebody that you are cool with," Tank said.

"It's cool," QT told him. "That's Kathy. Her nigga got locked up, got ten years in the Feds. He been down about eighteen months. Come on, let me introduce you to her."

As they were walking over to Kathy, she peeped them coming her way but tried to play it off like she was looking the other way.

When they got to her, QT said, "What's up, Kathy? What you doing out here? You know yo nigga ain't going to like that."

Kathy said, "I ain't with that nigga no more. I went to see that nigga and caught him with some hood rat bitches visiting him two times. I was going to stay down for the nigga but I ain't going to take that shit. To top it off, both of the stupid ass bitches had the nigga's name tattooed on their necks. I gave all that nigga's shit to his mama, moved out his house, and got my own spot."

QT said, "This is my people from Texas. He wanted to get at you. He good people, a real nigga."

With that, QT looked at Tank and said, "I'll be right over there talking to the homies." He pointed to a few niggas standing against the fence.

QT walked over to them, embraced them, and shook their hands. "What that mafia like, cuz?" he asked.

"What that Tank like?" they asked back.

They were Big Jess and Droopy from Nine Eight Main St Mafia.

Droopy said, "Cuz, where you been? We ain't saw you out here in a few months."

QT said, "You know how shit get at times. A nigga been tryin to get paid like you and Big Jess."

Big Jess said, "Nigga please, everybody knows who got Compton sewed up."

Droopy said, "On a more serious note, I heard about the half a ticket for the whereabouts of them slob ass niggas. I thought them niggas had skipped town."

QT said, "They did, but I think they are back in town now."

Droopy said, "Cuz, you know how we do it. Yo enemy is my enemy."

Big Jess nodded in agreement. "If we see the slob ass niggas, we are going to smoke they ass. What's up with Gangsta? I heard that he got action on his appeal and he will ce home soon."

QT said, "Yeah, cuz will ce home real soon. I'm going to give him a big coming home bash. I'll let ya'll know when and where."

Big Jess said, "I know it's going to ce off the hook. Just let us know and we there on deck."

Big Jess and Droopy were Gangsta's age. They had been tight with Gangsta for years. They got tight with QT through Gangsta.

Tank and Kathy were having a good conversation when one of Kathy's ex man's homie walked up and said, "What the fuck you think you doin?"

Kathy said, "Nigga, I ain't with yo homeboy no more and if I was, you don't run me. Nigga, you don't know me like that."

The nigga said, "Bitch, who in the fuck you think you are? Fuck you."

He acted like Tank wasn't even there. He didn't notice the look in Tank's eyes or his changing facial expression. Tank moved quickly and slapped the fuck out of the nigga. Before the nigga could react, Tank had the strap out and in his face.

As the nigga's homeboys started to pull out their straps, they were surrounded by QT and his homies with straps drawn. There were only four niggas with the nigga that Tank had slapped around and about forty of QT's niggas surrounded them with straps drawn.

QT said, "Nigga, you want to die over a female that ain't even yours or your homeboys? She told you that they wasn't together anymore, so what's the problem?"

The nigga was just as big as Tank and he said, "Cuz, I need a fair one. This nigga slapped me. I can't go for that."

QT said, "Tank, this one want to fight you one on one."

Tank said, "I wouldn't have it any other way. I need to get some frustration off."

He handed the 9mm to QT.

It wasn't even a fair fight. The nigga threw one punch at Tank and that was all he was able to get off. Tank sidestepped him, gave him a left hook to the body and a combination to the head. The nigga was knocked out while still on his feet. His homie caught him as he hit the ground.

QT walked up to one of the nigga's homies and said, "Yo homie got a fair one and really he was in violation becuz baby and yo homie ain't together no more. She wit my homie. I don't like getting into it with Crips so I hope this shit is over."

The homie answered, "Cuz, I didn't know what was going on I just saw yo homie slap my homie and draw down on him, that's why I drew down on him. Yeah, this shit is over and we ain't got no beef with ya'll."

They shook hands and QT walked back over to Tank and Kathy.

"Thanks for watching my back," Tank said.

"Cuz, we family and you are my guest. I always got yo back."

QT gave the 9mm back to Tank. He looked at Kathy and said, "He a good nigga, somebody you would want to get to know."

Kathy smiled and said, "I recognize the real when I see it."

QT and his homies kicked it on the Shaw until 11 p.m., then QT told them he was ready to roll. Almost all of his homies had females they had come up on.

Tank told QT that he was going home with Kathy. QT told Kathy to take care of his people and gave Tank his cell and house phone numbers. Too Cool had two females with him.

QT said, "So what are you going to do?"

Too Cool said, "Drop us off at a cool hotel and I'll just call you to pick me up sometime tomorrow."

QT told them to get in the car. They got back to Compton about midnight. QT put his cars up and dropped Too Cool and the two females off at the Hyatt Hotel by LAX. Nat had spent the day with QT's mom and sister Lisa. When QT got home, Nat was still up. She was in the bed watching TV.

When QT walked into the room, Nat said, "I know that you went out there and served those fools. I can't wait to have this baby so I can drive my car out there and serve them fools with you."

QT had taught Nat how to drive a Low Ride and hit the switches. He wanted to see her get out there with him serving fools but once she got pregnant QT told her she would have to wait until after the baby was born before she could ride in a Low Rider again.

He said, "You know I made my grand entrance and served those fools out there. You should have saw Too Cool and Tank — they were loving every moment of it. They even busted some broads and went home with them. Too Cool went to the hotel with two of them."

He lay down on the bed next to Nat. She pulled him close to her and said, "I'm glad you know to bring yo butt home becuz I will smoke a bitch over you."

QT smiled and said, "Oh, so you do love a nigga."

"Nigga, you know I love yo fine sexy ass."

She undid QT's pants and pulled his pants and boxers off. He slowly and tenderly made love to her. He loved her too and he wasn't about to let nothing nor anyone come between them. After he made sure she came, he came inside her and they fell asleep in each other's arms.

Kathy had bought herself a nice two bedroom condo in North Hollywood. She was a real estate agent. She hadn't been with anyone since her dude went to jail. Tank was just the kind of dude that Kathy was into: tall, dark, athletic, and sure about himself.

Tank didn't know what to expect. He hadn't ever been with a female from Cali. He also didn't want her to think that he was trying to rush her into bed. But then he thought about the situation and came to the conclusion that she wouldn't have brought him home if she wasn't going to fuck him, especially this late at night.

Kathy asked him if he wanted anything to drink and he said no, he was cool. He asked her if it was cool for him to blaze up a blunt. They were sitting in the living room and Kathy cut some music on. Anita Baker's "Rapture" was in the deck.

She said, "Yeah, it's cool, blaze it up and I'll be right back."

As she walked away, Tank watched her sexy ass sway from side to side. Tank blazed up the chronic. A few minutes later, Kathy came back in the living room with just her panties and bra on. She walked up to Tank, took the blunt from his hand, and took a drag as she got on her knees between his legs. She hit the blunt again and gave it back to Tank. She told him to stand up. When he did, she undid his pants and pulled them and his boxers down.

Tank didn't have the biggest dick that she had ever seen, or had, but to her it was the average size. It just seemed smaller because of how tall he was. She took him into her mouth, took her time and made love to his dick.

It wasn't like Tricia—she didn't take her time, she always rushed it. Tricia just made Tank cum fast so she could be through with him.

Kathy gave him the best head that he had ever had. When he came, Kathy swallowed every drop. She took him by the hand and led him to her bedroom.

Too Cool was in his hotel room butt naked with the two females that he hooked up with. While one was sucking his dick, the other one was sucking his balls and licking his ass. All three of them were high off chronic and ecstasy that the females had. They freaked until 4 a.m. then both of the females fell asleep in Too Cool's arms.

He lay there thinking these bitches were some real freaks—they even 69'd with each other. He hoped that Tank had good luck like he did.

Boss-T pulled up in front of Maniac's spot. He got out of the car and before he got to the door Maniac was out the front door and waiting for him on the porch.

Maniac said, "What's up, Blood?"

Boss-T said, "What's up, big homie? What are you up to?"

Maniac stepped off the porch and said, "I'm trying to hook up with that fine ass bitch Tracy tonight."

Boss-T said, "You and Sandy ain't together no more?"

"Yeah, she's in the pad but you know a nigga got to have a variety."

"What's up with Tracy's sister, Mia? She fine as a muthafucka too."

"Yeah, that bitch is fine. (Maniac knew that, that was his way in.) Shit, what's up, you want to hook up with them bitches later on tonight?"

Boss-T said, "Hell yeah. We can take them bitches out to eat then back to my spot. I just bought me a new truck yesterday. A Suburban. We can pick the bitches up in the truck. You know they golddiggers anyway. After we eat, we can toss them bitches up."

Maniac said, "Pick me up about eight tonight. I'll hook everything up with the bitches."

Boss-T said, "That will work, big homie. I'll see you tonight."

As Boss-T got in his Camaro and drove off, a smile came across Maniac's face. He thought to himself: Yeah, I'll have me a new truck in a few days too, sucka.

Maniac called Tracy and Mia and hooked up the date for eight thirty. He only had $1500 to his name but he didn't give a fuck. He would splurge tonight if he had to because within a couple of days, he would be back in the game.

At eight, Boss-T pulled up in a new Suburban he had picked up from the shop at seven. The shop had put 20" rims and tires on the truck and put in a new sound system.

When Maniac saw the truck he was really jealous but he played it off with a smile. He said, "Damn, Blood, this muthafucka is tight. That bitch Mia is going to be all on yo dick especially when she sees that Rolly (Rolex) that you sporting."

Boss-T said, "I been wanting to fuck that bitch ever since we were in junior high school. I just never got at her ass. I'm ready for her ass now."

When they got to Tracy's spot, her and Mia were standing outside waiting. Maniac got out to let Mia get in the front and him and Tracy got in the back.

Mia said, "What's up, Boss-T? It's about time you asked me out."

Boss-T said, "I was just waiting for the right time, you know, when I had my shit tight."

Mia was a fine bitch: bronze skin, long wavy black hair, slanted eyes, pretty face, and a bangin body. Her sister Tracy was just as fine. Maniac had been fucking Tracy off and on for the last two years.

They had dinner at the Outback Steakhouse in Torrance. After dinner, Boss-T took them to his spot at the Embassy Suites. His spot had two bedrooms so once they got there he took Mia to his room and Maniac and Tracy went to the other bedroom.

QT picked up Too Cool and Tank the next day. Both of them had smiles on their faces. He picked up Too Cool first since he was the closest to his house. When too Cool came out the hotel, the two females were right behind him.

QT said, "We got to go pick up Tank. I don't have time to drop them off."

He reached into his pocket and pulled out a hundred dollar bill and handed it to one of the females. "I'm sorry, baby, but we are in a hurry. You are going to have to call a cab."

She said, "It's cool. I'm just glad you didn't leave a bitch stranded."

He smiled and said, "Never that, baby. We are gentlemen."

She looked at Too Cool and said, "Don't forget to call us, daddy."

Too Cool said, "I'm a man of my word. Remember that."

QT pulled off and said, "Cuz, I'm surprised you still got some energy."

Too Cool said, "I wish I could have had that ordeal on tape. I could have made some money off of what went down in that room this morning."

QT laughed and said, "Cuz, you are a fool for real."

He picked Tank up from Kathy's condo. Kathy walked Tank down to QT's truck, kissed him, and told QT, "Thank you for hooking me up with this wonderful man."

QT said, "Damn, Tank. You got it like that."

Tank just smiled and said, "The pleasure was all mine."

QT took them back to his pad so they could change clothes. While they were there, he got a call from Goldie who told him one of Boss-T's homies got at him through one of Goldie's homies and said he knew where Boss-T was laying his head, but he didn't know where Nutt was. QT told Goldie to tell his hook-up to tell Maniac to tell him where the nigga was. He would get his money after the location was verified.

Goldie called back fifteen minutes later with the location. QT went in the den and told Too Cool and Tank, "We got a location on Boss-T. We going to get his ass tonight."

Tank asked, "What about Nutt and that bitch?"

"Nothing yet, but if Boss-T knows where they are, we will get it out of him before we smoke his ass."

Goldie picked QT, Tank, and Too Cool up in a van around 9 p.m. They went to the hotel that Boss-T was staying at. They parked and waited. Maniac had told them about the Camaro and the Suburban and where they were parked at.

They saw the Camaro parked so Boss-T had to be in the Suburban. They parked two spaces over from the Camaro so that Boss-T could park next to the Camaro. They were all strapped and all of them had on ski masks. The van had a dark tint on the windows and blinds so no one could see in but they could see out.

They sat in the van until 11:30 p.m. when they saw the Suburban pull up and park next to the Camaro. He had a female with him but that wasn't going to stop them from handling their business.

Boss-T wasn't paying his surroundings any attention. Since he had been back in L.A. he had completely forgot about QT being a threat to him.

Before he knew what was going on, QT and his people were out of the van. Boss-T had a gun to his head and Goldie had a gun to Mia's head with his hand over her mouth. He told her, "If you scream you are dead. We don't want you, we want him."

Both of them were put in the van and duct tape was put over their eyes and mouths. Boss-T thought that it was a jack taking place. He only had about $100,000 in his room. He had given the rest of the money to his sister to put up for him. He would gladly have given them the hundred grand.

QT took the tape off Mia's mouth and said, "You should watch the company that you keep. This nigga here is a piece of shit."

Boss-T was trying to remember if he knew the voice but he had never heard it before.

QT said, "We are going to let you go, Mia." He was looking at her ID. "But we know who you are and where you live so if you are smart, you will forget all about tonight. Don't make me regret letting you go. Now when we let you out, count to fifty before you take the tape off your eyes. Can you do that for us?"

Mia nodded her head up and down frantically.

"I don't hear you," he said. "You can speak."

"Yes, yes, I understand. Tonight never happened."

QT cut the tape off of her wrists and said, "I'm going to sit you in the back seat of his truck. The keys will be on the front seat. Remember, don't take the tape off your eyes until you count to fifty."

He helped her out of the van and into the back seat of the truck. He threw the keys on the front seat and warned her again, "Don't start counting until I close this door. And count slowly."

He closed the door, got back in the van, and Goldie pulled off headed for the abandoned steel factory on Alameda. As Goldie drove, they took the ski masks off.

QT reached over and snatched off the tape from Boss-T's eyes.

Boss-T couldn't believe that he was looking at QT and Tank in the same van.

Tank said, "What's wrong, nigga? You look like you have seen a ghost."

QT said, "You picked the wrong niggas to fuck with. You should have really done yo homework before you fucked with us. When we get to where we are going we are going to ask you some questions. I hope you have the right answers."

At the abandoned factory, the rest of the G-Code Mobb were already there waiting. Goldie pulled the van around to the back and then drove it inside the building. They took Boss-T out of the van and cut the tape off his wrists. They were about to put him in handcuffs when Tank walked up and took his Rolex rings and chain off of him.

"This don't belong to you," he said.

Boxer put the handcuffs on him and Boss-T was hung by the cuffs on a hook hanging from the ceiling.

When QT snatched the tape off his mouth, Boss-T knew that it was the end for him. He had gambled and lost. As tears ran down his face he just hoped it would be a fast death. All he ever wanted to be was a baller and be known. He wanted to be the man. Now he realized that being the man wasn't all that he thought it was. He thought: Well, I was a baller for a week and a half, and I did get to fuck Mia.

QT shattered his thoughts when he said, "Where is Nutt and that bitch staying at?"

At first, Boss-T was going to try and play it hard and go out like a gangster. He looked at QT and said, "Fuck you, Blood."

QT pulled a pair of wire cutters out of his pocket and reached up to Boss-T's hands. He cut off two fingers.

Boss-T screamed like a bitch.

After a few minutes went by, QT said, "After I finish yo fingers, I'm going to go to yo toes, and then yo dick and balls. You want to continue to play like you a gangsta?"

Boss-T said, "I swear on my mama I don't know where they are exactly. All I know is they are in the valley in a hotel until they buy a house out there."

QT looked at Tank and said, "It's yo call. What do you want to do?"

Tank said, "Fuck him. Let's smoke his ass."

QT pulled out his 9mm and the others did as well. QT fired the first shot. Everyone followed suit.

When Crip Crazy and Big Bam took him down from hanging on the hook, Tank said, "I ain't finished yet."

QT knew what he wanted to do. He went to the van and came back with a machete. He gave it to Tank.

Tank walked over to Boss-T's body and with one swing, the head was cut from the body. Tank picked up the severed head and put it in a pillowcase.

QT took the pillowcase from Tank and gave it to Lil Man. "Make sure it's sitting on his mama's front porch before the sun rises."

Goldie dropped QT, Too Cool, and Tank off at QT's house. The rest of the G-Code Mobb got rid of Boss-T's body and cleaned up the warehouse.

QT said, "More than likely, the hotel room will be in that bitch's name so I'm going to have Nat use one of our burnout phones and start calling all the hotels in the valley and ask if she's registered there. It might take a lil time, but we are going to get they ass."

QT told Nat what had went down and also told her about tracking Tricia down.

The next morning as QT, Nat, Tank, and Too Cool watched the

news, a reporter came on with breaking news saying a severed head was found on a porch in East Los Angeles. The victim's mother was the one who found the head when she opened her front door to take her usual morning walk. As of now, the reporter said, no one knew who could have done something so hideous.

QT cut off the TV and they all went out to breakfast.

As Nutt and Tricia watched the news, tears ran down his face. Boss-T was his homie. They had grown up together since elementary school and now he was gone just like Nacho, Ed Dog, and G-Rob.

Tricia said, "How did that nigga Tank find Boss-T? That's the same thang he did to the niggas that killed his brother."

Nutt said, "Pack up. We got to get out of here. Boss-T didn't know where we are out here, but he knew we were in the valley so we got to shake this spot."

Tricia said, "Where are we going?"

"Let's go out to Magic Mountain. That should be cool. I know they will think we skipped town once we got the word on Boss-T."

They packed and moved to Valencia by Magic Mountain. Boss-T's body was never found so he had to have a closed casket funeral. QT, Tank, Too Cool, and Goldie were posted in a van waiting for Nutt to come to Boss-T's funeral but he never showed up. It was like he had disappeared.

After a month went by Tank and Too Cool had to go home for a couple of weeks because it was time for Tasha to make her trip to New Orleans. Tank and Kathy had been seeing each other exclusively. Tank asked her if she would go back to Texas with him for a few weeks and she said yes. QT took them all to the airport and told them he would pick them up when they got back. Both Tank and Too Cool had bought convertible 64 Chevys, super clean, with hydraulics in them. QT taught them the basics of hitting the switches. They had the cars shipped back to their spots by car carrier.

Nat was due to give birth in a month and a half. Monica gave her a baby shower at QT's mom's house. It was a females' event but QT made a showing just to let Nat know that he would always be there for her. QT was still fucking Destiny and Tasha but they knew what time it was when it came to Nat.

Gangsta was due to come home in three and a half months. QT reserved the ball room at the Hyatt Hotel. He wanted Gangsta's coming home party to be the biggest and best ever. He ordered 200 bottles of Cristal, 200 bottles of Dom Perignon and 100 bottles of Moët. Not to mention the Hennessy and Remy Martin. He was going to have a king's throne on the stage and two bad bitches that would be dressed in thongs to bring out the king's crown to QT so he could crown Gangsta with it. All the music was going to be from the 60s, 70s, and 80s. QT was also going to surprise Gangsta's wife with a queen's tiara. It was going to be a grand event.

When Tank got home and Kathy saw how he was truly living, she was in shock. She had no idea that Tank was as wealthy as he was. He owned two night clubs and even though Tricia thought the beauty shops were hers, the property was in Tank's name. Kathy loved Tank's big beautiful house and, most of all, she had fallen in love with him.

The first thing they did when they arrived was to go shopping for a new bedroom set. It was delivered and set up the same day. Kathy helped Tank hire a housekeeper and two days later Tank had to leave to go to New Orleans to get with Too Cool. PJ had kept everything right so when Tank got home there were no problems. Tank told Kathy that he would only be gone for a day so she was to kick it and if she wanted anything that wasn't at the house, she was to call his sister Carla who would handle whatever it was she needed. If she wanted to go shopping, Tank left her $20,000 in the top left side dresser drawer. He kissed her goodbye and him and PJ left in two separate cars. Tank always had PJ take the money and bring the dope back while he followed him there and back.

Kathy's ex-man was in the game too but he wasn't on the same level as Tank. Kathy knew for a fact the most cash her ex ever had at one time was $600,000. Tank's car collection was worth more than that. His house had to be worth at least $3 million. Kathy wasn't a golddigger; she worked hard for her money. When she broke up with her ex she had $300,000 cash of his. She took every cent to his mother and gave her the keys to his house and his three cars.

Kathy cooked dinner, locked the house up, cut the house alarm on and talked on the phone to one of her friends from Cali.

The next day around 6 p.m., Tank and PJ pulled up in front of the house. Tank had work in two gym bags. He left one in the car with PJ and told him to get it to who was supposed to have it. He took the other gym bag in the house with him. Kathy met him as he came in the door. She immediately hugged and kissed him. He told her to wait there; he would be right back. Kathy wasn't new to the game—she knew what was going on. She also knew her place.

Tank took the gym bag down to the basement to his secret room and put it inside the safe. When he got back upstairs he told Kathy, "What do you want to do? You name it and you got it."

Kathy said, "I just want to be with you, baby. That's enough for me."

When she said that, Tank knew and felt in his heart that she was the one for him. He took her in his arms and kissed her. "I love you, Kathy."

Her eyes started to water as she said, "I love you too, Tank."

Tank called QT a few days later and told him he would be back in L.A. in two days. He also told QT he was in love with Kathy and wanted to marry her. QT congratulated him and said he was happy for them.

Two days later, Tank, Kathy, and Too Cool were back in L.A. QT picked them up from the airport and brought them to his house. He introduced Kathy to Nat and they hit it right off.

Tank had bought a ring before he left Texas but he hadn't asked Kathy to marry him yet. They were all having dinner at QT's house when Tank walked up to Kathy, got down on one knee, and said, "Baby, I love you with all my heart. I want to spend the rest of my life with you. Will you marry me?"

Kathy quickly said, "Yes, yes, yes, baby. I love you and I will marry you."

Everyone congratulated them and Too Cool said, "I guess I'm going to have to find me a wife too."

They all laughed and QT said, "Knowing you, you are going to have to move to Utah so you can have two or three wives."

Tank and Kathy set a wedding date for three months later. The wedding was going to be in Texas at Tank's house.

Maniac had received the money for giving up Boss-T's whereabouts. He was only given half of the money, which was $250,000, because Nutt wasn't there. There was still $250,000 for Nutt's whereabouts and Maniac was determined to collect that as well.

The only problem was, Nutt was no where to be found. Nobody had seen him, nor had he come to the neighborhood. Nat had tried to track Nutt and Tricia down by calling every hotel in the valley looking for them. It was Nutt's luck that when Nat called the hotel they had been staying in, that they already checked out. Since nobody had seen Nutt or Tricia, QT and Tank thought that maybe they fled to another state.

Tricia and Nutt had bought a house in Valencia by Magic Mountain. She opened up another beauty salon and Nutt was trying to figure out what he was going to do. He had never held a job in his life. All he'd ever done was sell dope, rob, and kidnap people for ransom. It was only a matter of time before he migrated back to the hood and to what he knew. Valencia was too quiet for him and there wasn't enough excitement around there. Tricia was happy; she had her house (which was in her name). She had her own hair salon and Nutt was keeping her physically satisfied so she was cool.

Tank was staying with Kathy at her condo and Too Cool was still staying with QT. Time passed quickly and before they knew it, Nat was in the den calling QT telling him it was time for her to go to the hospital.

QT grabbed Nat's bag and helped her to the car. Too Cool was excited too. He called Tank to tell him and Kathy that they were on their way to the hospital. Tank told him that he and Kathy were on their way too. QT called his mother and told her Nat was in labor and she told him that she and Lisa would meet them at the hospital.

Nat was taken to the labor room to be prepped. Once she was ready, QT, Lisa, and QT's mother were let into the delivery room. QT was at Nat's side, holding her hand, and talking to her. It didn't take long; twenty minutes after QT was let into the delivery room, Nat delivered a beautiful baby girl that weight 6 lbs, 9 oz.

As QT held his baby for the first time, he looked at her and was overwhelmed with love for her. They had decided to name the baby Cedric if it was a boy and LaShawn if it was a girl. So LaShawn it was.

QT took her to Nat and watched the tears come down her face as she saw and held their baby for the first time. QT's mother had called Nat's parents right after QT called her. They arrived at the hospital ten minutes after LaShawn. Too Cool surprised QT, Tank, and Nat's father with cigars. Everyone stayed at the hospital until they saw LaShawn and made sure she and her mother Nat were all right.

A day later, Nat and LaShawn were released from the hospital. QT and Too Cool were there the whole time. QT took Nat home and watched LaShawn while Nat, Lisa, QT's mom, Kathy, and Monica went shopping for the baby. They already had the baby bed, the cradle, Pampers, Similac milk, and a few baby outfits for a girl but most of the clothes they had were for a boy.

So as they went shopping, QT, Too Cool, Goldie, and Tank watched LaShawn. Rocc arrived at QT's house followed by all the members of the G-Code Mobb. They all came with presents and congratulations. Too Cool was almost as worse as QT when it came to LaShawn. He was like a mother hen watching over her lil chick.

When Nat and the rest of the girls got back it was a full house. QT's mom said, "Okay, let's go. It's time to go. Ya'll can come back tomorrow. We got to get the baby's room together and put all this stuff up."

They had bought bags and bags of clothes and different things for the baby. LaShawn was a real beauty; everyone who saw her fell in love with her. She looked just like Nat only she had QT's skin complexion.

A week before Gangsta got out of prison, QT hooked everything up for his coming home party. He passed out all the invites to the real niggas, playas, and gangstas. The females didn't need an invite as long as they were fine and dressed to impress.

Tonya, Gangsta's wife, went to pick him up from Folsom State Prison. She took him to QT's house where QT had a private party and dinner for him with just family, all the members of the G-Code Mobb, plus Tank and Kathy.

Everyone was glad to see Gangsta and he was glad to see them as well. He was introduced to Tank, Kathy, and Monica. He knew everyone else. He hadn't met Nat in person but he had talked to her many times on the phone. Gangsta was already solid when he went to jail but now he was ever bigger and cut up like someone had taken a chisel to his body.

Nat, Lisa, Kathy, Monica, and moms did all the cooking. They had fried and BBQ chicken, BBQ ribs and steak, macaroni and cheese, mustard greens, BBQ baked beans, corn, okra, cabbage, peach cobbler, and chocolate cake.

Everyone was in and out of the pool or chilling in the Jacuzzi and drinking Cristal or Dom. QT pulled Gangsta to the side and told him to take a ride with him real quick. They pulled up in front of a big six bedroom house with four baths, a family room, a basement, swimming pool, Jacuzzi, and a big back yard. There was a brand new 500 Benz and a new Ferrari in the driveway.

Gangsta asked, "Who lives here?"

QT threw him some keys and said, "You do. This is yours, the cars included. I also got eighteen million in cash for you. I already told the homies I'm stepping down. I already know that you ain't ready to get out the game so just always know I got yo back. We will discuss all this shit later. Come on, let me show you the house."

The house was beautiful inside and out. QT even had a secret lil room built like the one he had. It was already loaded with straps. There was also a million in cash.

QT said, "I didn't want to furnish it. I figured you and Tonya would want to do that together."

Gangsta said, "Tonya is going to love this house becuz I do. Good lookin out, lil bro. You did a hell of a job since a nigga was gone."

"Cuz, don't get sentimental on me. I just did what had to be done. The only thing you are going to have to do is find somebody else to take the dope to Too Cool. Cecuz baby that was doing it for me has retired."

"I got it covered. Just give me the rundown on how she was doing it."

QT said, "Later for that. Let's get back to yo party."

Gangsta's house was only three blocks away from QT's and one away from his mom's house.

When they got back to QT's pad, the food was about to be served. Everyone was just waiting on QT and Gangsta to get back.

LaShawn was now two months old and bossy as ever. She had been asleep but now she was awake and fussy.

When Nat brought her downstairs, Gangsta said, "Bring her to me. Let her uncle hold her."

Nat took her to Gangsta and when he saw her, he fell in love with her as well.

"QT, you going to have to put bars on her bedroom windows. And guard the front door with a shot gun to keep niggas away from her. She's a beauty."

QT said, "Wait til you have a daughter. You are going to have to do the same thang."

Gangsta got out of jail on a Wednesday. His big bash, coming home party was that Friday. Tonya loved the house and kept Gangsta busy helping her shop to furnish the house. He also went shopping for a new wardrobe and some new jewelry.

Chapter 14: Welcome Bacc

When Friday came, QT called Gangsta and told him to dress to impress because they were going to a party for one of their partners and to bring Tonya becuz he was bringing Nat.

Gangsta said "Cool" and that he would be at QT's pad about 9:30 p.m.

QT and Gangsta looked like a million bucks with their two-piece Armani suits on, with full length mink coats and the mink hats to match. They wore Gator shoes and top-of-the-line pieces of jewelry. Nat and Tonya had on different color Versace mini skirts with four-inch high heel pumps with waistline mink coats, and their pieces on as well. They were definitely dressed to impress.

Nat had bounced right back after she had her baby. Within five weeks she was back to normal looking beautiful as ever.

QT drove a new Lamborghini he had just bought and Gangsta drove his new Ferrari. They pulled up to the hotel and got their cars valeted at 10:20 p.m. When they walked into the hotel there were still a few hundred people trying to get into the ballroom. QT, Nat, Gangsta, and Tonya went straight to the front of the line. Goldie, Crip Crazy, and Big Bam was at the door.

As soon as they got inside, the lights came on, the music went off, and everyone turned to them and said, "Welcome home, Gangsta."

Everyone he knew and hadn't seen since he had been locked up came to personally welcome him home.

The lights went back off and the DJ put on one of his favorite songs, "Dazz" by Brick. Gangsta took his mink coat off and told Tonya to do the same. He gave them to Lil Man and told him to put them up. QT and Nat gave Lil Man their coats as well.

Rocc came over with a female that he had been kicking it with and all three brothers got their boogie on. They danced, mingled, and were having a great time. They had a whole corner reserved for them: Tha G-Code Mobb, Tank, Kathy, Too Cool, and whatever females he was with.

The DJ was jamming all 60s, 70s, and 80s cuts. He played Tina Marie, Anita Baker, The Moments, Chi-lites, Delfonics, Smokey, Prince, Alexander O'Neal, Cherell, Morris Day and the Time, Michael Jackson, Barry White, Teddy-P, Isley Brothers, One Way, Cameo, Gap Band, Zapp, Parliament Funkadelics, Bootsy and more. The only rap that was played was NWA and Grandmaster Flash and the Furious Five.

About 12:30 a.m. QT brought out the king's throne to the stage, cut the music off, and had Gangsta take his rightful place on the throne. Then he had two super fine females dressed in G-strings and bras bring out a king's crown on a blue velvet pillow and a queen's tiara for Tonya. Everyone was quiet as QT placed the crown on Gangsta's head and Nat placed the tiara on Tonya's head. The DJ put on "Return of the Mack." Everyone started clapping and cheering Gangsta on. It was a hell of a party; no one had ever done it like QT had done it for Gangsta. That party would be talked about for years and years to come.

Tank kicked back and enjoyed the atmosphere, the people, and the party. If you would have asked him six months ago about hooking up and kicking it with niggas from Cali, he would have told you to get the fuck out his face. Them Cali niggas be on some bullshit and he would only deal with them on his terms. But as he sat there observing the scene, he realized that it didn't matter where you were from, all real niggas basically were the same when it came to loyalty, respect, and honor.

A month later, QT, Nat, Gangsta, Tonya, and the members of the G-Code flew down to Texas for Tank and Kathy's wedding. QT, Nat, Goldie, Monica, Gangsta, Tonya, and Too Cool all stayed at Tank's house. QT and Nat brought LaShawn with them. QT's mom wanted to keep LaShawn with her while they went to the wedding but QT and Nat wasn't having it.

The other members of the G-Code Mobb stayed at a hotel paid for by Tank, with two limos at their service. They all got there a week before the wedding. Tank showed them the town and took them to his clubs every night. Tank was a good host and went out of this way to make sure that all his guests were having a good time. He even hooked up the ones that didn't bring a woman with them with a female while they were there. Everyone loved Tank's house and his Olympic size swimming pool. They also enjoyed getting away from the females and going down in the basement to just get high, chill, and shoot pool.

The wedding was beautiful. Tank's moms, sister, and other family members attended as well as his syndicate members and other hustlers, playas, and gangstas that he knew. The wedding was held outside in his backyard. Kathy's mother, father, and two brothers also attended. Tank's homie PJ was his best man and Kathy's long time home girl Tina was her maid of honor.

Tank's mother and sister never like Tricia but they instantly took a liking to Kathy. The reception was held at a hotel in Houston which lasted until 4 a.m. the next morning.

A day later, QT and his people went back to Cali and Tank and Kathy went on their honeymoon to Jamaica.

Nutt started slowly but surely coming back to L.A. on the low-down. He had even kicked it with Maniac a few times. Maniac tried to find out where Nutt was staying but Nutt never told him or anyone else where he lived. His family didn't even know where he lived.

Nutt and Maniac were rolling around in Nutt's new Corvette and decided to go to the Fox Hills Mall. Nutt wanted to go to Mensland to buy some new gear. As usual, he had his strap with him, a .45 automatic. Since Boss-T had been murdered, Nutt didn't go any-where without his strap.

While Nutt and Maniac were shopping in Mensland, QT and Nat were at the other end of the mall with LaShawn shopping for some baby shoes. She was growing fast as she was now six months old and feisty and loveable as ever. As they walked through the mall, QT had LaShawn in his arms.

Nat said, "You know you are spoiling that girl to the point that whenever she sees you or hears your voice she cries so you can pick her up."

"I know, baby, I'm going to always spoil both of my beautiful babies." He kissed Nat on the lips and added, "I love you, baby." Then he kissed LaShawn and said, "I love you too, baby."

Nat said, "We love you too, daddy."

QT said, "You keep talking like that we are going to have to go home and get naked."

Nat laughed and said, "I already had that in mind."

QT was strapped. He had a 9mm in the waistband of his pants in the middle of his back under his shirt. Nat also had a 9mm in her purse.

QT said, "We got what we came for. Let's go home. I want to give you a massage."

She smiled. "There's something on you I want to massage too."

They headed for the underground parking lot to their car.

Nutt and Maniac were already in the parking lot at Nutt's car when Nutt said, "Damn, Blood, I left my fucking cell phone on the counter when we bought this shit."

They put the bags of clothes and shoes in the car and started back towards the entrance to the mall. Just at that moment, Nat and QT were walking out the exit that was also the entrance depending on which way you were going.

Nutt saw them about a half a second before QT and Nat saw him and Maniac.

QT knew who Nutt was instantly. He also knew Maniac. By QT having LaShawn in his arms he wasn't able to get to his strap in time. Nat was holding the bags so she was slowed up as well.

Nutt instantly went for his strap and came up blasting. The first shot hit QT in his shoulder as he tried to shield LaShawn by turning his back to Nutt. He was hit in the back as well.

Without hesitating, Nat dropped the bags, pulled the 9mm out of her purse and jumped in front of QT. She got off one shot hitting Maniac in the arm.

Nutt shot Nat three times, once in the stomach and twice in the chest. Nutt and Maniac then turned and ran to the car and sped away.

QT was bleeding and hurt bad but LaShawn wasn't hit. As he turned around, his legs weakened and he fell to his knees. He saw Nat lying on the ground bleeding. He crawled to her and found she was still conscious.

Nat said, "I love you, daddy, take care of LaShawn."

QT held the baby in one hand and held Nat's head with the other. With tears in his eyes, he said, "Just stay awake, baby. You are going to be all right. We have so much to do together. Our baby needs you. I need you."

When the ambulance arrived, Nat was still alive. A civilian had taken LaShawn and was holding her while QT held Nat in his lap. They were all taken to the hospital.

"I finally got that bitch and that nigga!" Nutt said as they sped off. "They are the ones who killed Nacho, Ed Dog, and G-Rob. Fuck them muthafuckas. Blood, payback is a bitch, ain't it?"

Maniac said, "Blood, I'm hit, but it went straight through. Just drop me off at the pad. I'm cool."

After Nutt dropped Maniac off, Maniac was scared to death. He knew that QT knew him and he also knew that Gangsta was QT's brother and was out of jail. He hoped that QT was dead; that way, no one would know that he was with Nutt when that shit went down.

Nutt was happy he had finally got rid of QT and his bitch. He didn't have to hide anymore. They were dead and by now Tank had went back to Texas. Now he would be able to enjoy his money and life. He could open up a couple of chronic spots in the hood to maintain his way of living. Lately, he had been spending money and hadn't been bringing any in. He wasn't broke; he still had $700,000, but he knew eventually he would be if he didn't invest his money in something. He drove home with a smile on his face.

QT was unconscious for three days. Gangsta, Rocc, G-Moms, Lisa, and Tha G-Code Mobb were all at the hospital praying and hoping that he would pull through. When they got the call that QT and Nat had been shot, Too Cool, Tank, and Kathy had jumped on the first thang going to Cali and joined the others at the hospital.

No one on the street had heard anything about who gunned QT and Nat down. It was a miracle that the baby wasn't harmed.

When QT woke up, his mother, Lisa, Rocc, and Gangsta were in his room. Lisa was holding LaShawn. It took him a minute to focus clearly.

His moms asked, "Baby, can you hear me?"

QT said yes but he could barely talk. His throat was dry and he needed some water. After he was given some he felt better.

He said, "Where is Nat? I need her."

No one said anything. They couldn't even look him in the face. QT's mother was sitting next to him holding his hand.

He looked at his mother and asked, "Mama, how is Nat doing? I need to see her."

He sat up in bed and pulled the I.V. out of his arm trying to get out of the bed. Gangsta and Rocc rushed to his bedside to restrain him.

Once they had him in their grip, his mother said, "Baby, I'm sorry, but Nat didn't make it. She died yesterday."

QT snatched away from Rocc. He didn't believe it. Nat couldn't be dead. His love, his wife, his daughter's mother, the love of his life. QT was stronger than his brothers; he snatched away from Rocc, slid off the bed and pushed Gangsta off of him.

His mother started to yell, "Get him! Hold him! He's not well. Call the doctor."

As Gangsta and Rocc had QT back on the bed holding him down, tears ran down his face.

"No, no, no, not Nat! Why, why Nat? It should have been me. I'm the one that deserved it, not Nat."

As he cried and struggled to get free the doctor came and gave him a shot to calm him down. He was knocked out in about twenty seconds. The doctor put the I.V. back in his arm and put restraints on his wrists and legs so he couldn't get up once he awakened again.

Gangsta asked the doctor if restraining him was necessary and the doctor told him it was for the best until his wife's death was a reality to him.

As Lisa and QT's mother cried, Gangsta and Rocc silently swore to themselves that whoever did this to their brother would hurt fourscore.

When QT woke up six hours later to find his arms and legs bound, his first though was of Nat. He began to cry. No one had seen QT cry since he was eleven years old but his mom and Nat, and that was when Rocc was fighting for his life. All of them were already hurting because they all loved Nat. To see QT in so much psychological and mental pain made their pain much worse. They all tried to talk to him but he wouldn't say anything to anyone. All he did was lay there and cry and think of Nat.

The next day, the doctor took the restraints off. Still he said nothing. All he did was gesture for Lisa to let him hold his daughter. As he held his daughter, once he looked at her the tears came again. LaShawn looked just like Nat.

QT wouldn't talk to anyone. His family was starting to think that he was loosing it mentally. All he was doing was planning and plotting. Nutt didn't give a fuck about him, Nat, or their baby girl. If he wanted to play the game that way, then that's how it would be. QT wouldn't have any regard for mothers, fathers, sisters, or brothers. The only thing off limits to QT was kids. Maniac had it coming as well. That's the same nigga QT had paid $250,000 for Boss-T's whereabouts. QT knew he would set an example that would never be forgot.

Nutt and Maniac were running scared when they heard that QT had survived and that his wife had died. Maniac told Nutt about Gangsta and that he was QT's brother. This was something that Nutt didn't know. Nutt was scared but at the same time he felt safe because no one knew where he was—and he wasn't going back to L.A.

Maniac knew that they would be coming for him. He just didn't know when. He moved to North Hollywood with his woman and stayed out of the hood also thinking shit would blow over. The only person that knew where he lived was his mother. He told his woman Sandy not to tell anyone where they were. But her being a dumb bitch couldn't wait to flaunt their new condo to a couple of her girlfriends when Maniac wasn't home. Both of her girlfriends were golddiggers that fucked with niggas that were in the game.

Nat's funeral was large. All of her friends and family were there as well as QT's family and everybody that had love and respect for him. There were over a thousand people attending her funeral. Even Destiny and Tasha were mixed in with the crowd.

QT was released from the hospital on the morning of the funeral. He walked in last holding his daughter just behind his moms, Gangsta, Rocc, Lisa, Tonya, Goldie, Monica, Tank, Kathy, and Too Cool. QT had on a black Armani suit, a pair of black Gators, a black Godfather hat, and some black Armani glasses that looked like locs.

As he walked down the aisle of the church tears were already streaming down his face. When he got to the front of the church they all sat on the first bench next to Nat's mother and father. The preacher gave a good sermon, and then it was time for people to get up and say something. Monica, Kathy, Tonya, and a few others said good things about Nat.

QT was the last one to speak. He handed LaShawn to Nat's mother and walked up to the podium. It took him a minute to compose himself. Then he said, "I don't know if any of you believe in love at first sight but I do. The first time I laid eyes on Nat, it was a wrap. I fell in love with her instantly. I knew that she was the woman I wanted to spend my life with. Nat was beautiful inside and out. She was sweet, loving, generous, loyal, and had the biggest heart I've ever known. Nat taught me how to love. Before I met Nat, my life was in the wind with a destination I was certain would be displeasing. Nat gave my life purpose and a clear destination that we could be proud of. Nat was my best friend and her love for me was unconditional. She gave us a beautiful baby girl that looks just like her. I miss her so much and she will always be here in my heart. I love you, Nat, yesterday, today, tomorrow, and always. You were special, baby, one of a kind. Believe me, when I say this; I know that you are in heaven looking down on me right now. You know that I'm hurting and my heart is broken but you know me as well as anyone and I'm telling you right now, I got you, baby."

QT walked from the podium, took LaShawn from his Nat's mom, and sat down as tears streamed down his face. No one knew what QT meant when he said, "I'm telling you right now, I got you, baby." But all his homies and street niggas knew that he was saying that he was going to kill whoever had killed her.

As the organ played, the family sat as everyone viewed the body. The family wanted to go last because QT wasn't able to view Nat's body at the wake; he was still in the hospital. The family knew that he would want some time with her by himself. It took about forty-five minutes for everyone else to view Nat's body. After they were all outside, the family viewed the body for the last time. Nat's mother and father had to be carried out of the church they were so overcome with grief. QT handed LaShawn to his mother after everyone had walked out. QT was the last one.

When he saw her, he broke down crying uncontrollably. As she lay there she was so beautiful. It looked as if she was sleeping. QT softly kissed her on the lips and said, "I'm so sorry, baby, I was supposed to protect you. It should be me lying here, not you. Nat, I swear on my love for you, them niggas will be dead in a week. I'm so so sorry, baby. Please forgive me. There's so much we didn't get to do together and so many places we didn't get to see together. It wasn't supposed to end like this, baby, not for you and me. We were the ones that was supposed to get out the game and have more babies together and live a good life."

QT stood there another fifteen minutes pouring his heart out to Nat until his mother came back into the church and took him in her arms.

She said, "I know you hurting, baby, and it's going to hurt for a long time but some how you are going to get through this. Come on, baby, we have to go."

At the graveyard, QT stayed there until Nat was buried and the cemetery was closing. Gangsta, Rocc, Goldie, Tank, and Too Cool stayed there as well while QT sat next to Nat's grave rocking back and forth. He still hadn't told anyone who shot him and Nat.

When they were all in the limo on the way to QT's house, he finally spoke.

"It was that bitch ass nigga Nutt that killed Nat and shot me. Maniac's bitch ass was with him. I'm going to do this my way. A lot of muthafuckas may have to die and I don't give a fuck about killing them. I'm going to find out where them niggas are no matter who I got to kill. I just wanted to bury Nat first. My mission starts tonight at Nutt's mama's house. Then I'm going to Maniac's mama's house. All it's going to take is three of us, so who is it going to be?"

Before anyone could say anything, Gangsta said, "Me and Goldie."

Rocc blurted out, "Fuck that. I want to go too."

Gangsta told him, "In case anything goes wrong, we are going to need you out here to take care of the family."

Tank said, "I consider ya'll my family too, so what ever I can do just give the word and it's done."

Too Cool said, "Ya'll already know where I stand. Just tell me who you want dead and it's a done deal."

QT said, "I just need ya'll to look out for my brother Rocc and my family if anything goes wrong."

Tank said, "When you find out where Nutt and that bitch is, let me know. I know you want Nutt, but I got unfinished business with that bitch."

QT said, "Don't worry about nothing, I got you."

The limo driver dropped Rocc, Too Cool, and Tank off at QT's mother's house where everyone else that was close to the family had gone. QT, Gangsta, and Goldie were dropped off at QT's house. Goldie then left in his car to go get a throwaway van.

When QT and Gangsta went inside QT's house, Gangsta asked,

"You all right, lil bro? You strong enough for this shit that's about to go down?"

QT said, "Nothing could stop me from doing whatever it is that I got to do to get them niggas."

They changed clothes and put on black khakis, black sweatshirts, some black Chuck Taylors, and black ski masks. Gangsta had two .45 automatics and QT had two 9mm Berettas. Goldie got back at eight thirty and was dressed the same as QT and Gangsta.

They left at 10 p.m. and headed for Nutt's mama's house. As Goldie drove the van, QT said, "Everybody in the house is fair game except the kids. I want that nigga to hurt, to be scared, and to know that I'm coming for his bitch ass."

Goldie parked directly in front of the driveway. They got out of the van, walked to the front door, pulled the ski masks down over their faces, and QT kicked the door in. Nutt's mother and two of his brothers were sitting on the couch watching a movie. Nutt's brothers were ages 21 and 18.

QT, Goldie, and Gangster moved quickly into the house with guns drawn.

QT said, "Shut the fuck up and don't nobody move." He walked up to Nutt's youngest brother, put the gun to his head, and asked, "Who else is in the house?"

The mother answered, "My husband and my two granddaughters. Please don't hurt us, we don't have any money."

Gangsta and Goldie went to search the rest of the house. They came back with Nutt's father.

Gangsta said, "The two girls are asleep. I closed the door to the bedroom that they in."

QT said, "I'm only going to ask this question once and once only, so think about it before yo answer it. Where the fuck is Nutt?"

They all looked at QT and shook their heads from side to side saying they didn't know. QT walked up to the father, put the nina to his head and pulled the trigger. As his wife started to scream, Gangsta shot her twice in the head as well. The two brothers tried to get up and rush them but QT shot the younger one in the face and chest. Goldie shot the other one twice in the head.

"Let's get the fuck out of here," QT said.

They casually walked to the van and pulled off. Goldie drove six blocks over to Maniac's mother's house where he parked in front. They got out and went to the door. QT turned the knob and they all went in. The TV was on in the living room but no one was in sight. They walked through the house. The first bedroom they came to the door was closed but they could hear the bed moving and a female moaning.

QT gestured for Goldie and Gangsta to check the other two bedrooms. QT slowly opened the door. Maniac's brother was fucking a female who was bent over doggy style on the bed. They were so caught up in what they were doing they didn't notice QT standing there with a ski mask on, dressed in all black. QT cut the light on.

When the light came on, both of them turned and were shocked to see QT standing there with two guns pointed at them.

QT said, "If you scream or make any noise, I'm going to smoke both of you muthafuckas." He threw a roll of duct tape to the female and told her to tape her dude's hands and ankles together.

Once she'd done that, QT got the tape back and taped her hands and mouth up. Gangsta and Goldie came back with Maniac's mother. No one else was in the house.

QT snatched the female off the bed and said, "Thank God becuz tonight is yo lucky night." He told Goldie to take her to the back room and tape her legs up. QT held her close to him and whispered in her ear, "Don't leave that room for at least two hours or I will come back and smoke yo fine ass."

While Goldie took her to the back room, QT snatched the tape off Maniac's mother's mouth and asked, "Where is Maniac?"

"I don't know."

QT pulled a pair of wire cutters out of his pocket and went to her son and without hesitation cut his pinky finger off. He yelled and screamed but no one could hear him because of the tape covering his mouth. Tears ran down his face.

His mother cried out, "Please, please, don't hurt my baby no more!"

QT said, "I'm going to ask you one more time. Where is Maniac?

This time, after I cut his other pinky off, I'm going to cut your pinky finger off as well. You got ten seconds."

As QT walked toward her son, she blurted out, "He has a condo in North Hollywood."

She gave QT the address. Before QT walked out of the bedroom door, he turned and shot both of them twice in the head.

They got in the van and headed for North Hollywood.

"We got to get this nigga tonight," QT said. "If we don't he will probably skip town once he finds out his moms and brother are dead."

It was 1 a.m. by the time they found the condo. They couldn't just kick the door in because they were in North Hollywood and the neighbors would surely call the police. The garage was connected to the condo so QT went and checked it to see if it was unlocked. QT pulled on the garage door and it started to come up. They quickly went inside and let the door back down. The door that connected the garage to the condo was open. They crept inside and looked around. The first two bedrooms were empty.

When they got to the third room the door was open and they could see Maniac sleeping in bed with his woman. Gangsta crept up to the bed and put the .45 auto to his head. QT cut the light on and Goldie put his hand over Maniac's woman's mouth and told her if she screamed he would kill her. They could see the panic in Maniac's eyes but there was nothing that he could do. He had been caught slippin.

Goldie taped Maniac's woman's wrists, legs, and mouth up with duct tape. Then he taped Maniac's wrist and mouth up. QT told Goldie to go get the van and pull it up to the garage.

QT looked at Maniac's woman and said, "I would just lay there for a few hours if I was you. Don't make us have to come back. Sandy, you lucky I didn't smoke yo ass."

They put Maniac in the van and headed to Compton to the abandoned warehouse on Alameda. Goldie had his ski mask off because he was driving. In the back of the van, Maniac watched as QT and Gangsta pull off their ski masks. Once they did, he knew he was a dead man.

QT said, "Nigga, you a piece of shit. You gave yo own homeboy up for money. Then you end up being with the nigga that shot me with my daughter in my arms. Not to mention the muthafucka killed my wife." He backhanded Maniac like a bitch. "Nigga, you had to know that I would be coming to get yo ass."

Maniac knew that he had fucked up big time and there was no way out of the situation.

When they got to the warehouse, Maniac was taken out of the van and hung by handcuffs on a hook hanging from the ceiling.

QT said, "Make this easy on yourself, just tell me where Nutt is and I will kill you fast. You bullshit me and you are going to hurt real bad."

He snatched the tape off Maniac's mouth.

Maniac said in a rush, "I swear I don't know where that nigga live. That's why I was with him that day, trying to find out where he lived so I could tell you. You see I didn't have a strap that day. That nigga ain't told nobody where he's at. When I was in his car I saw a parking ticket from Valencia. That's got to be where that nigga is hiding out at."

QT told Gangsta to help take Maniac down. They put him back in the van then QT smiled at him and blasted him twice in the head. He had Goldie drop them off on Golden at Lil Man's Spot. He told Goldie to burn the van with Maniac's body inside of it. Then he told Lil Man to follow Goldie and pick him up. They also gave the straps to Goldie to get rid of.

QT and Gangsta used one of Lil Man's cars to go home.

Gangsta said, "What is that bitch's full name that's going with Nutt?"

QT answered, "Patricia Green. Why?"

"Because if that bitch and that nigga is in Valencia, then likely everything is in her name. I got a boy that can find anybody as long as I got a name."

"Handle that shit. I don't want that nigga to skip town on me."

QT dropped Gangsta off at home. He went home alone for the first time since the shooting. Once again, as he got undressed and lay in their bed, he thought of Nat and the tears came.

Nutt heard about the murders of his and Maniac's families when he called one of his home boys the next day. As he sat in his house, tears ran down his face. Ever since they had tried to jack QT and Nat, people close to him had died. Now both of his brothers and his mother and father were dead and Maniac was missing. Nutt knew that more than likely Maniac was dead as well.

The only thing he had in his favor was that no one knew where he was. If they did, he would also be dead. He had to figure out what he was going to do. He couldn't go back to Texas; that was a definite no-go. Basically, he had been in Cali all of his life until him and Boss-T went to Texas. Cali was all that he knew. Nutt hadn't told Tricia about shooting Nat and QT and he wasn't going to tell her about his family either.

Tricia was at her beauty salon. Nutt sat at home smoking chronic and drinking. He was in this shit all by himself. He knew that after the message QT sent by killing his and Maniac's families. There was no way that anybody was going to step up and help him; not even his homies from his neighborhood.

As he sat there, he thought about just taking the money he had left and his new Corvette and hitting the highway. At least, he would be alive. Fuck Tricia if she didn't want to leave with him. Yeah, that was exactly what he was going to do: leave Cali.

Two days later, Gangsta walked into QT's house and found him sitting in the den playing with LaShawn. His moms and sister Lisa were there as well. They had basically moved in because they didn't want QT to be alone. Gangsta greeted his mom and Lisa each with a kiss and a hug. He told QT that he had to talk to him.

QT gave LaShawn to his sister and QT and Gangsta walked out the sliding doors of the den to the back yard.

Gangsta said, "Cuz, I know where that nigga and that bitch are."

"Where dem muthafuckas at?"

"They have a house in Valencia. Tricia also have a beauty salon that's in her name there as well. The house, the business, and the cars are all in her name. That nigga Nutt has to cee there with her."

QT said, "Tonight, me, you, and Tank, we got a hot date with that bitch ass nigga. The bitch is Tank's; he can handle her. We will leave around one this afternoon so we won't have to be in that rush hour traffic. That gives us about three hours to get ready."

QT called Tank and gave him the good news. Tank told QT he would be at his house in an hour.

QT thought to himself: Finally, I can kill this nigga and end this shit. Finally, Nat will be able to rest in peace.

Destiny and Tasha had been constantly paging QT but he hadn't called either of them back. He knew that they were concerned for him and LaShawn but he wasn't ready to talk to them. Not until his unfinished business had been finished. He knew that eventually he would get with one of them because LaShawn would need a mother figure. But not now; he was still grieving Nat. For now, his mom and sister would have to do.

Tricia closed her shop at 8 p.m. and went straight home. When she got in the house, she quickly undressed and got in the shower. She didn't know that QT, Tank, and Gangsta were also in the house until Tank walked in the bathroom and opened the shower door.

Tricia couldn't believe her eyes. How could he have found her?

"Tank, baby, I was going to call you," she said with fear in her voice. "I just needed some time by myself."

She didn't know that her whole episode with Nutt at Tank's house had been recorded.

Tank grabbed her by her hair and snatched her out of the shower. He dragged her naked into her bedroom where QT and Gangsta were. Tank slapped her and pushed her down on the floor in front of the bed. He turned the TV and the VCR on and put the tape in.

"Watch this tape you scandalous bitch, then tell me if you deserve to die."

Neither QT nor Gangsta had seen the tape before, and they watched as well. As Tricia watched, she cried like a baby because she knew that Tank was going to kill her.

When the tape ended, Tank said, "I would have given you anything you wanted. That money you took from me wasn't nothing; that was crumbs. It ain't about the money, you and that bitch ass nigga totally disrespected me to the fullest. Ain't no need of crying. You wasn't crying when you was fuckin and suckin that nigga's dick in my house, in my bed."

Tank pulled out a .45 auto with a silencer and shot Tricia three times in the chest and once in the stomach. Then he pulled out a machete and cut off her head. He sat the head in the middle of the bed.

QT hit the eject button on the VCR and handed the tape to Tank.

Gangsta said, "One down and one to go."

QT closed the bathroom door and left the shower running so when Nutt got home he would think that Tricia was in the bathroom.

Nutt made it home around 11 p.m. He had been preparing to leave and he had decided not to tell Tricia he was leaving. He was just going to fuck the shit out of her that night and when she came home from her salon the next day he would be gone.

When he walked in the house he heard the water running so he thought he would get naked and join her in the shower. He got naked right in front of the bathroom door. He had two .45 automatics which he laid on the floor first.

Gangsta and Tank watched him from the bedroom that was closest to the bathroom. As soon as Nutt went in the bathroom, QT, Tank, and Gangsta quietly stepped out of the bedroom. QT kicked Nutt's straps to the side.

Nutt opened the shower door but found that the shower was empty. He said out loud, "What in the fuck is going on?"

He turned around and suddenly found himself facing QT, Gangsta, and Tank who stood in the doorway with guns pointed at him.

QT said, 'Remember me, muthafucka? Bring yo punk ass on out here."

Nutt came out of the bathroom and Gangsta quickly duct taped his hands behind his back.

Tank walked up to Nutt and said, "I got a surprise for you." He pushed Nutt towards his bedroom. He opened the door and pushed Nutt inside.

When Tank cut the light on, Nutt saw Tricia's head on the bed and her bloody body on the floor. Nutt cried out and fell to his knees and began to beg for his life. He was a killer with a pistol — that's why he always kept one — but he was a coward without one.

QT slapped him like a bitch.

"All the shit you've done you could at least die like a man, oh, but you ain't a man without a strap," QT said. "I don't want to hear this bitch ass nigga cry and beg."

Gangsta put duct tape over Nutt's mouth. QT then proceeded to cut all of Nutt's fingers and toes off as he screamed in pain. No one could hear his cries because of the tape covering his mouth. Then QT shot Nutt between the eyes. Tank cut the head off, and his dick, and put it in his mouth. He sat Nutt's head next to Tricia's.

The three men crept out of the house as quietly as they had come in.

Tank said, "Now this shit is over."

QT said, "Yeah, now Nat can rest in peace."

Tank and Kathy flew back to Texas and Too Cool flew to New Orleans. QT and Gangsta took them to the airport and they all said their goodbyes. They said they would see each other again soon.

When QT and Gangsta got back in the car, Gangsta said, "So are you still going to step down from tha G-Code Mobb? You can still sit on the board and be my right hand man."

QT said, "Naw, I'm cool. I got to take care of LaShawn. I owe that to Nat, myself, and her. I have to run my business and take over Nat's. I got $25 million stashed that Uncle Sam don't know about, and $6 million that's in the bank legally. I'm cool. Between the businesses and LaShawn, I don't have time for nothing else."

Two months later, Gangsta had taken over the Tha G-Code Mobb. Goldie stepped down and he and Monica were expecting their first child. Over in Inglewood, QT was sitting at his desk in his office at his shop when Destiny walked in his office. He stood up and she walked up to him and gave him a long hug.

"I'm truly sorry about Natalie. I've been paging you like crazy. I want to be here for you and LaShawn. No strings attached. I just want to be here for you."

"I meant to call you back but I wasn't ready to talk to anyone plus I was feeling guilty for cheating on Nat."

Destiny said, "So how are you really doing, baby?"

QT said, "I'm managing but I still miss her so much. Sometimes I be at home and LaShawn may start crying and I'll call out for Nat to get her."

Destiny hugged QT and said, "I'm here for you, baby. I was going to quit my job this week anyway because I want to be here for you and not have to worry about those assholes at work questioning me."

As Destiny was holding QT's hand, Tasha walked in.

She ignored Destiny and walked straight up to QT and kissed him on the cheek. "I couldn't wait any longer to see you. I've been stressed out the game wondering and worrying about you."

QT sat down behind his desk and told both of them to have a seat. He introduced them to each other and said, "You are the only other women that I've been with besides Nat. I love both of you and I'm not going to choose one over the other. So I will understand if one or both of you decides you don't want anything else to do with me. I would hope that we all could be friends for now."

Both of them told QT that they would do whatever it took as long as they could be with him. QT gave them his address and told them to be at his house at 6 p.m. He wanted them to meet his daughter, but for now, he wasn't ready for a relationship.

They both kissed QT on the cheek and said they would see him that evening.

QT picked LaShawn up from his mom's house. He had told his moms and sister that he was going to be all right three weeks earlier and that they could move back home. He would drop LaShawn off to them every morning on his way to work and he would pick her up no later than 5 p.m. during the week.

When they got to QT's house, Tasha and Destiny looked beautiful. They instantly fell in love with LaShawn and got down on the floor and played with her. Neither Tasha nor Destiny wanted to share QT but they would do whatever it took to please him.

He said, "I hope that someone is going to feed me. I'm starving."

Destiny and Tasha jumped up and headed for the kitchen. QT put LaShawn in her playpen and said, "We can all cook dinner together."

After they cooked, they all sat down and ate dinner together. Tasha and Destiny started to loosen up with each other and actually saw that the other was a cool person.

Destiny went to work the next day to resign. But before she could, Special Agent White called a meeting. As everyone on the task force sat around waiting and wondering what the meeting was going to be about, Destiny was thinking about QT and LaShawn and how she could win him over to her and her only.

Agent White walked into the briefing room and said, "I think we finally got a break. As we all know, after QT's wife was killed he stepped down from his organization. So now his brother Gangsta is back out and is running things again. There was a drug bust in Long Beach two days ago and the guy that was busted gave us some very important information on the organization.

"It's call the "G-Code Mobb" and there are six generals under Gangsta. All of them have their own areas of distributing drugs. Also, all of them export drugs out of state as well. This guy has just admitted to the existence of the G-Code Mobb in the last month and a half. He did time with Gangsta in Folsom where they became tight. He's given me the other names of the G-Code members. They meet twice a month at Gangsta's house. Our guy is a three strikes candidate and he doesn't want to go back to jail so he's agreed to work with us.

"At their next meeting, I'm going to send him in there wired for sound. With a man on the inside, it shouldn't take us long to take all of them down. Maybe some of them will talk and give us something on QT as well."

As Destiny sat there, she knew she could not resign, not now. She had to warn QT; she had to protect him and LaShawn.

Agent White said, "This operation will be called 'Operation G-Code.' This time, we have the upper hand."

Agent White sat back down with a big smile on his face.

To Be Continued …

Real Talk by Fredrick Staves

This book, by no means, was written to glorify drugs, gangs, or the street lifestyle. Period. By reading my books, I pray that the reader realizes that there are only three things that can happen to anyone who chooses this lifestyle: you will go to jail, you will end up paralyzed, or you will be murdered.

It's real easy to do the wrong thing or make the wrong choices in life, but we must realize and understand that there are consequences that we must face when we choose to do wrong. Most of us can not or will not accept those consequences when everything goes all bad.

Everyone wants to live a good life and have the finer things that come with it. We must understand that we as individuals are responsible for our lives and the choices we make.

We all know right from wrong. I chose to do the wrong things for over thirty years. I can count on two hands the homies that I grew up with that are still around and half of them are crack heads. Ninety eight percent of the homies I grew up with are dead, on death row, or have life sentences in prison.

I know now that I haven't been lucky; I've been blessed.

The world doesn't consist of the neighborhood, city, or state that we are from. The world is a big place and I want to see as much of it as I can.

I choose now to do what's right: be a father to my children, a husband to my wife, and an asset to the community, but first and foremost, be a man of God.

So the next time you know you are going to do what's wrong, step back, think about it, and choose to do what's right. A real man is not afraid to make the right choice.

Also Available:

Gangsta: Some Talk It I Live It

$19.95

Send checks or money orders to:

OG Publishing
PO Box 211 Rialto CA 92377

All book orders require $2.06 in taxes (Cal only)
plus $4.00 for shipping and handling.

Visit our website: OGOriginalGangsta.com